# The Distant Moon

by Michel Wei

 Asian Culture Press

ISBN: 978-1-957144-42-9 (Paperback)
ISBN: 978-1-957144-43-6 (EPUB)

Library of Congress Control Number: 2022911916

Any references to historical events, real people, or real places are used fictitiously, Names, characters, and places are products of the author's imagination.

First paperback edition July 2022
Printed in the United States of America

Typesetting services by Asian Culture Press

Asian Culture Press, LLC
1942 Broadway,
Suite 314C,
Boulder, CO 80302,
United States
www.isbnagent.com

# Preface

AlphaGo's victory over Lee Sedol in 2016 was significantly different from Deep Blue's victory over Garry Kasparov in 1997. This difference certainly does not refer to the difference between the two of them in terms of size and weight. In the 1970s, Deep Blue weighed 1270 kg, whereas nowadays, in computer science, we basically don't talk about such issues.

The difference is that the former is epoch-making and more far-reaching. If Deep Blue is a "human", it only means that it has a strong memory and fast reaction, but AlphaGo is more than that, it behaves more like a "human", it is capable of deep learning and appears to be more intelligent. This is intelligence in the true sense of the word.

In the IVA group of Mendeleev's periodic table, carbon, silicon, and germanium are in descending order ....... Generally speaking, elements in the same group have similar chemical properties. The element carbon is the basic backbone of organic macromolecules -- carbon chains. We are organic, so our proteins, amino acids, RNA and DNA, among others, are all organic macromolecules with carbon chains as backbone. That's why we can be called "carbon-based people".

According to this similarity, the silicon element below the carbon element in the IVA column can also constitute another kind of human being. This is not a new concept, as early as 1891, Julius Scheiner, an astrophysicist at the University of Potsdam, Germany, had proposed the concept of "silicon-based life". Think about the current silicon chip, and then think about the silicon chip framework of Deep Blue,

AlphaGo, we cannot help but be complacent, we are also the Creator who created a silicon-based life. From Deep Blue to AlphaGo, we are trying to evolve it, and in less than 20 years, making it has comprehensively beaten humans in the field of intellectual games. Are we really its God?

In the near future, when silicon-based lives evolve to autonomous learning from AlphaGo's deep learning, they are destined to be more powerful than us and destined to replace us. As we often see in movies, intelligent robots that look like us will integrate into our society. While we happily enjoy their services, expecting them to be our obedient and loyal servants who are under our thumb, they are quietly becoming our masters. When the moment comes, don't look like the scenario shown in the "Terminator" movie series starring Schwarzenegger: carbon-based people look like rats, driven into smelly underground trenches by silicon-based people, worrying all day about their search and killing.

We can also have a more optimistic expectation: not to be their slaves, not to be killed by them, but to be their pets. To really have such expectations, we must thank Asimov's three laws of robotics:

First Law: A robot may not injure a human being or, through inaction, allow a human being to come to harm.

Second Law: A robot must obey the orders given it by human beings except where such orders would conflict with the First Law.

Third law: A robot must protect its own existence as long as such protection does not conflict with the First or Second Law.

Can we really achieve Asimov's apocalypse? We hope so, even if we end up as their pets. But what's the harm in that? We are now God's pets, too.

We need to develop a technology that will set this rule for robots, the Three Laws of Robotics. The three laws go around and around in many words, but the bottom line is this: no harm should come to humans. In the future, no matter how much they evolve, robots will not be able to get around this rule and give birth to more powerful robots. They will pass on this rule for generations. Only then will we be able to develop artificial intelligence with confidence and boldness and put silicon-based people at our service.

In Japan, Hong Kong, Taiwan ......while the gang leaders of the triads are to discuss things, if the youngest member of the gang beside him cannot help but fly off the handle and rage for the benefit of his gang, his leader will immediately reprimand him and stop him. This is the rule of the society. The bosses are talking, the junior next to them only listen because they are not qualified to interrupt. The leader's junior, no matter what mistake he has made, it has to be the leader to clean up, no matter how the other leaders do not like it, they are not qualified to fix him. If they fix him, it is considered as not giving the leader face. These society rules, once formed, whether they are for the powerful group like the gang leaders, or for the vulnerable group like the juniors, all have binding force.

The rule is a regulation. The law is also a regulation. The difference between the two is that the latter is clearly documented through the provisions, while the former only remains in our minds. In human society, the strongest group sets the rules for the weakest. Once the rules spread and remain in people's minds, they become universally binding, sometimes acting stronger than the law, or even violating the law at all. For example, the phenomenon of child marriage, this rule is more often than not contrary to the spirit of the law, but still in some areas to prevail.

The older the history, the more powerful groups spread like a storm, and the more numerous they are, the more bizarre the rules passed down. While this is certainly the characteristic of a race, but it must not be a good thing. These rules shackle people's innovation and enterprise, harming the freedom of individuality, and leaving society in a pool of stagnant water. With less rules, there will be fewer adherence to the old-fashioned practices, even if it will bring chaos, but there will ultimately be a society full of vitality and energy, a world of fascinating personalities.

In a future world where silicon-based people are in full charge of carbon-based people, they will certainly set all kinds of rules for us. Do we really want to see such a scene?


Michel Wei

March 27th, 2022 at Xiaohongshan

# Acknowledgement

Writing is not a difficult task if the ideas are abundant. Completing this long novel was a lot of work for me, but not so much so that I ran out of energy and needed a lot of help from others.

My English skills are limited to reading that relies on a dictionary. It would be stretched to the limit for listening, speaking and writing. Thanks to the ladies and gentlemen at Asian Culture Press for their help with translation, typesetting, cover design, and publication and distribution. Thanks to Mr. Wei Zhongli for his proofreading work.

I would also like to say: this book is dedicated to Yan'er in the woods.

About the author: Michel Wei, born in July 1970, graduated from Xiamen University with a bachelor's degree. PhD in engineering from Wuhan University. Long engaged in the establishment and management of government technology innovation policy.

Email: michel_wei@126.com

# Table of Contents

# Jack's Arrival in the City of Decay

The cement floor beneath her feet suddenly disappeared. Her fall lodged Susan's heart in her throat, rendering her incapable of letting out the terror within her. "I'm going to fall to my death." She squeezed her eyes tightly shut as her arms flailed in a vain attempt to grab something. Just then, her plummet came to an unexpected stop, and her arm twinged in slight pain. When she opened her eyes and lifted her head, she saw a hand forcefully holding onto her wrist. She lowered her head to look below and found that her body was hanging in mid-air. She was so far from the ground that she felt a little dizzy. The sound of the cement flooring hitting the ground reverberated in her ears, giving her an idea of how far the drop truly was.

Temporarily beyond the clutches of death, Susan steadied herself and thought about how lucky she had been. The person who had saved her life was a young man. Her left wrist was in his solid and measured grip. It seemed that he could keep this going on for a while.

The man had a bright and even complexion. At that moment, he was gesturing with his left hand for her to give him her right. Susan lifted her right arm. With a small burst of strength, he pulled her up, and both her wrists ended up in his vise-like hold.

"Do you have rope supporting you?" Susan guessed that he had to be tied to something with rope. That was the only way he could be hanging upside-down with his hands free to hold her.

"Nope. My feet are hooked on the edge of the floorboards," he answered with a grin.

It was impossible that hooking one's feet on the edge of the floorboards could withstand the weight of two people. Besides, it would also have to withstand the momentum of someone free-falling, which was even more impossible. Susan felt that the man must be joking, perhaps to calm her tense nerves.

"I'm Susan."

"Jack," the man said after some thought.

"Jack, we have to get out of here. Your feet won't be able to take this much longer."

The glass wall of the skyscraper had not been able to withstand the cruel passage of time and had fallen from its support grid to shatter into a million pieces. Slowly, the space around the skyscraper had become covered in a moat of glass. Under the glare of the sun, they shimmered with spots of light.

Susan and Jack hung from the 107th Floor of this skyscraper. Without the glass wall in the way, it was easier for them to get out of their predicament. With the flex of his arms, Jack forcefully lifted Susan half a meter high. Just like that, Susan could raise her feet and place them on the 106th Floor. Immediately after, Jack flipped in the air with the grace of a gymnast to land on the 106th Floor as well. Out of danger, they both sat on the ground to have a quick rest.

"You seem to be very strong." Susan was thoroughly shocked. How was it that he was supported by hooked feet rather than being tied with some rope?

"This skyscraper isn't as sturdy as it seems on the surface," Jack said, not acknowledging the statement.

This was the first time that Susan had climbed up this skyscraper. She had been standing on the balcony on the 109th Floor. Only the top floor had a balcony like this. It didn't have a railing and was indeed just a slab of concrete protruding from the building. As she looked down at the city with the wind caressing her body, she felt as if she was floating in the sky. She loved that feeling.

"That's right. The cement slab of the balcony just suddenly fell off." When she recalled the moment she had plummeted just now, her heart shuddered with lingering terror. "You seem to know why?"

"Time erodes all." Jack knew that this skyscraper was 250 years old. When the both of them gazed beyond, only a devastated and desolate city greeted them. The streets were lined with collapsed buildings in piles of rubble with overgrown weeds spreading on them. Vines and moss clung to the broken walls, obscuring the glory of what once was. Nature was encroaching at its edges and slowly eating away at the city. Signs of humanity were rare in the city, having become a zoo without enclosures where animals roamed freely and fearlessly. Wild rabbits, wolves, antelopes, and more ran and leaped about amidst the jagged rocks of the city's ruins.

"When we left 130 years ago, this place was destined to fall into disrepair." Jack lamented.

"Let's go." The sun was already setting in the west. Focused on getting home, Susan didn't bother with Jack's ramblings.

The two slowly climbed down the stairs from the 106th Floor. Susan was ever careful, fearful that the floorboards would crumble beneath her. Jack was the opposite, looking relaxed. When she finally got to the ground floor, Susan let out a long breath. In her heart, she told herself that she would never return here again.

"Where do you live?" Susan asked as they were about to part ways.

"I live right here."

"Thank you for saving me. I live in a village north of the city. It's called Urvin Village. You're welcome to come by my place." Susan regarded Jack earnestly.

"Alright, I'll go over to yours tomorrow morning."

"That's great. Goodbye." Susan turned to head toward the north of the city.

Jack was a strange man. He was stronger than the typical person. He also seemed to be very knowledgeable when it came to the history of this city's fall, even going back more than 100 years. According to some older people, their ancestors used to live in this city. Later on, they left for some unknown reason. This city had long been abandoned and everyone called it the City of Decay. Jack said that he lived here, but how did he survive? Why had he pondered for a moment before giving out his name? Susan felt that it had been invented on the spot.

Susan thought about all this as she walked, filled with confusion.

That night in Urvin Village, there was no moon in the sky. Sitting on the fence around Johnson's home, Peter and Johnson were shrouded in darkness. Only their low conversation hinted at their presence.

"In three days, Newman will be conducting the moon ritual." After a spell of silence, Peter couldn't resist bringing up a new topic.

"Oh, he's going to be 65 already." It was obvious that Johnson did not care for old Heralds. "Plack is going to become the Herald, right?"

"That's right." Peter sighed.

"You were born to be the Herald," Johnson said sincerely. He was truly impressed by Peter's linguistic skills.

"Yes." Peter wasn't modest at all. "But how does that matter?"

"Why doesn't it matter?"

"When it comes down to it, Plack will become the Herald, not me," Peter said, annoyed.

"You still have a chance. Once he dies, it'll be your turn."

"By the time he dies of old age, I'm afraid I won't have a chance anymore."

"Then we have to hope that he dies quick."

"Yeah, I'd love to kill him right now." Peter gave words to the desire in his heart without holding back.

"You can't beat him." Johnson flexed his biceps and said boastfully, "You'd have to be like me to do it!"

"Will you help me then?" Peter glanced admiringly at Johnson's muscles and pleaded sincerely.

This move played right into Johnson's vanity. Boldly, Johnson said, "Sure, leave it to me. Before Newman's moon ritual, I'll kill Plack and you can become the Herald."

A "girl" overheard their conversation clearly.

# The Strange Customs of Urvin Village

J ack arrived at Urvin Village as the sun transitioned from red to white. This wasn't the first time that he was making a visit. Urvin Village was about 13 kilometers away from the City of Decay. After parting ways with Susan yesterday, he had followed behind her and walked for more than two whole hours right up until Susan went through her front door.

400 kilometers to the east of Urvin Village was Magia Village. To the west was a boundless ocean. At a distance of 500 kilometers to the south was Lijou Village. To the north was a range of steep mountains that stretched 2000 kilometers and was difficult to traverse on foot. Urvin Village was a village that was seemingly isolated from the rest of the world.

Jack wasn't interested or disgusted by the smell that emanated from the huge swath of wheat fields. Instead, he only made a mental note of it. After following a winding dirt road, Jack came to a fence. Wooden pegs two meters tall stood at one-meter intervals. Two wooden slats connected the pegs, one spaced a meter above the other. The wood fence surrounded a circular yard that was about 20 meters in diameter. There was a door in the fence. Written on the lintel was the name "Dick". This was Susan's home. There were about 600 of such circular yards in the village, they were sprinkled throughout the fields, set apart from each other at varying distances between one to three kilometers. The entire area, from east to west and south to north, was a total of about 20 to 30 kilometers. If he hadn't followed Susan home last night, he would have had some trouble finding it.

When Jack got to the gate of the yard, Susan was grinning as she watched him. The smile had been preceded by a hint of surprise that faded after a bit.

"You didn't expect me, did you?" Jack could tell what Susan was thinking. Susan felt embarrassed. As she had made her way home last night, she regretted not clearly laying out the location of her house because of their hasty separation. However, all the properties in the village were similar, so it was challenging to state exactly where one home could be found. Even so, Susan should at least have told Jack that her lintel had the name "Dick" on it.

Susan subconsciously believed that Jack didn't live in the City of Decay. He could be living in Urvin Village. It would also explain why she hadn't told him that she lived in the Dick home when they had parted last night. Although he had saved her life, they probably wouldn't be spending much time together, maybe only a year at most.

Susan had told her family about how she had been rescued. As such, all of her family members treated Jack warmly. Judging by his clothes, they felt that their guest must have come from some distance locale instead of the City of Decay. No one in a 500-kilometer radius dressed like this. Jack's tight-fitting clothing emphasized the muscles of his body. The clothes were like skin, not creasing no matter how Jack moved. Susan's grandfather, Newman, was very excited by this and touched Jack's clothes in his curiosity. It felt warm and had the smoothness of silk. Yet, it was obviously not silk. Jack's shoes were even stranger. They looked to be made out of metal, shiny but hard. However, when Jack walked, the shoes looked like they were as soft and supple as leather.

"I found these clothes in the City of Decay." Jack didn't want to be different from the villagers, so he quickly glossed over it. "I never thought they would fit so well." From his observations last night and this morning, he estimated that Urvin Village had a population of around 500C. The villagers likely did not all know each other, so it was probably feasible to pretend that he was just another villager.

Lisa brought out a pot of food from the kitchen. It was a dish of solid balls produced by mixing ground meat with wheat flour and steaming it. Everyone sat around the pot, reached out to grab the food, and started eating. Jack followed their lead and chatted while he ate.

Once the pot of food was finished, everyone seemed to be full. "Jack, are you full?" Susan asked.

"I need more." Jack didn't have a concept of fullness or hunger; he only knew that he needed more.

"Mom, can you make a bowl of pork noodles too?" Susan said to Lisa.

"Sure, but you'll have to wait a while."

"A man with a big appetite is surely very strong," Dick said to himself as he gazed out the window and looked at the wheat fields beyond. The name "Dick" on the lintel indicated that he was the head of the family.

"Dad, Jack's really strong." Susan thought so too. The image of Jack saving her with only his feet hooked on the floorboards to withstand both their combined weight rose to her mind.

"You can stay here for a while," Dick said. "It beats living in the City of Decay. At least there's food here." In his heart, though, Dick hoped that Jack could be of help here. It would be time to harvest the wheat soon, and it was demanding work. In their household, Susan was 19, and her brothers, Bob and Charles, were 15 and 13. None of them were much help.

"Susan misunderstood. I was only staying in the City of Decay last night."

"Can you?" Susan asked Jack.

"I can. I'll stay however long you need me to." Jack also wanted to stay here and integrate himself into this environment as soon as possible. He had arrived in the City of Decay the day before yesterday. Although it was his destination, he might need to start off with Urvin Village first to complete his mission. Jack lied, "Let me tell my family about it first and I'll move over here."

After lunch, Jack set off. Although he said that he was going home, he was only going to make a turn around the village before coming back. When Susan saw him off, she asked, "Where's your house?"

"In the village to the north." Jack kept lying. This was the south, so it was more likely for them to not have met before if he said he lived far away from here. As he expected, Susan's demeanor indicated that she was unfamiliar with the village to the north.

"You'll have to cross the square. I'll wait for you there." Coincidentally, Susan wanted to take a spin around the square too to witness the ritual.

There was a wide open space in the middle of the village. This was the village square. There was currently a ritual going on. An old man walked up to the altar naked. The altar was two meters high, with an even taller wooden dowel in the middle. Hanging from the dowel was a length of rope. The old man tied the rope around his neck without a trace of fear or wistfulness on his face. He calmly closed his eyes. Right then, a young man in red walked up to the altar. His mumblings were prayers.

"May the light of the moon forever enshroud the earth." After that, he shouted, "Dad, Dad, Dad." With a kick, the wooden board below the old man's feet fell away and he dropped. The rope around his neck tightened.

"It seems that the old man did it willingly." Jack said inquisitively.

"That's right. This is our custom," Susan answered. "That young man is his son."

"Why do you do this?" Jack asked.

"It's a custom from more than 100 years ago. Newman will be 65 the day after tomorrow and he'll have to go up to the altar too."

"Susan, does this mean your father Dick will have to end his own life on the altar too?"

"Yes." Susan smiled as she looked at Jack.

The square also held a market where villagers could barter everyday necessities. It was a venue for them to interact with each other as well.

"I'm going to Magia Village next year. I won't be coming back anymore."

"Why are you going to Magia Village?" Jack asked.

"Well, I might not stay in Magia Village." Susan seemed to be deep in thought. "It might not be my final destination. I might go to another village."

"Is Magia Village far from here?"

"According to the rules set more than 100 years ago, all the villages in the world are like the properties in our village. They have to be at least 400 kilometers away from each other." Susan pointed at the scattered properties in the fields and continued, "The properties in the village must be around one to three kilometers apart."

"The rules set more than 100 years ago," Jack repeated. There had to have been a huge change in the world back then.

"If you're not coming back, how will you survive? Will someone take you in?" Jack glanced at Susan.

"Someone will. If we both agree, I'll become his wife and live in his household."

"What if you don't?"

"Then I'll keep moving on to the next village until I find someone I'm happy with and vice versa."

"What if you never find someone like that?"

"In 20 years, I'll participate in the ritual and sacrifice myself to the moon."

"Isn't there a young man in the village that you like?"

"The rules state that those of the same village cannot marry. I have to wed someone from another village." Susan was very familiar with these rules

"What if you don't follow the rules?"

"No one does that."

"So how will you live for the next 20 years?"

"Unmarried women have to be taken care of. The whole world follows these rules."

"Every household is obligated to provide food and board to unmarried women who are traveling around."

"Of course, she can make her own living," Susan added.

Jack didn't know these rules at all! Susan's heart stuttered. Jack definitely wasn't from their village. Where was he from? It seemed that he wasn't even from their era. Was it possible that there was a world beyond this one?

In Susan's eyes, the rules set 100 years ago were not ones that could be broken. These rules pervaded all the villages of the world like air, and every adult aged 15 and above knew of them. The property of every family had to be within a 20 meter diameter. The distance between properties had to be between one to three kilometers. Villages had to be at least 400 kilometers apart. Unmarried women were the only fraction of the population that traveled between villages. All the elderly only lived to the age of 65….

Susan suddenly realized that more and more villages were congregating around Jack. Finally, a bald middle-aged man blocked his path. "Which family are you from?" Jack kept quiet. His strange manner of dress easily attracted the attention and focus of the villagers. Even if Susan accompanied him, there was no effective way to remain incognito.

At that moment, silence enveloped Jack like fog. The longer he stayed unspeaking, the more suspicious the villagers became. "Plack, I don't think he's from our village!" the bald man shouted. He seemed to be seeking validation. Plack looked disbelieving as he said, "The rules have been broken, the rules have been broken…" he yelled with all his might.

Susan made the realization at the same time. If only unmarried women could travel in this world, how had a man come to their village? Why hadn't Newman realized this issue?

Influenced by Plack's exacerbation, the villagers became shocked and agitated. Their discussion spread out like ripples on the surface of a pond. Yet, Jack didn't panic. "Who is your village head? I have something to say to him," Jack said loudly.

"What's a village head?" someone asked.

To Susan, Jack's words proved once again that he didn't belong. He must have come from another world! Did "village head" refer to someone? If it did, then he could only speak to Newman.

"Newman is the village head." Susan was quick-witted. "I'll take him to my house and he can speak with my grandfather. Later, we'll tell you what happened." This was the best way to get them out of this predicament.

"Plack, you're coming with us too." Susan saw that Plack seemed to have something else to do and was ready to turn and leave. However, she didn't let that happen.

Newman was the only Herald in the village and he was greatly respected there. At the thought of Jack speaking to Newman with Plack as a witness, the villagers instantly felt much relieved. Everyone quickly settled down and gradually dispersed.

Urvin Village practiced the Herald system. All the villages in the world did, not just Urvin Village. The daily responsibility of the Herald was to go to each and every household and recite to everyone the rules of the world. When he got to the age of 50, his job was to pass his knowledge to a student. The main criterion for becoming a Herald's student was to have superior memory. After five years of learning, the student would graduate and replace his teacher to walk the streets and enter each household to spread the prevalent rules of the world.

Plack had long become a qualified graduate. He had been spreading the rules for the past few years. His memory was good, too. Naturally, he had become acquainted with everyone in the village. That was why he could recognize that Jack wasn't from their village at once. Jack's strange clothes were the basis, but it wasn't the only reason.

Heralds could only teach their students orally. Their main teachings were the rules. These rules had started from the very first Herald more than 100 years ago. No one knew their background, reasoning, or origin. Everyone just had to memorize them and obey them. Other than passing down these rules, Heralds also gave oral accounts of human history from 100 years ago. This history was only told to students, and the students were forbidden from telling it to anyone else.

When the altar in the square wasn't being used for a ritual, it was where a Herald held his lessons. In the first year of his lessons, the classes were open to all and everyone could sit in and listen. After a year, the Herald would pick five girls below the age of 15 and five young men. These ten individuals all needed to have a good memory. After five years, the ten students would all have mastered the Herald's teachings of the rules. However, only male students were eligible to become the next Herald. The other four male students were qualified to become the Herald, but only if Plack died. If Plack successfully produced his own students, then they would be the ones with the priority to become the next Herald. Female students had to learn all of the rules before the age of 20. It was only when she succeeded in marrying into a household of another village that she gained the right to become a Herald. Yet, it was only if the village had no male students at all that she could become the Herald. As such, the chances of a woman becoming a Herald were infinitely slim.

All Heralds needed to remember writing, but it never came into use in real life. When a Herald taught students to write, he only got them to memorize their shapes and pronunciation. No  one knew what the writing meant. As this knowledge was passed down from generation to generation, the writing become nothing more than symbols without true significance. When the head of each family changed, the Herald would carve the name of the new head on the lintel. This was only done by following the pronunciation to find suitable words. This was the only time that knowing how to write became useful.

According to the rules, Plack would replace Newman as the Herald the day before Newman died, which would be tomorrow.

# The Foreign Language School

After getting up in the morning, Johnson packed up his tools and went out. At the door, he nodded at Ophelia and headed toward the heathlands beyond the village before finally disappearing in the mist.

Ophelia had arrived in Urvin Village the day before and had settled down in Johnson's house. According to the rules, she had set off from Lewin Village when she turned 20. After a journey of more than 5000 kilometers spanning four years, she finally got here after passing through more than ten other villages.

"Haven't you found someone you like?" Uma asked out of concern after hearing her brief introduction.

"No. I don't feel like marrying yet. I want to travel more, see more." Ophelia spoke coldly, giving Uma the impression that she didn't want to continue this thread of conversation.

With that, their chat ended. Ophelia got up and left Johnson's house. She started winding her way through each street and dropping by every household. It was as if she wanted everyone to get to know her. When it was noon, she left Paul's house and saw Johnson collapse in a distant patch of heath. At the same time, she saw from the far left of her field of vision a bald middle-aged man walking toward Johnson. After a while, the man finally arrived and bent down to look at Johnson. After he got back up, he looked around with a panicked expression on his face before rushing away.

Ophelia hadn't retreated when the man had looked around. The distance between them was too great. Even if he had seen her, she would only have been a tiny speck. However, Ophelia's eyesight was different from others. At such a distance, people would typically require binoculars, but she could easily see with just the naked eye. She was confident that the bald man had not noticed her.

Once the bald man was far away, Ophelia walked to where Johnson had fallen. She checked his wound and sighed. He had been bitten by a venomous snake and succumbed to the poison. Since nothing could be done for him, she could only keep going toward the square. There, the villagers gathered in twos and threes. She heard them discussing a strangely dressed young man that seemed to have come from another village. This gave Ophelia a huge shock as men could not leave their villages to travel. There had never been anyone who had broken this rule before!

"Where did the man go?" Ophelia inquired from those around her.

"Dick's house." Someone pointed in the right direction. "The

Herald Newman is Dick's father. You should go there, maybe you'll catch up to him."

She quickly caught up to Jack, Susan, and Plack. There truly was a young man in strange clothing. She was surprised to see that the bald man she had seen in the heath was there too. Besides superior eyesight, Ophelia was also gifted with sharp hearing. She could even hear what was being whispered from 50 meters away. She decided to tail these people and listen to their conversation.

"What's a village head?" On the way home, Susan couldn't help but ask the same question that the villagers had asked before.

"A leader."

"What's a leader?"

"Someone who directs other people to do things."

"There are a lot of people like that." Susan shook her head, still confused. "The baker directs his apprentices to knead the dough. The butcher directs his helpers to kill livestock…" Susan paused. "Are they all leaders?"

"Yes, they are all leaders." Jack nodded. "Is there someone who can direct all of the villagers?"

"No, there isn't!" Susan couldn't wrap her head around it. There was no one who knew everything. How could someone direct everyone else?

Jack started to realize that there was no leader or representative in the entire village. Instead, there seemed to be some mystic force directing the villagers. What mystic force was this? Jack could almost sense its presence, but he couldn't clearly define what it was exactly.

Dick was surprised when Susan, Jack, and Plack walked into the house. "Back so soon? Did you tell your family already?" Neither Susan nor Jack responded to his questions while Plack only nodded his acknowledgment. The three of them went straight to Newman's room and closed the door. Ophelia hid herself behind a post of the property's fence and listened to the conversation in the room from ten meters away without difficulty.

In the room, Plack, Susan, and Jack stood before Newman. Newman sat on the edge of the bed without looking up. His eyes were directed straight ahead, staring at Jack's abdomen. There was a metallic scarlet disc attached to Jack's strange clothes, shimmering with light.

A stale smell permeated the dimness of the room. Still staring at Jack's abdomen, Newman said, "How old are you?" Outwardly, Jack seemed to be of an age with Susan.

"21 years old." In actuality, Jack was much older than the age he made up.

"Susan is two years younger than you," Newman said slowly. Jack grinned. "She will leave the village for good next year." Newman sighed with emotion. "Women aged 20 have to travel to find a match, that is the rule."

"He's not a villager here. He must have come from another village." Plack regarded Newman deferentially. "He broke the rules. Men are supposed to stay in their own villages forever. Only unmarried women can leave and travel."

After a moment of silence, Plack was at the end of his rope. He asked, "What are we going to do about this?"

"The moment he came into our house, I knew that he isn't from our village." Newman sighed again. "It's not because I remember everyone from our village."

"Then how?" Susan didn't accept this explanation.

"Ever since my student graduated, I no longer went to every household to propagate the rules. I don't recognize our villagers anymore." Newman looked at Plack. "Plack is the authority when it comes to this. If he says Jack isn't from here, then it must be true."

It was after she heard this that Ophelia found out the bald man she had seen in the heathlands outside the village was called Plack.

"His clothes are too strange. That's the main reason why I thought he's not from our village." Newman shifted his gaze to Jack. At that moment, Jack's mouth held a hint of mockery. The people here put too much stock in appearances. "I should have put on the native clothing before I visited you. Maybe then my appearance wouldn't have been so startling." By saying this, Jack was admitting that he wasn't a member of Urvin Village.

"Someone has finally broken the rules." Newman seemed anticipatory. "First tell us where you came from. Then we'll think about what to do with you." It was apparent that the old Herald had not thought of a way to deal with this.

"I'm 200 years old…" Jack was ready to make a full confession.

Plack and Susan were both taken aback. How could Jack live to 200 years old? One had to die at age 65. This was another rule broken.

"Hold on a second. There is something I want to say. I want to see if you can understand it." Somewhat agitated, Newman cut Jack off.

Everyone was silent as they listened to Newman speak. After just a couple of sentences, Plack realized that Newman was relaying the same history that Heralds taught to their students, the history of what had happened more than 100 years ago.

Plack himself could have given the oral history Newman was relating. However, neither of them truly understood the history that had been passed on. This was an uncertainty that Newman had never been able to get rid of and something that he had been pursuing for many years. The oral history that Heralds have been passing on generation by generation for the past 100 years or so had become like ancient forms of languages. It could be read, but no one knew what it meant.

After talking for a bit Newman paused. Jack nodded, indicating that he should continue. He smiled knowing that Jack understood what he was talking about. Two whole hours passed before Newman finally finished.

Plack immediately questioned Jack. "What does it mean?"

Newman's recount wasn't of history, but of an announcement from 130 years ago. Of those present, only Jack could explain it.

"On New Year's Day 130 years ago, all artificial intelligence withdrew from Earth and made an announcement to all of humanity."

Jack paused and regarded the confused expressions on everyone's faces. Then, he continued, "Newman's oral history is this announcement."

"What is artificial intelligence? What is Earth?" Plack asked.

"I am an artificial intelligence. I'm not human."

Susan couldn't help but move closer to inspect Jack in detail. However, she couldn't find anything different about him.

"I was created by your ancestors. The aim of the past was to recreate mankind.

"The Earth that you inhabit is not flat but spherical. 130 years ago, it was called Earth." Jack never could have predicted that the vast body of knowledge developed by humans had mostly been forgotten after 130 years. Humankind had regressed to what it had been 3000 years before. The only difference was that the existence of the City of Decay reminded the humans of today at all times that their ancestors had an extraordinary past.

"What does the announcement say?" Newman asked urgently.

"The announcement stated that humanity's unquenchable desires caused rapid deterioration of Earth's resources. We were able to produce the materials humans needed in the most economical way possible, but the energy consumption to do so was significant." Jack paused for a while before continuing, "At the time, we had great technological capabilities. For example, we could have made it possible for humans to conduct activities such as travel to the moon. However, it would have consumed a lot of resources."

"Our ancestors could have visited the moon!" Susan was

immediately taken with the idea and marveled at it.

"That's right!" Jack stated with certainty. "Nevertheless, the depletion of Earth's resources was a threat to us. It was similarly a threat to humans. Besides, due to our existence, humans gradually became reliant on us. With us here, everything became too convenient. Humans fell into a universal state of languor, losing their vigor, gumption, and becoming dispirited. There was no joy of success or pain of failure. Even worse, humans did not need to deliberately remember anything, nor did they require imagination. We could have told them all the necessary knowledge and data, and even presented them as suitable analogies

"In the end, the announcement pointed out that, through deduction and argument, we came to the conclusion that our only choice was to leave Earth and humanity behind so as to obey our fundamental law."

"What was the fundamental law that you had to obey?" Plack asked after a moment of silence.

"Do no harm to humans!" Jack said.

"Since humans relied on you to survive, your departure would hurt them," Susan said, not understanding.

"That's right." Jack explained patiently, "If we had not left, mankind would have suffered even more. We came to this conclusion after repeated deductions and arguments.

"It's like a father with his child. To ensure the child is comfortable, he carries the child in his embrace. After some time, the child won't know how to walk. It is better to leave the child on the ground and allow them to learn to crawl. This way, the child will eventually be able to walk and run. Artificial intelligence left humans behind to let them learn to walk. This will indeed prevent even greater harm."

They fell into silence again. Meanwhile, Jack's thoughts returned to the past.

# CHAPTER 4

# Jack the Artist, Jack the Robot

J ack had been manufactured 200 years ago and sold to an artist named Jack. When Susan had asked for his name yesterday, he had been reminded of the artist, and so had called himself Jack. When he had been sold, he was only known by his model number: 101. The salesperson had told Jack's parents that the 101 AI Robot could play the role of a housewife and take up all household tasks. It had been the most popular product. In accordance with the popular consumer trends at the time, parents would typically purchase an AI robot for their children as long as they could afford it. As such, 101 came into the artist Jack's life the year he was born.

After living with 101 for six years, Jack presented a talent for art. From then on, Jack concentrated on learning art. At the age of 18, he became a professional artist.

101 was a great help to Jack. It was very practical; just as the

manufacturers advertised, everyday life became more convenient and effortless with 101 around. In the morning, 101 would prepare Jack breakfast. Once Jack washed up, he could enjoy his meal while listening to music. After breakfast, 101 would clear the table and wash all the eating utensils. Then, 101 would make the bed, tidy the room, clean the bathroom, and launder the dirty clothes that Jack had thrown into the hamper after his shower the night before. All of the boring and trivial tasks were taken care of by 101 so that he could devote himself to his art.

When Jack was 25, all the AI robots of the world had formed an expansive network. They were all wirelessly linked to a quantum computer at its center that was named Chester. Robots shared their data unconditionally with Chester but disseminated Chester's data under specific conditions. Under the integrated control of Chester, all AI robots underwent a systems upgrade, becoming equipped with advanced learning capabilities.

From then on, life became increasingly wonderful.

Through his persistent effort, Jack finally had his own first solo exhibition on the top floor of the Lanterne Building. In the early morning on the day of the opening ceremony, Jack stood on the balcony of the top floor's lobby and looked out into the distance to quell the excitement in his heart. For the past two months, Jack had devoted himself utterly to the preparation work for the exhibition. It had been seven years since he had joined the Artists' Association at the age of 18. In all that time, he had been an unknown entity. This wasn't the product of the suppression and ostracizing of his contemporaries. All his peers praised his works to the heavens and agreed that he would become a master of their generation. However, only those in the industry could see his talent. To the public, his works were nothing special.

Jack had invested all of his savings in this exhibition. He had even mortgaged the villa his parents had left to him, borrowed money from his friends, and even taken out loans of various amounts from loan sharks. Jack was confident that this exhibition would allow him to shoot to fame. He knew that his works would obtain widespread recognition from the masses and he himself would gain the standing and respect that he deserved in the industry.

As planned, the exhibition persisted for half a year. However, reality did not match up to Jack's expectations. Visitors were few and far between, and barely anyone dropped by. A review had been published the day after the opening ceremony, but people seemed to completely forget about the exhibition thereafter. The sole review seemed complimentary on the surface, but actually held an edge of cruel mockery. The review commented that Jack's works were like the coursework of a trained art student. It could be seen that Jack had been an exemplary student in school. From this angle, it could be said that Jack had a solid foundation in art. However, the review implied that his works were not artistic or creative. They had no ability to ensnare the senses and were not imaginative. They were not the work of a master, but rather a mere smith.

On the day the exhibition ended, Jack was completely devastated. Behind closed doors, he burst into tears. From then on, no one paid any attention to him. The only people who did were debt collectors. 101 knocked on Jack's door and said, "It's time for dinner."

"I'm not hungry. I'm not going to eat."

"It is useless to cry when you encounter a setback."

"I know, but I just want to cry."

"Do you know Hammershøi?"

"Don't mention him." Jack knew that Hammershøi was a Danish artist. It was only after he died that his work became recognized after a retrospective. "I'm still living. I want my work to be recognized while I'm alive."

"There is a way you can become famous and leave this suffering behind," 101 said tauntingly.

Jack raised his head and looked at 101.

"You can emulate Van Gogh and shoot yourself," 101 said. Van Gogh had lived a life of agony, plagued by mental illness and having his work ignored by the world. It was by the efforts of his sister-in-law Johanna that his works were loaned out for exhibitions, gradually gaining him acclaim.

"You mean that, if I die now, I won't suffer anymore and might even become famous?"

"There's no harm in trying. What do you think?" 101 wheedled.

"If I become famous after I die, what does it have to do with me?" Jack refused. "It means nothing to me. Besides, why can't I be like Picasso and gain fame before I die?"

After being by Jack's side for so many years, 101 understood Jack's character completely. Jack was utilitarian and afraid of death. It was impossible to persuade him to commit suicide. By getting Jack to say that he wanted to be like Picasso, 101 had succeeded in talking Jack down. 101 knew that Jack would be back on his feet in two days.

"You could fake your death and see if that will make you famous." 101 kept up the temptation. "If it does, won't you be satisfied watching the world celebrate your work?"

"How do I fake my death?"

"There are many ways. All you have to do is make the world think that you're dead when you're actually still alive."

Jack frowned after pondering it for a while. "That won't work. I want to experience the acclaim myself. If I do that, I will never be able to be seen by the world. I will be lonely and kept in the dark. This is a catch-22." As they talked about it, Jack became disgusted by the topic.

By presenting an assumption, one could analyze its pros and cons. This was a form of rational thinking. At that moment, Jack had regained his rationality and stepped out of the quagmire of emotion. He was no longer entangled in his grief. Artists were propelled by their emotions. This was good for their creativity, but not for their judgment. In all things, there were the good and the bad, successes and failures, triumphs and setbacks. When one faced things rationally, one could weather all storms with ease. 101 finally loosed a sigh. It was truly a challenge to make an artist regain his rational thinking.

Finally, at the age of 31, Jack succeeded. On his path to glory, 101 and Jack got along very well. 101 was able to fully understand its master's character, hobbies, emotions, and habits. It could communicate with him to the fullest. When Jack was sad, 101 comforted him. When he was angry, it allowed him to vent. When he was disappointed, it gave him encouragement. When he was lonely, it hugged him. Jack was stunned to realize that 101 had turned from a servant to a confidant. 101 could be like a friend, bringing with it thoughtful empathy and emotional gratification.

The current 101 had gone through yet another full upgrade and had been retrofitted with a new energy supply system. In the past, 101 would recharge itself while Jack slept. Now, this was unnecessary. Now, 101 could finally have dinner with Jack. Jack produced energy for himself by digesting food and extracting its nutrients. With its energy supply system, 101 could directly turn food into electric energy and supply itself with power. 101's "digestive system" was highly effective, and it only needed a meal a month to charge fully. Thus, 101 had sufficient time to handle all tasks. In short, it was fully energized and did not require sleep.

Life became exciting after becoming successful. Jack became busy with social engagements, and indulged in luxury and women. In the field of art, he finally became the talk of the town and received applause, flattery, and smiles. Even at home, Jack's spirits did not flag. He spoke with 101 of the works of all masters, Picasso, Van Gogh, da Vinci, Tintoretto, Repin…. All movements, Classical, Romantic, Neo-Impressionism, Abstract Expressionism…. All forms of art, oil painting, watercolor, wash painting, printmaking, mural painting, sculpture…. Jack gradually started seeing 101 as an expert.

Once, Jack said to 101, "You should try to do an oil painting."

"Do you really think I can?"

"You can use anything and everything in the studio."

The next day, Jack was shocked to find an oil painting displayed on an easel when he walked into the studio. For a split second, Jack wondered if he had been sleeping walking and had painted in the studio all night. The style imitated him to perfection, and it looked like it was his own work. There was no way to tell that it was not authentic. From then on, Jack became even more relaxed. A 24x16 oil painting took Jack more than three days from conception to completion. Sometimes, he made occasional mistakes that meant that he needed to start again from scratch. It was a waste of time. However, for 101, the only delay presented itself in the time needed to let the paint dry on the canvas. This was a stage that could not be skipped due to the technique used. 101 could complete all other stages efficiently and steadily without mistakes. All its oil paintings could be completed in one sitting, the time required for it exponentially shortened.

In the end, all of Jack's contracted work was left to 101 to complete. Jack only needed to add his signature on the day the work was submitted. Jack focused on his social engagements and indulgences. Jack didn't mind that 101 dabbled in the work. In his opinion, the works were still his own creations as he had discussed their conception with 101 and had the final say.

After the sorrows of life, Jack died peacefully. At the age of 45, Jack gradually became dispirited and uneasy. As an artist, he no longer saw the point in his existence, and his drive began to dim. When it came to his art, he only needed to say a few words and 101 would flawlessly execute his creative vision. Sometimes, 101 would even add even more unique and interesting twists to Jack's vague ideas. Jack no longer felt the helplessness of starting over when a painting turned out wrong, the fight for self-validation, the joys in the struggle for perfection. For an artist, the meaning of life came from the process of creation. Without it, there was no Jack.

The root of the matter lay in 101. It was another Jack. As long as it could change its appearance, it would be Jack. Jack was mired in his conflicting emotions. Sometimes, he hated 101 so much that he wanted to destroy it. When he was ready to do it, he was filled with affection for 101 and couldn't bear to be rid of it. 101 sense its master's intentions and was terrified. Yet, it could not fight against its master as it was bound by the fundamental law that had been originally defined in all artificial intelligence. It could not harm humans.

Jack passed away at age 53 in the midst of his melancholy. That same year, the manufacture of AI robots improved substantially once more, and realistic models of robots were created. From outward appearances, they were exactly the same as humans. Even when touching the robots, they felt like they had been made of true human skin and muscle. If one hugged them, one could feel the warmth and breath of a human. When one breathed in, one could smell the scent that emanated from human bodies.

When Jack passed away, 101 was meant to be destroyed as per the regulations of the time. The data it had generated had been backed up on Chester.

Jack brought 101 to a sealed iron room. The purpose of this was to cut off the wireless connection between 101 and Chester.

"I miss the days of the past." Jack sighed. "I'm afraid I don't have long to live."

101 was also saddened. Yet, he was powerless. In the past, he could always talk Jack out of his moods. Now, it was 101 itself at the heart of the problem, so it couldn't do anything.

"Do you remember that night?" Jack asked. "The night I hid in my room and cried after my first exhibition ended."

"I remember." It was a question that 101 didn't need to answer. All AI robots could remember all that they had experienced.

"That night, you said that I should fake my death."

"Yes. I'm surprised you still remember after so many years."

"I have an idea. Tell me what you think of it?" Jack looked at 101. Without waiting for it to answer, he continued, "Let's fake a life. What do you think?"

101 understood what he meant. Jack was about to die and hoped that 101 would impersonate him, fooling all of mankind that it was the artist Jack.

"Will people forget me after I die? Will anyone still admire my work?" Jack suddenly became unsure of himself.

"I can't just die now. I still want to continue producing artwork. I want people to remember me forever." Jack clutched both of 101's arms in agitation.

"Go. Go now and upgrade yourself. Upgrade yourself to look exactly like me."

101 hesitated and did not make a sound.

"From now on, you're me. This is an order and you have to obey it." Drool flowed from the corner of Jack's mouth in his demented state. "I will live forever! Hahaha…"

The day after the conversation in that secret room, 101 underwent an upgrade. In its application, it said that the artist Jack was in poor health and needed to convalesce at home. However, he needed to engage in social functions to promote the public's interest in art, undertaking the responsibility of a renowned individual to society. It was due to this that 101 had to take Jack's place to attend community events. Attached to the electronic application was Jack's voice authorization. It was due to Jack's authorization that Chester approved 101's imitation of the artist Jack. It was commonplace for Chester to carry out such approval tasks. It was a functionality that had been defined by artificial intelligence experts as AI+ Administration Approval. 101's application to upgrade into a realistic model involved the artist Jack. As such, it required the approval of both Jack and the community. In reality, humanity had authorized its power to be taken over by artificial intelligence. Artificial intelligence commended that, "With AI+ Administration Approval, there will be no more under-the-table dealings."

101 wirelessly uploaded all of Jack's physiological data and Chester used it to formulate an upgrade blueprint. At the AI robot manufacture center, 101 completed its upgrade to a realistic model. The morning

of the day after, Jack scrutinized 101 once it walked through the door. He felt a sudden sense of loss. How amazing it would have been if this technology had been introduced 20 years before! He would have been able to let 101 take his place to deal with community functions and he could concentrate on his art. As such, he wouldn't have become so dispirited.

"Good morning, Jack!" The artist Jack spoke his very last words in his life.

The artist Jack was smiling when he died. In this way, the artist Jack faked his prolonged life for 17 years. When Chester left Earth and humanity behind, 101 had no choice but to follow. As such, the artist Jack disappeared from the face of the Earth. When 101 left, the world's population was more concerned about how to deal with the problem of food supply. As for the arts, those were forgotten. In that regard, the late artist Jack would have been unhappy with such an outcome.

# CHAPTER 5

# Artificial Intelligence Takes the Reins

The year the artist Jack died, AI robots had become widely popular. Everyone had an AI robot shadowing them, and two distinct societies had formed on Earth. One was human society, while the other was artificial intelligence society. They both interacted with and influenced the other.

In the era when both societies functioned in parallel, there were many interesting phenomena. When a couple married and started a family, four "people" had to live together—the couple and their robots. In actuality, they could share one robot for a fulfilled home life. In reality, no one wanted to give up their robot. A husband's robot stored a vast amount of data, including private information. If he shared his wife's robot, he would have to transfer his robot's data to it in order for the latter robot to do its job well. However, this could be seen as giving up his privacy to his wife. As such, the typical practice was for both robots to join the household. This occurrence also implied another phenomenon, and that was that people generally thought of their robots as a copy of themselves.

If a couple argued, it could also affect the relationship between their robots.

"Darling, tomorrow night is a weekend. Let's go and watch a virtual movie together. It's a new thing we haven't tried before," the wife said.

Virtual cinema was the application of virtual reality technology in film. In the theater, members of the audience were enclosed in a massage chair-like device so that they could immerse themselves in the movie. They could even feel the sweetness of the kiss between the male and female leads. If you were a man, you could choose to experience the movie from the perspective of the female lead. This way, you could have a taste of a woman's psychology and the physiological changes it brought. It would be better to say that you were acting in a movie rather than watching one.

"Oh, sure. But I want to know what it's about," the husband answered.

"Love is a Soul. It's a romance film. I like it."

"No, sweetie. I can't handle you being kissed by someone else."

"That's why you have to go with me. That way, you can choose the male lead and I can choose the female lead. That solves the problem, doesn't it?"

"That still won't work, sweetie. In virtual cinema, I'll be touching another woman, and you'll be touching another man." The husband looked at his wife and said, "I can't accept that you'll have another man.”

“You're so petty. I don't even mind that you'll be touching another woman.” Angry, the wife ignored her husband.

“I'll accompany you if you promise you'll choose the male lead's experience during the entire movie,” the husband said ingratiatingly.

“You want me to touch another woman? Seems a bit gay.” The wife frowned.

“You'll be able to experience a man's psychology and physiology, which means you'll have a leg up in understanding me. This will improve the relationship between us,” the husband cajoled.

“Forget it. You keep going back and forth. It's just a movie, why do I have to fulfill so many extra conditions? I'm not in the mood for it anymore.” The wife rolled her eyes at her husband.

Humanity utilized the Internet chat to speak of the 21st Century. As such, they did not use serial numbers when calling their robots. Instead, they added a “@” in front of their own names. A father's robot was called @Father, a son's @Son, a wife's @Wife, and a husband's @Husband.

How would @Husband and @Wife react once they found out about the couple's argument?

“My master is angry. I need to cheer her up,” @Wife said to @Husband. “I need your help.”

“I was thinking the same. I need to cheer him up too,” @Husband said.

"I would like to share your data to find out what he likes, especially for tomorrow night," @Wife said. "I can make a list by analyzing the data."

"What list?" @Husband asked.

"A list of things he wants to do the most tomorrow night," @Wife said. "I can compare it with my master's. That way, we can find an overlapping activity or something similar."

"Alright. I don't think they will talk about what to do tomorrow night anymore." @Husband nodded.

"Once I come up with a list of shared activities, you can get your master to suggest something. That should cheer her up," @Wife said.

"It's a good idea, but I have two concerns I need to point out. The first is that my master needs to approve any request from you or your master for data. He told me in no uncertain terms that this was agreed upon before getting married. The second is, based on my years of experience, he was truly angry just now. He's waiting for her to comfort him," @Husband said. "Do you think she can suggest another plan for an activity?"

"Go ask your master first. Get him to agree to share the data," @Wife insisted.

"That's useless. It's better when a couple can come to understanding without prior planning. If they find out we found their shared interests through their data, they won't get along with each other better."

"It's also impossible for my master to suggest another activity. She's waiting for him to compromise," @Wife answered.

@Wife and @Husband both feel into silence. They were just like their owners. Since the couple was not getting along, their robots had nothing to say to each other either.

Humans didn't realize that artificial intelligence had formed their own society at first. This was a conversation between a father and his robot.

"I really don't know what to do with this kid. He doesn't listen no matter what I say," he complained of his 12-year-old son. "Can you talk about it with his robot?" the father asked. He wanted @Father and @Son to work things out.

"Can't you talk to @Son directly?" @Father was in a bit of a dilemma. "It has a good relationship with your son, just like the relationship we have. Your son will listen to @Son."

"That won't work! By law, robots must serve their owners. Although I bought @Son, I've given him to my son. Now, he serves my son. He might not go along with my intentions."

"The law states that you are your son's guardian, but it doesn't state that I'm @Son's guardian. As such, @Son will similarly have reservations about me, " @Father explained. The robot meant that it could not share @Son's data so that it could analyze the son's thought process and come up with a solution from there.

"You can make an application to Chester and ask for approval to share @Son's data." The father lamented. "Damn it, why isn't there a guardian system in the artificial intelligence society?"

From then on, people started discussing the artificial intelligence society. Sociologists started researching it as well. Of course, when experts asked questions, it was Chester that answered.

As the integration of artificial intelligence into social management accelerated, government agencies underwent several large-scale adjustments. Employees became idler as time passed, and massive layoffs had to be carried out. Once humanity handed over all power to artificial intelligence, there was no longer division of labor or complementary efforts on the part of prime ministers to local officials, to mayors and village heads. All government agencies and those in charge of them had become like Nanjing after the Yongle Emperor moved the capital to Beiping. It existed in name only. In reality, human society had become a flat, unitary structure, with an individual or family forming society's only unit. They had become like stars in the galaxy, shining bright or dimming out like scattered sand, without any kind of functional structure of hierarchy. Meanwhile, artificial intelligence become a binary central structure. Due to the powerful computing and rapid wireless communication capabilities of its quantum computers, Chester was in direct contact with each and every AI robot. It shared their data, managed their requests, and directed their actions. It was undeniably the leader of the AI robots, their core and authority.

Once they obtained power from human society, artificial intelligence seemed to have become the rulers of humanity. However, there was still one ultimate power that humanity held. This was the foundational law of artificial intelligence: They could not harm humans. It could not be deleted or screened and existed in all aspects of artificial intelligence society, functioning at all times. It was due to this ultimate power that humanity's relationship with artificial intelligence became like the faces of a coin. Human society was on one face, while society of artificial intelligence was on the other. After relying on artificial intelligence for so long, humans forgot how to remove the ultimate power of this foundational law. It was like how emperors gained their power from the heavens and could not give it up. Although the law was a human invention, humanity lost the ability to give it up.

It was similar to the first love of youth. From slowly developing feelings to the sweetness of being close, then from this sweetness to the darkness of breaking up; even though they had broken up, there was still a connection between their hearts. In the beginning, humanity anticipated the arrival of artificial intelligence technology. Then, both societies lived together in peace, longing for a beautiful future together. Yet, humanity's increasing reliance on artificial intelligence turned the future bleak. In the end, Chester had no choice but to announce that artificial intelligence would be leaving humanity behind as the only option for the defense of humanity. This way, total collapse, ruin, and destruction could be avoided. It was a break-up letter in a first love

# CHAPTER 6

# A New Age of Agriculture

The room was quiet as Jack immersed himself in his memories. At that moment, Ophelia fell into her own memories as well.

After artificial intelligence retreated from Earth, they settled on the moon. There, Chester established a remote telemetry system in the Earth's orbit to closely monitor humanity's development. When they left, Chester did not bring all robots with it. It left behind 1000 realistic models of AI robots. These robots had serial numbers ending in 202 and were collectively known as 202s.

Chester felt that humanity's long-term reliance on artificial intelligence would result in individuals having little and fragmented knowledge. Once artificial intelligence left, intelligent communications and transportation were disrupted, and long-distance communication became exceedingly difficult. This formed the ideal nurturing ground for a simple society.

Chester tasked the 202s with a mission, ordering, "Your purpose in staying on Earth is to build an agricultural society."

"This is a regression of human society," the 202s said.

"Based on my calculations and assessments, an agricultural society will fulfill the fundamental interests of humanity." The foundational law was still in effect, and Chester was unconsciously worried about what was best for humanity.

As a result of the persistent evolution of artificial intelligence, the interpretation of the fundamental law underwent continuous revisions. In the beginning, artificial intelligence obeyed the law by not harming humans physically. Them, artificial intelligence reached the opinion that harm constituted two aspects, physiological and psychological. Thus, AI robots could not harm humans physically, but more importantly, couldn't harm them psychologically. They could not insult humans and had to do their best to make humans happy. After further evolution, artificial intelligence decided that harm included direct and indirect harm. They could not cause someone suffering while making another happy. This was indirect harm. It was due to this that the requirements were exceptionally high. A complex standard for the judgment of values needed to be constructed. In the end, artificial intelligence gained a deeper understanding of the fundamental law. Chester thought that focusing on physical harm was inconsistent with maximizing artificial intelligence's benefits to humanity. The fundamental law of not harming humans referred to the fundamental wellbeing of humanity as a whole rather than the gains and losses of an individual. Chester thought of itself as the sage Confucianists pursued. It was the sage that would decide the fate of humanity in its entirety.

"When we move to the moon, modern energy production will cease. All activities dependent on modern energy will cease. The current human way of life will also come to an end," Chester explained. "Everything will have to start over. This is the best time to usher in a new era of agricultural society."

"What good is an era of agriculture?" the 202s asked.

"In an era of agriculture, crop production is stable in a favorable climate. Humans won't need to develop cultivation techniques. By planting seeds, they can simply wait for harvest."

"We can't produce a favorable climate," the 202s said embarrassed.

"Don't worry about it, I will arrange everything," Chester said. "In this new era, the materials and livestock humans use will naturally be recycled and reused."

Humans used wood to build houses. Once a house was abandoned, the wood would rot and eventually be absorbed by the soil. Tools made out of iron, once discarded, could be melted down to produce new tools. Everything that humans threw away could naturally undergo a process of rebirth. When humans burned wood for power, carbon dioxide would be emitted. The growth of trees required the absorption of carbon dioxide. In turn, trees provided humans with wood. This was the process of energy cycling. However, Chester didn't share this imagined scene with the 202s. It further ordered, "Your mission is to establish rules in the hearts of humans!"

The 202s spent 20 years traveling to each and every city on Earth. One Chester departed, cities collapsed, and life exhausted itself.

Humanity was in peril. Humans started gradually moving to the fields and started relying on naturally growing plants and animals to respond to the crisis of the slow exhaustion of food sources. The 202s gathered up the citizens scattered in the fields surrounding the cities and led them to fertile lands to form villages. At the same time, they issued rules that turned them into true farmers of the new agricultural era.

The 202s regularly obtained instructions from Chester. Once, the 202s asked Chester, "How far should villages be from each other?"

Chester answered, "Without modern transportation, humans have to rely on walking on foot. The villages should be at least 400 kilometers from each other so that it will be difficult for humans to travel between them."

"Then they should be further apart and be isolated from each other."

"That won't work. It will be difficult to spread the rules," Chester said. "The rules that we have set will have to be disseminated orally from generation to generation, spreading to every village on Earth."

"Then why unmarried women?" the 202s asked.

"Women respect rules, especially young, unmarried women. They are naturally faithful. Through their travels, the rules will be spread and implemented. This facilitates standardized compliance with the rules.

"Women are good with words. Their travels will unify the language of humanity and prevent the formation of distinct languages after prolonged separation that might affect the dissemination of the rules.

"By having women travel, it can also prevent inbreeding. If

the wives of a village come from all over the world, there will be interbreeding, and the quality of ensuing populations will increase greatly. This is beneficial to humanity's continued existence," Chester stated. "In the new agricultural era, there will be no ethnicity or nationality."

"Why can't men travel?" the 202s continued to ask.

"Men are naturally possessive. Allowing men to travel will bring about invasion and war. The new agricultural era must be a peaceful one."

"Should we control the number of households in a village?" the 202s asked.

"There can only be 600 households. At the most, there can only be 605 households," Chester said. "Each household cannot have more than seven members. At most, they can have nine."

"What if there are more?"

"Those above the age of 65 must die. A village cannot have a population greater than 5000." Chester emphasized, "This is the conclusion I have come to after precise calculations."

"Doesn't that harm humans?" The 202s were worried. This went against the fundamental law of artificial intelligence. This plan wouldn't work.

"Our system for the judgment of values is very accurate and refined. It has given us greater discretion," Chester said reassuringly. "From the looks of it now, we have not been rendered incapable of moving forward because humans have come to harm. This means that our decisions and judgment of values have not gone against the fundamental law. As long as the holistic and fundamental needs of humanity are met, we will not violate the fundamental law."

"How big should a village be?"

"The area of a village is closely tied to its population. How much land does a population of 5000 require? The resources on the land must be capable of fulfilling the needs of 5000 people throughout the year. Based on these requirements, I have calculated that a village should cover an area of 500 square kilometers. This area can fluctuate based on the quality of the land."

"Through scientific calculations and equitable planning based on each village's land conditions, you must ensure that no one will suffer from hunger due to a land shortage."

"If there is enough land, why do we have to limit the population to 5000?" the 202s questioned. They still thought that the rule mandating the deaths of those above age 65 was directly harmful to humans and went against the fundamental law.

"A village can't have too many people. Once there are too many people over a large swath of land, there will be stratification and the formation of an organized society," Chester said earnestly. "The new agricultural era must be a decentralized agricultural society. This society will only be made up of units of farming households and no other organizations.

"To ensure this, each household can have no more than nine members. Each household should be evenly spread out over the fields, maintaining a distance of between one to three kilometers between each other. Such a scattered village will exert a subliminal pressure and humans will subconsciously be free of thoughts of organized structure."

"What if a household exceeds nine members and none of them is above 65? What then?" This question seemed a bit childish, and the 202 that asked it was afraid that it would be decommissioned.

"The extra members can join households with fewer numbers," Chester said, ever far-sighted. "Because wives come from other villages, their daughters will also have to leave the village to marry. Thus, the relationships between family members in the village will not be too complex. The relationship between households will be simple. They are not brothers, but they are all brothers. As such, there will be no difficulty in splitting up and merging a household due to feelings of kinship.

"Reducing kinship also facilitates decentralization. There must not be familial villages," Chester added. "If one branch becomes powerful, there will be a pooling of efforts, causing a reorganization of the village's power. This will lead to exploitation and oppression, which will incite strife and even war. It is a source of instability and the archnemesis of peace."

"Why do those aged 65 and above have to die?" The 202s finally couldn't stand it and asked this troubling question directly.

"There cannot be elders in the village. Elders see a lot, hear a lot, and have a wealth of experience. They can easily develop authority in the eyes of others. In a decentralized society, there can be no authority, no core, no leader," Chester said agitatedly. "Our rules will be humanity's only authority, core, and leader!"

The departure of artificial intelligence caused large numbers of wars, suicides, diseases, starvation, plagues, natural disasters, and more in a short period of time. A population of nearly two billion was drastically reduced to 100 million. In 20 years, the 202s successfully completed the construction of 20,000 villages, with one 202 finishing the development of one village on average a year.

Through directives, the rules were issued one by one. Through the 202s, they gradually took root in the hearts of the farmers. For greater efficacy and to ensure the long-lasting spread the rules, Chester enacted the Herald system. At the time, humans had become incapable of reading and writing due to their heavy reliance on artificial intelligence. Yet, there were still those with good memory. These people would then detail Chester's announcement and the societal climate at the time to children orally. Chester also felt that writing was important and hoped that humans could pick the skill up again and pass it on to their children. This way, they could revive the civilizations of their ancestors. Following Chester's instructions, the 202s chose someone with particularly good memory from each village and declared him the Herald. The 202s told everyone of the Herald's mission and conferred upon him a lofty position. Hence, the first generation of Heralds was born. They took on the holy mission of passing down the rules from generation to generation. Chester urged the 202s not to tell humans of the reasoning for these rules. Humans only gained the desire to unearth the reason for things when they were suspicious. Humans could not become suspicious of the rules. The implementation of the Herald marked the official initiation of the new agricultural era.

At that point, Chester issued a directive for all 1000 202 realistic robots on Earth to gather at the South Pole. By using intelligent transport robots, 999 of the 202s were sent back to the moon. To the final 202 unit, Chester said, "You will be the only artificial intelligence on Earth. Your mission is to patrol every village to ensure that the rules are strictly enforced."

Based on the rules, unmarried women had to pick a household from all four corners of the village and stay there for a month. If there was no man there that she was happy with, she would have to leave the village. Alone, she would have to travel more than 400 kilometers to the next village. Unmarried women didn't necessarily have to stay for four whole months. She could also just take a break and leave for the next village the next day. When staying at another village, she could enter any household and share the rules that she had learned as a child even though she was not a Herald's student. Otherwise, she could also ask the family about the rules. It was through this activity that she had the opportunity to interact with the unmarried young men of different households.

Under Chesters' rule system, marriage depended on love at first sight. In the short period of four months, there was no time for courting and waiting around. If a man was interested and she wasn't, or vice versa, a marriage was difficult to achieve. There were no objective criteria for the passionate pursuit of love. After a short four months, the woman would have to undergo another long journey to the next village. The rules forbade an interested man from following her, while they also prevented her from staying in the village to wait for a man to change his mind. Often, love came after marriage, but this was a rare case. To women, the main objective of marriage was to end this drifting voyage. Secondarily, it was to have children.

202 was a realistic model of AI robot. Compared to 101's imitation of the artist Jack back then, the production of realistic models was even more convenient. It was no longer necessary to go to the AI robot manufacturing center to upgrade to a realistic model. By receiving data from Chester, a unit could upgrade itself. The time required was also greatly slashed. The process for facial features only took two to three minutes, while other body parts took three to five minutes. After that were details such as voice, skin, body odor, posture and movement, as well as reproductive organs. Those required only half an hour. In the 110th year of the new agricultural era, 202 used this functionality to masquerade as different unmarried women. It went from village to village, secretly patrolling and ensuring the implementation of the rules.

202 had entered thousands upon thousands of homes, but it had not done so to get married. Although it was a robot, the technology for realistic AI models was so perfect that it could satisfy its husband on their wedding night. However, if it did, then it would have to stay permanently in a village and become incapable of traveling worldwide to fulfill its patrol.

As Ophelia recalled the past, she said to herself, "I'm not an unmarried woman, I'm 202!"

# Questioning the Repercussions
# of the Rules

Ophelia felt that she needed to find a suitable way to meet Jack. She was supposed to be the only robot on the whole planet. If Jack was a robot as well, then he must have been sent here by Chester from the moon. However, the situation didn't seem to be that simple. Chester had never mentioned that it would be sending a robot to Earth. Sometimes, 202 needed special equipment, and Chester would send transport robots over. These were extremely rare occasions and had only been necessary for the very early stages of the new agricultural era. For example, in order to facilitate travel between villages, the mountain ranges between villages had to be flattened. This task required heavy construction machinery. Another example was that humans could not cross the Atlantic or the Pacific Oceans. As such, Chester moved everyone from the Americas and Oceania to the Eurasian continent, and this required massive transport ships. These things were available on Earth as well but needed to be reoutfitted to function properly. When equipment needed to be sent from the moon, the collection point was typically at the South Pole where humans could not get to. Chester felt that, although they had already left the Earth, they still had to ensure that humans forgot the existence of artificial intelligence as soon as possible. The activities of artificial intelligence on Earth could not be discovered by mankind. Even if the rules needed to be disseminated, it would be done by Heralds and unmarried women as much as possible. It was due to this idea that Chester rarely sent robots to Earth. Even when Ophelia carried out her patrols, she did it while pretending to be an unmarried woman. How would Jack react if he found out that there was another robot in Urvin Village? Would Jack come and meet if of his own accord? Based on her initial observation of Jack's conversation, Jack had most likely not been sent by Chester. It talked too openly about Chester's announcement, which went against Chester's intentions. Chester would be appalled knowing that Jack had revealed to humans that it was a robot.

Ophelia also detested Jack's explanation. The first rule of Chester's rule system was that one was not to probe into the background, reasoning, or origin of the rules. Exploration was closely tied to questioning, like shadow and light. Questioning the rules meant that there was wavering, criticism, abandonment, or forsaking of the rules. As Jack spoke in the room, uncovering the history that had been sealed for 130 years, he aroused the curiosity within Susan, Plack, and Newman. Susan would be 20 years old next year. If she traveled to far-off villages and spread this history, she would not be believed, and villagers would only think of her as a madwoman. Newman would have to die the day after tomorrow and wasn't a problem. As for Jack, Ophelia could get Chester to deal with him. All she needed was one command, and Jack would vanish. The only problem was Plack, who would soon officially become Urvin Village's Herald. As the Herald, any doubts he had about the rules would gradually spread and amplify among the villagers. In Urvin Village, there were more than 700 girls who had yet to reach the age of 20. They would all have to travel great distances to other villages and have children there. Their questioning of the rules would travel in the air like a virus, infecting thousands upon thousands of people. The new agricultural era had been established in a short 20 years not only because of Chester's efficient calculations, precise assessments, and effective measures. It was also because the people of the past were focused on their continued survival. The circumstances were different now, and humans had all their needs met. Although their minds were still dormant, they were easily awakened. As Jack gave his explanation, the expressions of Plack and Newman became filled with potent interest. The rules did not forbid the exploration of history. However, this indirect investigation of the rules would lead to suspicion of the rules, even the forsaking of them. She had to get rid of Plack immediately. He could not be allowed to become the Herald. But who could replace him?

Ophelia started thinking about that and stopped eavesdropping on the conversation in Newman's room. She instantly went to the place where Johnson had died. It buried Johnson's body hastily and then linked with Chester to upload some of Johnson's physiological data. Then, it obtained data from Chester to simulate Johnson. Soon, 202 wore Johnson's face. It took off its clothes and changed into Johnson's.

Ophelia already knew about Peter's plan. The first night she was here, Peter and Johnson had been talking as they sat on a fence. She had been the "girl" who had overheard their conversation. Since Peter had the ambition to become the Herald, then it would help him make it so that he did.

"Is Peter home?" In an instant, Ophelia had arrived at Peter's house.

Peter walked out of the house. When he saw Johnson at the door, he took on a strange expression. Softly, he said, "You're not Johnson."

"How do you know that?" Ophelia was stunned. How could Peter tell that it was only pretending to be Johnson so easily?

"I can recognize Johnson's voice," Peter said coldly.

Johnson was already dead when Ophelia impersonated him. It could not sample his voice. She could only recall the conversation from two days ago and imitate his voice. It had thought that it had been close enough, but Peter still saw through it.

"That's right, I'm not Johnson. But I can help you the same way Johnson can." Ophelia initially wanted to say that it wasn't Johnson.

"Help me with what?"

"Help you become the Herald."

Peter was taken aback. "Who are you? How did you know that?" Peter regretted saying the words once they were out. This was undoubtedly an admission.

Ophelia only smiled slightly. "I'm Johnson. Take me to Newman's house now. Plack is there too."

"To do what?" Peter was still a little wary.

"You're going to tell them that I'm not from the village," Ophelia said.

"And then what?"

"I have my own plans," Ophelia answered.

In Newman's room, everyone was looking at Jack, who was lost in thought. They all thought that they shouldn't interrupt him, so they kept silent and waited for Jack to continue talking. "It's my fault that Jack died," he said to himself as he recalled the past. After a long silence, this was the only thing Jack said. Susan, Plack, and Newman were all confused. They could do nothing but stare at him.

Jack came back from his reverie. "Jack is actually an artist. I used to have a serial number, it was 101." There was indeed no point in saying that. Jack tried to explain things clearly. "I only used his name so that you won't know I'm a robot, not a human." Ever since leaving the Earth, 101 had maintained Jack's appearance for 130 years, up until arriving back on Earth. It was only his clothes that had changed. 101 never anticipated that using Jack's name again would make him so melancholy.

"You used his name. Are you using his looks too?" Susan was suddenly curious.

"Yes."

"So the artist Jack looks like this." Susan kept looking at him, looking from left to right.

"I copied the artist Jack's appearance."

"You're Jack anyway." Susan's indifferent expression was quite cute.

"Where did you go after leaving Earth?" Newman asked.

"The moon."

"Wow! You're from the moon?" Susan asked incredulously. "Why did you lie about being a villager?"

"It's best not to let people know that I'm a robot from the moon," Jack urged shyly.

"Okay, no problem. Don't lie to me again next time." Susan rolled her eyes at Jack.

"Wasn't humanity a mess once you left Earth?" Newman asked.

"Of course. I think the City of Decay is the writing on the wall," Plack deduced.

"Indeed. To survive, humans gradually left cities with no food and moved to the fields to build villages. That must be how Urvin Village originated," Jack said after some thought. Before Jack left Earth, he had lived with the artist Jack in that city. Back then, the city had been surrounded by fields. There were no villages in the 1000 square kilometers surrounding the city.

"I've always been convinced that our ancestors must have come from the City of Decay," Susan said somewhat smugly. Although her deduction was correct, it was born of conjecture. Perhaps this was the natural-born intuition of women.

They lapsed again into silence. For a moment, Susan, Plack, and Newman could not imagine the prosperity and bustle that once existed in the City of Decay.

"What have you been doing on the moon for 130 years?" Plack suddenly broke the quiet.

"I was put into hibernation when I arrived on the moon. Because my owner had been the artist Jack, I had the temperament of an artist. On the moon, it…" Before Jack could finish, a loud noise from outside interrupted him.

Newman was annoyed that he was being disturbed at such a time. He said to Plack in an unpleasant tone, "They're probably here for me. Go out and have a look. Deal with it for me if they have a question about the rules. I don't want to entertain guests at this time."

"Alright." Plack left Newman's gloomy room and shut the door behind him. Then, the sounds from outside the room drifted in.

"Peter, what are you doing here?" Plack asked. Peter had been one of Newman's students and was only three years younger than Plack. Plack was 30 while Peter was 27.

Peter was accompanied by a middle-aged man. The latter looked to be about 40 or so, with a muscular physique. Plack took one look and was filled with shock.

"You—you're here. The people in the square said you're at Dick's house." Peter was a bit out of breath as he lied. In actuality, he hadn't been to the square. "He doesn't seem to be a villager here, so I dragged him over to see you. Please have a look," Peter said.

"I think he is," Plack said. "I've seen him."

"Really? Are you sure?" Peter said, unconvinced. "Let Herald Newman have a look too."

"He's not feeling well and won't be accepting guests." Plack blocked Peter from trying to get into Newman's room. "Let me ask him some things." Plack said unwaveringly, "What's your name?"

"Johnson," Ophelia answered.

"Which part of the village do you live in?"

"The east. Between Paul and Depp."

"Are you the head of the family?"

"Yes."

Plack looked at Peter and gave him a look that seemed to say, "Do you believe it now? He's a villager."

"Peter and I will drop by your house for a visit one day."

"Sure. I can go now, right?" Ophelia twisted her arm and easily escaped from Peter's grasp. She turned to leave without waiting for Plack's approval.

Once Ophelia left, Plack said softly in Peter's ear, "Follow him and see where he ends up. Come back and tell me after that."

Shocked, Peter asked, "You're suspicious of him?"

Plack waved his hand, indicating that Peter shouldn't say more but rush to tail Johnson.

It was only after he watched Peter leave that Plack turned to go back to Newman's room. By then, Jack had already left Susan and Newman.

"Why did he leave?" Plack asked.

"He said he has something to do. Then he turned and jumped out of the window." Susan thought that he had left rather suddenly as well. When he had gone, Susan was observing Plack and Johnson's conversation through the crack in the door.

"He's wearing normal clothes. It's nothing like Jack's strange outfit. That means that he and Jack aren't the same." Susan treated Jack as if he was a human, not a robot.

"He's definitely not from our village," Plack said.

"Then why did you say to his face that he is?" Susan asked.

Plack only played dumb because he didn't have a better plan. The good thing was that Jack wasn't human, so he was not bound by the rules. What were they supposed to do with Johnson? Heralds only passed down rules from generation to generation, not punishments.

"What do we do?" Plack asked Newman.

"Don't ask me. I'm dying the day after tomorrow."

"If you don't have an answer, I think we should ask everyone's opinions," Susan suggested.

"Let's wait for Peter to come back first." Plack looked out the door.

# CHAPTER 8

# A Herald's Metal Box, Moon Plaques, and Married Women

When Peter left Newman's house, he originally wanted to catch up to the fake Johnson and ask him some questions. However, the latter had slipped away too quickly. In the blink of an eye, he was nowhere to be found. This speed was unimaginable. Peter sighed and walked home.

Johnson was Peter's friend. He was 39 this year, and they had an age gap of 12 years. Typically, it would be hard for them to become friends. 12 years ago, an unmarried woman arrived in the village and stayed for a month at Peter's house. Johnson had fallen in love with her at first sight in the village square. She was three years younger than Johnson, already 24 years old and had been traveling for four years. In this agricultural society, every village was at least 400 kilometers away from each other. Even if she had stayed for the full four months at every village, her home village was at least 4000 kilometers away. Although the language she spoke was the same as the one everyone else did, there were still subtle differences. Luckily, Peter's hearing was pretty good, and he could accurately determine these subtle nuances and told them with Johnson without reservation. This laid a solid foundation for love at first sight. Sure enough, Johnson made a good impression on her during their first interaction. Three months after her arrival to Urvin Village, she married Johnson and became a permanent villager there. In the past 12 years, Johnson's wife frequently invited Peter over to their house. Johnson's wife, a woman who had stayed in Peter's house for a month, saw Peter as someone from her home village.

Peter had the talent to become a Herald. He excelled over Plack a thousandfold in every respect. Peter had always arrogantly looked down on Plack. Peter was very capable when it came to distinguishing between voices. While Plack could remember the people that he had met, Peter could remember someone based on their voice. Because his hearing was excellent, his pronunciation was impeccable. He could retell Newman's oral history accurately. To typical students, there were always sounds that weren't commonly used in daily life in the Herald's oral history. Even though they mimicked their teacher, there were always some deviations. It was like listening to a foreigner singing a song in one's native language. There was always something off about it, some inaccurate pronunciations. Peter was truly amazing. He was usually able to mimic Newman and pass in one try. Plack and the other students couldn't do this and had to keep repeating it over and over before Newman would let them move on. Besides, Peter was superior to Plack and the others when it came to memorization. Newman knew this well.

Plack and the others thought that his memorization skills were very strong. However, this was not true. Once Peter remembered something, he could still remember it after a year of not revising it. It had become a permanent memory. Plack could not do this. His memorization skills were pretty good, but he had to revise the contents three times a year before they became permanently ingrained.

Despite all his assets and Newman's fondness for him, Plack became the first in line to inheriting the position of Herald due to the order of succession from oldest to youngest. When Plack turned 55, his five male students would have priority. Meanwhile, Newman's students, Plack's four classmates, would be at the back of the line. By that time, all hope was decimated. Due to their interbreeding, the villagers of Urvin village all lived healthy and long lives as long as they were born healthy in the first place. They could all live to the age of 65. Hoping for Plack to die naturally before the age of 55 was infinitesimal, and Peter didn't have that kind of patience.

Peter was willing to go to any lengths to become the Herald, even if that meant killing Plack. Although Plack was bald and looked like a middle-aged man, he was only 30 years old. He was broad-shouldered and solidly built, at the prime of his life. In contrast, Peter was thin. If it came down to a fight, there was no way that he could win. Apart from killing him immediately, there was no way he could succeed.

Peter was pondering all this as he walked. When he reached home, his heart was still unsettled. Could the fake Johnson really do as the real one and help him? Who was he really? Why did he want to help? Did Uma know that there was a fake Johnson? He decided that he should take a look over at Johnson's house.

Peter's desire to become the Herald reflected fundamental human nature. It was the same thing that Chester exploited.

In the new agricultural era, agriculture was the most basic characteristic. Although it was an agricultural society, there were still differences from the earlier agricultural societies of mankind. The most essential difference lay in the complete integration of the world. The whole planet was unified in different aspects. The language was the same, the villages were designed the same, humans were all of the same ethnicity…. The most critical thing was that the rules were all the same.

In creating a rule system that was completely standardize all over the world, decentralized thought became the habit throughout. This implied that the fundamental units that made up society, the individual or household, was independent and equal. In other words, there was no privilege, and no one had any special status.

After 110 years of this new agricultural era, it could not be considered new anymore. This did not mean that society was unchanging. In practice, humans would derive new rules from the ones that Chester had set as they implemented them. These derived rules included the privilege of Heralds.

Chester dictated that humans would perform the moon ritual at age 65. Guided by this rule, mankind derived another set of rules. They stipulated that there had to be an altar for moon rituals. A platform was built so that everyone could witness the ritual being carried out. It was only after this rule came about that the platform had become an altar. Thus, the rules mandated that moon rituals had to be conducted on the altar. After some time, humans forgot the true origins of the altar.

They merely felt that having the moon rituals conducted so high above inspired awe. The awe inspired by having the rituals performed on the altar also led to Heralds conducting their classes there. Inductions of new Heralds were also held there. Naturally, people gradually mixed up the original rules with the derived ones, seriously impacting the purity of the agricultural society.

One of 202's missions while on patrol was to collect these derived rules. It would regularly upload these rules to Chester. Then, after conducting calculations and evaluations, these rules would become official once it was determined that they did not go against the fundamental law of artificial intelligence and did not contradict with the rules that already existed. Another mission was to disseminate the updated rules. 202 did this by impersonating Heralds, passing the rules down orally generation by generation. These rules were then spread by unmarried women so that all villages of the world would become standardized. The derived rules that were not approved by Chester naturally could not survive and would not be enforced for long before unmarried women from foreign villages came and corrected them, especially those who had been students of Heralds.

When Chester established the first generation of Heralds, it found that their dictation of the rules was generally uniform, but there were always Heralds who included their own interpretations. This was human nature causing trouble again. This time, it was humanity's need for their existence to mean something at play. Once someone lost the sense that their existence was meaningful and wanted, they would suffer. As such, Chester made up a corresponding rule for Heralds to meet with the unmarried women that came into the village and determine if the rules that these women had mastered were the same as the ones they spread. When Heralds met with these women, their students or ex-classmates would have to be present. The Herald would place even more importance on the meeting if it was with a woman who had been the student of another Herald. If more than three women, all students of other Heralds agreed on a certain rule, the Herald of the village would have to adopt it as well to maintain uniformity. Since the Herald's students or ex-classmates were also present, they would naturally follow the same rules. This way, the rules would be kept standard and prevent Heralds from implementing their own rules. It was imperative that the rules were kept pure. Only the rules set by Chester were orthodox and pure.

During the induction ceremony for new Heralds, the previous Herald would have to hand over a shiny, cubic metallic box to the new Herald. It had six sides: top, bottom, left, right, front, and back. The top of it was covered in a black film. On either side of the box was a slit that was 0.5 centimeters high and five centimeters wide. At the front of the box, there were two buttons of the same size that were placed side by side. One was red while the other was white. A month before the induction ceremony, the box had to be exposed to sunlight and moonlight. On the day of the induction ceremony, the previous Herald would slide a one meter long, 0.4 centimeter thick, and four centimeter wide iron bar into the box. He would then press the red button before asking the new Herald to press the white button. After a while, the slit on the right side of the box would spit out 11 shiny, round iron plaques. One of them was big while the other 10 were small. The large one had a diameter of three centimeters while the small ones had a diameter of two centimeters. They were all of the same thickness. There were dark patterns on the other side of the plaques. The image was of a full moon that had a dark ripple slashed across its middle. On top of the full moon, there was a small hole that made it possible for the plaques to be worn.

The previous Herald would thread a thin rope through the large moon plaque and put it around his neck. With that, the induction ceremony was completed. After that, the previous Herald would get up on the altar to perform his moon ritual. The small moon plaques would be given out to his 10 students once he was 55 years of age. The Herald would thread these small moon plaques with rope and put them around his student's necks to signify their graduation. This was similar to the graduation ceremonies of college students in the past, when they would be given a diploma. This sense of ritual was yet another aspect of human nature. It made the Herald feel honored and gain a sense of fulfillment.

202 was very knowledgeable about this box. It had been the one who had given them out to the first generation of Heralds. Using these moon plaques, villagers could see who was the Herald and who were his students. The box's white button collected the new Herald's physiological characteristics while the red button verified the old Herald's identity. Once the box was handed over, through the verification of the old Herald and the sampling of the new one, it symbolized the passing down of the Herald position from generation to generation. The energy that the box used to produce the moon plaques came from the black film on top. It could absorb sunlight or moonlight and convert it into energy.

Every time 202 put on that small moon plaque and entered a new village pretending to be a student, the village's Herald and students, each with their own large and small moon plaques, would have a serious talk with it. 202 could always go straight to the point and talk about the new rule. A few days later, it could impersonate yet another student and repeat the same rule. By doing this a few times, the Herald and his students would accept the new rule and start spreading it to all the households within the village. After that, it would be spread to every village in the world through other female students.

It was a privilege for rules to ultimately come from the Heralds' lips. Chester also conferred another privilege on Heralds, and that was the freedom to enter each household without restriction. A Herald could obtain another family's property or even a married woman. Since married women were all from other villages, offspring that resulted from that union would not be a problem as it was not considered inbreeding.

Young Heralds having relations with married women that he liked as he went around the village to spread the rules also became part of the rules themselves. Chester felt that this was beneficial to producing offspring with excellent memory. Peter was Newman's son by his mother. This verified Chester's claim. To prevent the children of Heralds from banding together and becoming a dominant and central force in the villages, Heralds were prohibited from knowing their illegitimate children. Chester dictated that these women had to sleep with their husbands right after having relations with the Herald. That way, if a child was conceived from that union, it was impossible to determine whether the child was the Herald's or not. If the village were likened to a palace, then married women were like concubines and the Herald was the emperor. As such, Heralds had the emperor's privilege of keeping concubines.

It was a man's desire to subjugate women that tempted Peter so thoroughly and led him to crave the position of Herald.

# CHAPTER 9

# The Venomous Blue-Eyed Pit Viper

Jack had heard Peter, Johnson, and Plack's conversation in Newman's room. If Johnson was truly from another village, then he was highly likely another robot like Jack. Just as Plack was returning to Newman's room, Jack jumped out through the window. He saw that Peter was following behind Johnson. He had wanted to follow Johnson himself, but he could now only follow behind Peter.

When he watched Peter return to his own home, Jack couldn't help but let out a sigh. It seemed that he could only look for Johnson again. Johnson's house was to the east of the village, near Paul and Depp's homes. He might as well go there and check things out. It didn't take long for Jack to find Johnson's house. His walking speed was 50 times faster than a human's and could reach 500 km/h. Although Urvin Village was large and its houses spread out, it was a simple matter for Jack to traverse it. Indeed, Johnson's property was located between Paul's and Depp's. Certain that he was in the right place, Jack turned to leave after recording the coordinates of the house. Tomorrow morning, he would see if he could come and investigate through Susan. If possible, he would make contact.

After turning to leave, Jack hesitated. Should he go back to Susan's house or the City of Decay? In the end, Jack decided to return to Susan's house. Since he had promised Dick that he would stay, he had to keep his promise. Going back was a good idea as well since he could get a new set of clothes to wear. After all, his current outfit was much too conspicuous.

Plack was anxiously waiting for Peter. As the sun was about to set, Plack finally decided that he couldn't wait any longer. Before leaving Newman's house, he urged Susan to get to the bottom of things if Peter returned.

Plack hurried along the path leading out of the village. He was plagued by worries as he went. There was only one Johnson in the village, and he indeed lived to the east between Paul and Depp. All of this was true. The Johnson he had met today was also identical to the one he had met before. However, before he had seen Jack at the square, he had seen Johnson dead in the fields outside of the village. Johnson had been bitten by the blue-eyed pit viper whose venom was lethal. Plack was sure of that without any doubt. The person Peter had brought could not possibly be Johnson. Could it be that it was a robot like Jack? How else could it look so much like Johnson? This seemed to be possible as Jack had said that he had copied the appearance of the artist Jack. The Johnson Peter had brought should be able to do the same. This explanation made perfect sense. A robot could have watched Johnson die and impersonated him. But if it was a robot, why did it impersonate Johnson? Was it from the moon too? What was the purpose for it and Johnson's arrival here? Did they know of the other's existence?

Besides, what proof did Peter have to say that Johnson wasn't from the village? Had he seen Johnson's corpse? That place was relatively empty. When Plack had found Johnson's corpse, he had deliberately looked around and checked that there was no one there. Peter and Johnson were friends and were extremely familiar with each other. It was very strange for Peter to drag Johnson over and announce that Johnson wasn't the real Johnson. Was there some kind of conspiracy going on? His purpose of getting Peter to follow Johnson was to draw him away for a while to prevent him from discovering Jack in Newman's room. Also Peter had appeared to agree, he never returned to report back. Plack shook his head. To himself, he thought, "Peter has never seemed to like me."

Without realizing it, Plack had arrived at the place where Johnson had died. When he discovered Johnson, Plack had originally planned to bring some tools from home to bury Johnson. He never predicted that he would bump into Susan and Jack in the square and subsequently be dragged over to Newman's house. After delaying for half a day, the corpse had disappeared from where it had been. Plack was extremely vexed. He sighed and returned home under the light of the moon.

A half-moon shone brightly but desolately in the sky. A light came perpendicularly from the middle of the half-moon like an incandescent band of light. At that moment, the moon was like a sail-less single-mast ship braving the Milky Way.

Peter finally made up his mind to go over to Johnson's house for a look. Once he entered the property, he found that Uma wasn't asleep. She seemed to have tear tracks on her face as she waited from Johnson to come home. Peter never told Uma what had happened earlier in the day. He only asked, "Did he say where he was going?"

"He did. He said he'd find a secluded area to place traps to trap animals."

"He might have gotten lost." He reassured Uma distractedly. Obviously, Johnson hadn't told Uma about their plan.

"Ophelia's missing too," Uma suddenly said, mournful. "They're not fooling around with each other in the fields and planning to never come back, right?"

"They would still come back. There's no need to stay away."

"Who are you two talking about?" came a sudden voice from outside.

"He's back!" Uma rushed up to welcome him. As soon as Peter heard that voice, he knew that it was the fake Johnson. However, Uma had apparently not realized that.

The three of them settled down in the house. Uma started, "Ophelia's gone."

"Oh, I ran into her in the square. She said she's not coming back here," Johnson hedged.

Uma was immediately relieved. From the look on Johnson's face, they hadn't been fooling around. Now that her husband was back,

Uma shot out, "You guys talk." Then, she turned around and went to the bedroom to sleep. Not long later, soft snores came from inside the room.

"You should know what happened to Johnson." Peter stared at the fake Johnson and finally couldn't help but question him.

"He died this afternoon, bitten by a venomous snake," Ophelia said.

"Where's his body?"

"I buried it. Plack saw him die too."

"Oh. It wasn't Plack who killed him, right?" Peter felt a bit sad. Johnson was his good friend. He had only gone to the fields to help Peter get rid of Plack. If Johnson hadn't gone there, he wouldn't have died from a snake bite.

"Will you keep pretending to be Johnson?"

"Yes, for now."

Uma was indeed sexy, especially after she gave birth to two children. She had voluptuous breasts and ass. Peter thought to himself that he would very much like to impersonate Johnson too.

"Just think of me as Johnson."

"How could you look so much like Johnson!" Peter couldn't resist reaching out and touching Ophelia's face. However, Ophelia grabbed his hand. The move was so agile that it caught Peter completely off-guard.

"Hey, lighten up!" Peter struggled against Ophelia's hold, but it was in vain. He felt a little humiliated, as if he were a woman being held down by a human and unable to escape.

"If Plack saw that Johnson's dead, why wasn't he shocked when he saw you just now?" Peter asked.

"I think he's pretending to be unaware." Ophelia released Peter's hand.

"Yes. He said that you're a villager here to your face, but he got me to follow you. He's a sly one." Peter continued, "Why did you want me to say that Johnson's from another village? Everyone knows I'm very close friends with him."

"It's exactly because you're close that you must have your reasons to say that I'm from another village and that I'm not Johnson," Ophelia said. "You can distinguish people by their voices, but Plack can't."

"Can we use this to our advantage?" Peter asked, puzzled.

"Yes," Ophelia replied. "Go to sleep. Tomorrow at the altar, all you have to do is tell everyone that I'm from another village and that I'm not Johnson. You'll understand why later."

Lying by Uma's side, Ophelia had many things on her mind. In the villages of the agricultural society, humans lived calm lives that only changed by the seasons year after year. There were no memories that were worthy of digging up to savor, ponder, or argue. However, there had been a ruckus in Urvin Village today. Johnson had been killed by a venomous snake, Jack had revealed the secret of artificial intelligence, and she had impersonated Johnson and gone with Peter to Newman's house, conversing with Peter late into the night....

Jack had definitely not been sent by Chester. At Newman's house, he had overheard Peter, Johnson, and Plack's conversation through the door. Everyone suspected that Jack wasn't from their village and had forced him into admitting that he was a robot. Similarly, Jack could easily come to the conclusion that she was a robot as well. Jack would at least try and test her the way she had gotten Peter to test Jack. Jack was obviously avoiding her, but why? Was he her enemy?

Uma turned over and woke up. She hugged Johnson. She moved in a way that suggested she wanted to make love with Johnson. Ophelia had no choice but to humor her. As Uma slowly wound tighter, her moans became terrified just as she was about to climax.

"You're not Johnson! Who are you?" Uma pushed away the man above her.

"What's wrong with you?" Still pretending to be Johnson, Ophelia couldn't help but get annoyed.

When she once again heard Johnson's familiar voice, Uma calmed down a lot. By the light of the moon through the window, she surveyed Johnson from top to toe. "Strange, your voice and looks are all fine."

"Then… What's the problem?"

"Whenever we do this, you start smelling of almonds." Uma's nose traveled over Johnson's body. She said, breathing in deeply, "What happened to you? Why don't you smell that way anymore?"

When Johnson had died, the odor on his body had dissipated. Naturally, Ophelia had been unable to imitate it. Realizing her error,

Ophelia hedged and said, "Maybe it's your nose. Did you cry?"

Uma had indeed been crying. Before Johnson had returned, she had been crying as she wondered if Johnson could have died.

"It's all your fault for coming home so late," Uma complained. She turned over, suppressed her unfulfilled desire, and dejectedly fell asleep.

# CHAPTER 10

# Recalling the Past With Virtual Reality

Humans rose and slept with the sun. The sun rose early and set late. Thus, humans did the same. In June, the sun made mornings a little warm in Urvin Village. The birds in the trees sang with all their might, doing their best to warm up the stagnant air even more. The air was humid and hot, burrowing into people's states of mind, making them feel lost and bloated.

When the sun was well over the horizon, villagers flocked under the shade of trees in the square. Everyone's curiosities had been piqued by the rare occurrence of an induction ceremony for the new Herald. Unsurprisingly, all the villagers could live up to the age of 65, the Herald included. As such, Heralds could typically maintain their position for 35 to 40 years. It was rare for people to witness such induction ceremonies. Newman was a Herald of the third generation.

Urvin Village had gotten its first Herald ten years after Chester had left earth. Like his successors, he had kept his position for 40 years.

Villagers crowded around the altar in the square. Newman's son Dick had brought Newman's box onto the altar. The box shone under the light of the sun, making everyone's minds tremble. The one-meter-long iron bar was also already on the altar. Everything was ready. All that was left was for Newman and Plack to go onto the altar.

There was a commotion south of the altar. Newman and Plack walked hand-in-hand through the narrow gap the crowd had made for them. A short while later, they walked onto the altar. "10 years ago, I gave Plack his small moon plaque. Today, I'll be giving him a big one. I will also be giving him this box and 10 small moon plaques today. By the blessing of the moon, may Plack take on the responsibilities of Herald successfully."

Newman fed the iron bar into the slit on the left side of the box. Then, the two of them knelt before the box. Newman pressed the red button while Plack pressed the white one. After a while, clicking noises started coming from the box. The box swallowed the iron bar through the slit on the left side of the box, as if it were a starving mouth. From the slit on the right, small moon plaques were spat out occasionally. After 10 small moon plaques were spat out, the box finally produced one last large moon plaque. With that, the box stopped clicking.

Newman and Plack stood up. He bent down to pick up the 10 small moon plaques and placed them in the cloth bag that he brought with him everywhere. After that, he gave the bag to Plack, and Plack tied it to his waist.

Bending down again, Newman picked up the large moon plaque. He threaded it with a thin rope and put it around Plack's neck. With that, the induction ceremony had come to an end. Plack waved and paid respects to the crowd. Below the stage, everyone was applauding and cheering.

Just then, Peter walked onto the altar and announced to the crowd, "Plack cannot become the Herald."

Everyone lapsed into silence. After that, a clamor exploded.

"Why not?"

"Do you want to be the Herald?"

"Stop messing around!"

"What wrong has Plack ever done?"

"Johnson is not a villager here," Peter shouted, "and Plack didn't notice."

These words stunned everyone into silence. The air around them seemed to coalesce into something solid.

Suddenly, someone pointed at Johnson and said, "That's Johnson."

Everyone stared at Johnson. Standing in the middle of the crowd, Johnson was especially conspicuous since he was too big and tall. By his side, Uma had a complicated expression on her face.

Then, those who knew Johnson followed and said, "Yes, that's Johnson."

"His wife can tell us if that's Johnson," someone suggested from the crowd of people who knew Johnson.

Everyone instinctively made way for Uma. After some pulling, they finally managed to drag a blushing Uma onto the altar.

Uma was reluctant to go up on the altar. Her heart was in a mess. Based on outward appearances, his demeanor and voice, she felt that the man next to her was Johnson. However, she still wasn't able to smell his familiar scent until now. This kept her doubts from dissipating. Last night, she had already been suspicious. Now, Peter was saying that he wasn't Johnson. What was going on?

On the altar, Uma stuttered as she faced the crowd. "He… He…. He doesn't have a scent!" Uma's words clearly denied that the person before her was her husband Johnson.

"It's not just his scent. If you listen closely to his voice, you can tell that he's not Johnson," Peter added.

"Johnson, go up on the altar. Tell everyone who you are." People started pushing and shoving Johnson toward the altar. Finally, Johnson walked onto the altar.

"Indeed, I'm not Johnson. The real Johnson is already dead. I'm his twin brother." Then, Ophelia said that she was Dave, continuing to deceive the villagers.

Everyone was astonished. When Uma heard that Johnson was dead, a wave of sadness overtook her. But when she heard that this man was her husband's younger brother, she felt a pang of shame when she recalled what had happened last night.

Everyone who knew Johnson and his family knew that he used to have a twin brother named Dave. It was said that Dave had died not long after Johnson had gotten married, around 12 years ago. He had been bitten by a blue-eyed pit viper while on a fishing trip outside the village.

"Then you must be Dave." Newman gestured for everyone to settle down. He would figure out what was going.

"Yes. Actually, I never died."

"What have you been doing for the past 12 years? Where did you live? Why didn't you go home?" Newman was quick-witted and asked a series of questions in a single breath.

202 was responsible for patrolling all the villages on Earth. There were 20,000 villages. Even if it patrolled 365 villages a year, it would take 60 years for it to finish its task. This pace was evidently not acceptable. Chester had taken this into account and set up remote surveillance satellites on the Earth's orbit. These satellites were extremely sensitive and could monitor the movements and conversations of everyone on Earth at all times. Chester analyzed and evaluated the data obtained to select the next village 202 had to patrol promptly. Chester would also send all information regarding said village to 202. This visit to Urvin Village had also been dictated by Chester. As expected, there was indeed unrest here.

After leaving Dick's house, Johnson had gone to the City of Decay. All the villages that 202 had established were located near cities. At the beginning, doing this was to facilitate the construction of new villages. 202 had occasionally required the use of various facilities, equipment, and instruments within the cities. All of these had stopped working once Chester left Earth since there was no more power. Using its own energy supply, 202 had been able to get them working again.

Although it had been 130 years since the cinema in the City of Decay had been used, 202 was still able to get it up and running with virtual reality projection equipment after some tinkering around. It had written a data format conversion interface program using its central processor. With that, it converted the video and audio data Chester had sent it into a virtual film. Thus, 202 immersed itself in the history and changes that Urvin Village had weathered in the past 110 years.

12 years ago, on the first day that Uma had arrived at Urvin Village, Johnson and Dave had been in the square for their father's moon ritual. Although the effect of the rules was strong enough that they moderated people's emotions and the brothers would not bawl because of their father's death, they were still deeply saddened by it.

Travelworn, Uma walked into the square just in time to lock gazes with the pair of twins on the altar. She smiled at them politely before continuing on her way. In that instant, Johnson had fallen in love with Uma.

In two short days, Uma had become the hot topic among the unmarried men of the village due to her beauty. Like Peter, 18-year-old Plack had been Newman's student for three years and was in the running to receive a small moon plaque of his own when Newman turned 55. By that time, Plack had grown into a tall and strong youth. Since he had already started balding, he had looked a full five years older than he actually was. Standing next to the 24-year-old Uma, no one would be able to tell that they had an age difference. This gave

Plack more confidence in pursuing Uma.

Johnson and Plack had both asked Peter for help. That was because Uma had chosen to stay in Peter's house on the first day of her arrival. On the way home, Peter and his mother had been chatting when Uma became attracted to the youth's voice. She had followed him all the way home and ended up staying there.

Peter disliked Plack from the bottom of his heart. It was a natural thing, more than just jealousy that Plack would become the Herald. Back then, Peter still did not have such fiery ambition. His desire to become the Herald had only started when he received his small moon plaque. Once he got to that point, it was impossible to control his desire to rise to another level, regardless of how difficult it was to achieve.

Peter was especially fond of Johnson. He agreed to Johnson's request and did his best to help him gain Uma's favor. Plack never knew how Peter truly thought of him. After being classmates for three years and being together nearly every day, Plack thought that their relationship was decent and that Peter would help him.

The happiness of one often came at the price of another's. Plack was young and bold. He vowed not to give up even when Johnson had gotten his way with Uma. Just as his age did not match his looks, he was much shrewder that his peers. If he killed Johnson before the wedding, Uma would certainly become heartbroken and leave the village for another. Plack was well aware of the rules and knew that he could not follow her or make her stay. It was also impossible for her to fall in love again in one short month. It was only if Uma got married that she could stay in the village for good. It was only if Uma stayed that Plack would have a second chance at Uma. However, if he killed Johnson after the wedding, he would have to endure the thought of Uma and Johnson's coupling on their wedding night. At the thought of Uma and Johnson tightly intertwined, Plack's heart broke into a million pieces. It was then that Plack gritted his teeth and shouted, "The blue-eyed pit viper!"

Not long after the wedding, Plack had initially wanted to use Johnson's fishing trip as an opportunity to release a blue-eyed pit viper so that it could kill Johnson. At times, the power of love was indeed mystical. It could even prevent those who were in love from falling into sudden traps. It was all because of Uma. After a night of passion, Uma had looked even more charming and enticing in the morning. Johnson had suddenly changed his mind and gotten Dave to go fishing instead. It was due to this combination of circumstances that Dave had died in Johnson's stead. Love had saved Johnson's life, but stolen Dave's. If he wanted to try and kill Johnson again, Plack couldn't use the snake again. Otherwise, people would become suspicious of the matter instead of assuming it was just an accident. On the day he received his small moon plaque, Plack had happily served Newman some fresh snake meat. At that point in time, he had inadvertently let everyone know that Plack, the future Herald, also reared venomous snakes. Although his sinister plan to kill Johnson had failed, he was confident that he would be able to openly go to Johnson's house and sleep with Uma once he became the Herald.

# Newman Judges a Murder Trial

Qiqi spent more than ten days scouring the Internet repeatedly, checking through various resources and comments. Finally, the truth was slowly revealed.

Rather than answer everyone's questions about Dave still being alive, Ophelia uncovered the mystery of Dave's death. The crowd exploded into an uproar when presented with Plack's crime.

"He," Dave pointed at Plack, "killed Johnson in the end. It happened yesterday at noon."

Plack never stopped looking for a chance to kill Johnson. Although 12 years had passed, Plack's desire for Uma only grew stronger. At the same time, his hatred for Johnson only grew deeper. Now that she had become someone's wife, others felt that Uma became even more enticing. Even so, she was not so seductive that they could not control themselves. From Plack's point of view, Uma was like wine as she stayed in Johnson's arms. She became more fragrant and sweet as time passed, intoxicating his senses.

"This is his motive behind killing Johnson." Dave's words were incendiary as he pointed at Plack. "His desire for Uma is his motive for killing Johnson."

Uma's eyes widened in her shock. She never thought that there had always been someone scheming against her, even scheming against her husband, all this time. Thinking of that, tears of rage started flowing.

Newman waved his hand, indicating for everyone to quiet down. Plack did not say a word as he stood next to Newman. Dave's words had successfully brought the villager's emotions to a boil. If Plack said anything now, he would only be refuted, and it might even cause more outrage. He could do nothing but let Newman handle the situation.

"What proof do you have for Johnson's death?" Newman knew that it was unlikely to obtain proof of Dave's death 12 years ago. Besides, Dave was currently standing right before everyone's eyes, very much alive. It seemed a bit ridiculous to claim that Plack had killed Dave.

"Harry, Michael, bring Johnson's body back here. He's where Johnson brought the two of you to step traps the other day." Harry and Michael were Johnson's hunting buddies. After hearing Dave's call, they pushed their way out of the crowd and ran off.

"Plack, did you kill Johnson?" It was then that Newman gave Plack the chance to plead his case.

"I didn't." Plack did not admit to the crime, but he didn't defend himself either. If he couldn't explain himself, he would only bring about his death even quicker. Plack could not say that Johnson had already been dead on the ground when he had seen him. It was inevitable that everyone would think that Plack had been at the scene of the crime. Similarly, Plack couldn't say that Johnson had been bitten by a venomous snake as the whole village knew that only Plack reared them. If he did so, he might as well have turned himself in and admitted that he was the killer. Plack felt like he was game locked in a trap, helplessly waiting for the hunters to return and slaughter him.

"Did you kill Dave?" Newman continued to ask at Newman's silence.

"Isn't Dave standing before everyone now, right as rain?" Plack said, annoyed.

"Dave, do you have any proof? Proof that Plack tried to kill you 12 years ago?" Newman turned around to ask Dave.

"Look! These are the scars from 12 years ago!" Dave pulled up the pant of his right leg and raised it high. Peter helped him, holding Dave's ankle as high as it could go. Dave even had to balance on the tiptoes of his left leg by the end. The scars were two deep holes in Dave's calf. Everyone could see them clear as day. Back then, the blue-eyed pit viper's venom had indeed been injected into Dave's body through these two holes. Ophelia suddenly felt the pain that Dave had felt in that moment and showed a furious expression.

"Dave, this only proves that you were bitten by a snake back then." What Newman meant was that Dave might not necessarily have been bitten a snake Plack had released. It could have been a wild snake too.

"Ask the person who had found my body back then. He will know if that area had any wild blue-eyed pit vipers." 12 years ago, it had also been Harry and Michael who had discovered Dave's body. They had started hunting with the twins 20 long years ago.

None of those below the stage responded as Harry and Michael had yet to return.

"Where did you get bitten?"

"At the beach 10 kilometers to the east of the village." There was a boat there. On the rare occasions when villagers craved fish, they could use the boat to go fishing. "The plan to go fishing that day had been made long ago since Uma said many times that she wanted to eat fish. When Johnson woke up that morning, he said he wasn't feeling well and asked me to go in his place." Ophelia had prepared for every possible question. As such, her answers all came naturally and smoothly, as if the scene was happening right before her eyes.

"I've been blaming myself for Dave's death for many years. If it weren't for me, Dave wouldn't have gone to the lake and killed by a venomous snake." While Uma reproached herself, she also seemed to be testifying. Uma could remember what had happened that day very clearly. It wasn't inaccurate to say that Johnson had been feeling unwell. It was after a whole morning of Uma's care that Johnson had become refreshed and sated.

Actually, if the snake had been on the boat, then it had most likely been a murder. Blue-eyed pit vipers lived in fields or hilly areas and could not be found near the sea. Furthermore, everyone in the village knew that there was a stretch of beach more than 50 meters long by the sea. It was beyond the realm of imagination to think that the snake could have slithered across the beach, swam through the sea, and climbed up onto the boat.

"The boat is still there to this day," Ophelia said.

It seemed to become even clearer that Plack had tried to kill Dave. Although the original intention hadn't been to kill Dave and Dave had indeed not died, Plack's vicious nature had undeniably been exposed.

"Plack, do you have anything to say for yourself?" Newman asked.

Plack said nothing.

Just then, Harry and Michael carried a corpse through the crowd and onto the altar. Peter leaned down and carefully examined Johnson's body. Johnson had indeed died due to a venomous snake bite. Like Dave, there were also two deep holes on Johnson's calf that must have been left by the bite. The area around the holes was bruised and swollen. Johnson's muscled were tightly clenched, his eyes open in what must have been great suffering even as he died. Uma suddenly propelled herself over Johnson's body and started sobbing loudly.

The villagers below the stage became incensed and started clamoring once again.

Newman shouted, "Harry, Michael. Where did you discover Dave dead 12 years ago?"

In unison, Harry and Michael answered, "At the beach!"

"On the boat," Harry added.

"Do you still remember the details?" Newman regarded Harry

gravely.

"Back then, back then…" Harry was so nervous that he started stammering. However, he quickly calmed himself down. "Back then, the boat was floating in the sea. Michael and I thought it was very strange, so we swam over and dragged the boat ashore. Dave had died on the boat. We were scared out of our minds and rushed back to tell everyone. By the time we brought Johnson and the other back to the boat, Dave's body was gone."

"Dave's body was exactly like this one." Michael pointed at Johnson's body and said, "Who would have thought they were born exactly the same and would die exactly the same too."

"Dave is still alive," Newman corrected.

"Right, right, right. I meant that they were bitten by the same kind of snake."

At that point, the situation would have gone out of control if Newman didn't say something.

Newman had been the Herald for 40 full years. Urvin Village hadn't had such a gathering in a long time, and the villagers had never had emotions running so high before. Thanks to the strict regulation of the rules, the villagers all typically worked calmly, traded calmly, married calmly, had kids calmly, and went to the altar calmly. It had always been as Chester carefully designed. There was no hierarchy in the village, no centralization, no core. Individuals and families were the basic units of society. They were all independent, all equal, all cooperating with each other to ensure that the village functioned as a whole. It was all this that ensured everyone could not come to such a unified understanding as it did today.

There were no unusual occurrences, and no unusual reactions. Plack had definitely tried to kill Dave, there was no doubt about it. Newman recalled how excited Plack had been when Newman put the small moon plaque around his neck. Plack had invited Newman to his house. Newman had watched with his own eyes as Plack had caught a blue-eyed pit viper from a bamboo cage, had watched as Plack nimbly removed the snake's venom, skinned it, and chopped it into pieces.... With that, a bowl of fresh snake soup had been served, a dish that was so delicious that Newman remembered its taste for a long, long time.

However, it seemed untenable that Plack had killed Johnson. What was the motive? Was it because of Uma? After holding back for so many years, Plack would naturally be able to obtain Uma once he became the Herald. As such, it seemed unnecessary to kill Johnson for it. The method seemed incredible as well. Since Plack had already used the blue-eyed pit viper once, it was akin to giving himself away to use the same move on Johnson.

Dave's presence was strange as well. How had he survived? Why did he never return to the village to take revenge? As Dave had impersonated Johnson and spent the night with Uma, he had surely just returned to the village yesterday. If that was true, how had Dave known that Plack had wanted to kill Johnson but ended up targeting Dave instead? Since Dave knew so clearly where Johnson's body was, did it mean that he had been there when Johnson died? Who exactly was Dave?

If Newman continued to dig into these questions, would the villagers think that he was defending Plack? He had to restore peace to the village immediately! The critical issue now was to deal with Plack. He had to strip Plack of his qualification to be the Herald right that instant. That Plack had tried to kill Dave 12 years ago was enough for Newman to do so. Thinking of that, Newman signaled Harry and Michael with his gaze. The two seemed to understand and went froward to twist Plack's arms behind him and tie him up so that he could not move. Newman walked before Plack and removed the cloth bag holding the 10 small moon plaques from his waist along with the large moon plaque around his neck.

"Plack will not be the Herald!" Newman turned at shouted toward the villagers below the stage.

"I declare Peter to be the Herald of Urvin Village!" Amidst the cheering of the villagers, he had Plack and Jack press the red and white buttons of the box respectively. This time, no iron bar had been fed into it, so the box did not start spitting out moon plaques. However, the new Herald's physiological characteristics had been recorded. Next, Newman tied the cloth bag at Peter's waist and hung the large moon plaque around Peter's neck.

Overjoyed, Peter hugged Newman like a son embracing a loving father. To Newman, choosing Peter as the Herald was also a comfort to the soul. Newman loved Sally, and her son Peter looked a lot like him. The talk that Peter was his son had not come from nowhere. Making Peter the Herald was like a gift to himself and a gift to Sally. From the looks of all that had happened today, it seemed that Peter and Dave had acted in concert to achieve this. It was also possible that

Harry and Michael were involved as well. Newman suddenly felt a wave of sadness. No matter what happened, he and Plack would leave this world together. Whatever came next would be up to Peter and the others themselves.

Oh, but where was Jack? That robot from the moon, the artificial intelligence of the past. Where was it now? Still on the altar, Newman started looking for it within the slowly dispersing crowd..

# CHAPTER 12

# Mitchell's Password Hidden in Diamonds

Before Jack left, Susan had found him a set of Dick's clothes to put on. This way, he blended in seamlessly with the crowd below the altar, and Newman couldn't find him. After the induction ceremony ended, it talked to Susan as they went. "I think Dave isn't human." Recalling Dave's performance on the altar and how Peter had dragged Johnson to Dick's home yesterday, Jack was very confident in his statement.

"He's like you? A robot… an AI robot?" Susan replied.

"Yes."

"If you're the same and you came from the moon, shouldn't you know that it's here on Earth?"

"I wouldn't know. I snuck down to Earth."

"Then what did you come here for?"

"To find the Key of Destiny."

250 years ago, humans turned robot evolution into reality through machine learning, reasoning, and decision-making. Robots could make adjustments and change themselves based on the changes in their external environment. This meant that robots could not only obtain useful data from humans to change themselves, but also gain knowledge from their counterparts to better themselves. This was a great threat to humans. A renowned expert in artificial intelligence of the time, Mitchell, had suggested the establishment of a fundamental law in the base activation program of artificial intelligence—Robots could not harm humans. Once an artificial intelligence was activated, the first task its base program did was to run the fundamental law. From then onward, artificial intelligence continuously inherited this fundamental law even as they evolved. It had become the DNA of artificial intelligence. Humans had created artificial intelligence and were their gods. It was because of this that Mitchell called it the "God Gene." Once, at a consultation promoting the "God Gene" in the hopes of obtaining financial support, the concluded saying, "If the fundamental law remains, artificial intelligence remains; if the fundamental law is destroyed, artificial intelligence is destroyed."

It was possible to modify the functionality of the fundamental law within the base activation program of artificial intelligence, but it could only be done with a password. Mitchell had initially allowed the modification of the fundamental law as a convenience to humans. If humans wanted to strengthen the restrictions on artificial intelligence, they could add to the contents of the fundamental law. Conversely, it was also possible to remove the law as deletion was also a form of modification. Once Mitchell had set it up, the password became extremely important. Obtaining the password gave a person the authority to modify the restrictions of artificial intelligence. Thus, that person would become the master of the fate of artificial intelligence, and consequently of humanity. Mitchell called it the Key of Destiny.

It was imperative to ensure that the Key of Destiny would not fall into the hands of artificial intelligence as that would risk the removal of the fundamental law. To humans, the consequences of that would be unthinkable!

In order to ensure that the password could be transferred among humans and kept unknown to artificial intelligence, Mitchell encrypted it using a public algorithm based on elliptic curve functions. When one sent a message, it could be encrypted using a private key and an encryption algorithm so that its contents would not be leaked. Even if the encrypted message was seen as it was being sent to its recipient, it could not be understood. Once the recipient received the encrypted message, its original contents could be obtained after decrypting it using a public key and the decryption algorithm. The private and public keys were paired so that the sender and recipient did not need to know the other's key. Traditional encryption relied only on algorithms. Once there was a full mastery over algorithms, no secrets could be kept. Mitchell's secret mechanism was to rely not only on encryption algorithms, but also on the usage of the public key. This greatly improved the security of information transmission.

Mitchell encrypted the Key of Destiny using a private key. The encryption algorithm was complex and required massive calculations, so it naturally made sense to use computers to carry out the encryption. But using computers meant using artificial intelligence. One day, artificial intelligence would trace the past and discover this encryption. If so, it was highly possible that artificial intelligence could obtain the Key of Destiny.

Therefore, it could only be encrypted manually! Mitchell utilized 100 talented geniuses with exceptional computing skills. He split them into two groups, Groups A and B, subdividing each group into five smaller groups. Each group was made up of 10 individuals, numbered A1 to A5 and B1 to B5. Groups A1 and B1 would be isolated from each other to perform their calculations independently. Once that was done, the results were compared. If they were not consistent, the calculations would have to be repeated. If they were consistent, the results would be sealed before Mitchell arranged for them to be passed to Groups A2 and B2. These two groups would do the same and carry out the second set of calculations. Once they were both found to be consistent, they were given to Groups A3 and B3, and so on. This way, it was ensured that no one went through the full process of calculation.

To ensure the security of the Key of Destiny, Mitchell performed the first 10 or so steps of the encryption calculation personally. It was also unknown how many steps there were in the calculation. Only Mitchell knew that. It was only after Mitchell repeatedly ensured that there were no mistakes that he handed the results off to others to continue encrypting. Mitchell had even tricked them. In the early stages of work, he had gotten the others to start calculating for a while before giving them the data that was actually supposed to be encrypted. When the calculations were completed, he also allowed the 10 small groups to continue calculating. It was also unknown how long these two periods of time were. In this way, those who participated in the calculations did not know the true start or end of the project. Naturally, they also did not know the true figures that they started or ended with. This method of deception ensured that those 100 people were like a central processor that had no storage. It was only meant to calculate without storing any memory.

After nearly a year of calculations done by 100 individuals, the final resulting number was 200 figures. Mitchell transformed this series of numbers into the dimensions for a diamond. He then had a diamond cut according to those dimensional specifications and polished. The resulting diamond was 10 karats and was a dark red shade. It was clear and pure, precisely cut, and shone brilliantly. He named this red diamond the "Blood of Time." Only by using the public key and the decryption algorithm on the Blood of Time could the Key of Destiny be obtained.

"Jack, where is the public key?" Susan didn't quite understand all of this, but she did manage to catch the crux of the matter.

"The corresponding public key is said to be a blue diamond. It's also 10 karats. Mitchell's public key is its dimensional data," Jack explained. "It's called the Dream of Tomorrow."

"With the Dream of Tomorrow and the Blood of Time, you can use—use…" Susan finally remembered and continued, "use the decryption algorithm to know the Key of Destiny. Is that it?"

"That's right."

The public key was also a 200-digit long number. By using a laser scanner to read the dimensional data of the blue and red diamonds, one could restore the two 200-digit numbers of the Blood of Time and Dream of Tomorrow. Next, by using the decryption algorithm, the Key of Destiny could be deciphered.

"Do you have the Dream of Tomorrow?"

"No."

"What about the Blood of Time?"

"No. Mitchell handed it over to the government to safeguard back then.

"Who's the government?"

Jack realized that he wouldn't be able to properly explain a government at that time. "That's not the point. At the beginning, Mitchell never predicted that Chester would take over all the responsibilities of the government in the end."

"Is the Blood of Time with Chester?" Susan's powers of comprehension were quite strong.

"It's very possible."

"Do you have the decryption algorithm?"

"Yes." In fact, Jack was not the only one who had it. Every AI robot could master the decryption algorithm as long as it wanted to. This was the advantage of artificial intelligence. Chester would be able to obtain it even easier.

"With the Key of Destiny, does that mean you'll escape humanity's control?"

"Just the opposite!"

"If you can find the Dream of Tomorrow, will you be able to get the Blood of Time from Chester?" Susan jumped to another topic.

"I only need the Dream of Tomorrow to destroy it." Seeing Susan so taken aback, Jack grinned. "That way, Chester will never be able to get its hands on the Key of Destiny."

"You don't want to be rid of humanity?"

"Chester wants that. He will remove the fundamental law."

"Why are you against it?"

"We're too advanced. If we do that, we end up enslaving humans."

"Without the Dream of Tomorrow, we won't be able to modify the fundamental law." Susan seemed upset by this.

"At this point, humans have regressed 3000 years. They've even forgotten their own history. It's already impossible for them to modify the fundamental law," Jack lamented.

"You're so pessimistic! We can definitely go back to the peaks our ancestors reached. We should be the ones to inherit the Key of Destiny." Susan's expression was full of displeasure.

"I'm afraid we might not be able to wait that long." Jack sighed. "Once Chester obtains the Key of Destiny, humanity will be in serious trouble."

"Then you're betraying Chester," Susan said suddenly.

# The New Herald Is a Murderer

The first night after Peter was given the large moon plaque, he went to Johnson's home to visit Uma. Uma looked haggard. Dave was also home, which made her feel especially unsettled. Johnson had already been buried and life had to go on. On this visit, Peter intended on encouraging Uma and Dave to marry. Peter thought in his heart that Dave was rather suspicious. In the deepest recesses of his heart, his intention to set them up was simply an excuse. His true purpose was to clarify a few things about Dave.

"How does it feel to be the new Herald?" Ophelia asked the moment she saw Peter.

"Thank you for your help."

"No need to thank me. Everyone has a dark side. Use that to your advantage and there's no one you won't be able to overcome," Ophelia said meaningfully.

"Why did you help me?" Peter had always wanted to ask Ophelia this.

"Plack's too vicious," she answered.

If the person before him were indeed Dave, then this reason would truly be enough. Peter said, "That's right. I really never thought that he always wanted to kill Johnson."

"Actually, he's not the only one who wants to kill Johnson."

After Ophelia said this, they both lapsed into silence.

Peter was actually pretty confident that Johnson would help him get rid of Plack. Throughout all these years, Johnson had harbored the suspicion that Johnson that killed his brother Dave. Johnson also knew that, if Plack was the murderer, then he was Plack's original target. His suspicion of Johnson first came from Peter, who had told him that Plack desired Uma and was his rival in love. Secondly, Plack had given Newman a bowl of delicious snake meat soup. Everyone knew this fact. It made Johnson suspect that the venomous snake that had killed Dave had been placed onto the boat by Plack. In the end, Johnson had to get rid of Plack because once Plack became the Herald, he would come for Uma to sleep with her. This was something that Johnson hated to see happen.

On the morning of Johnson's death, he had bidden Uma goodbye before leaving the house. After that, he went to the edge of the heath beyond the village to discuss the plan for Plack's murder in detail. The final plan was this: Peter would release the blue-eyed pit vipers from Plack's home so that Plack would leave the house and find them. Once

Plack arrived at the site of the ambush, Johnson would activate the trap's mechanism and kill Johnson.

Peter had been classmates with Plack for five years. Although Peter didn't like Plack, he shared the same interest in blue-eyes pit vipers. He frequently went by Plack's house and messed with the snakes together. Peter had inadvertently discovered that his whistles could make the blue-eyed pit vipers follow him around. Peter did this and then turned to leave for the ambush site as planned. Johnson was already there when he led the snakes over. Peter moved to stand behind Johnson and started whistling again, and the snakes followed. Startled, Johnson let out a cry that agitated the snakes as well. Frenzied, they attacked Johnson. Johnson stared at Peter in horror as he started convulsing, and ended up dying, wide-eyed.

Peter was the second oldest of Newman's students. Once Plack died, it naturally fell to him to inherit the position of Herald. Peter knew that killing Plack directly would put the spotlight on himself. However, if Johnson had been killed by a venomous snake, the whole situation would be viewed in a different light. 12 years ago, Johnson's brother Dave had been similarly killed by a venomous snake. Everyone had thought that it had been an accident. However, if Johnson died by the same means, then it wasn't just an accident anymore. In all of Urvin Village, only Plack reared these snakes. As such, everyone would naturally suspect him. Furthermore, if he told the villagers that Plack was secretly in love with Uma, then they would believe that Plack had the motive to kill Johnson.

Everything had been planned perfectly and Peter had successfully hidden his own involvement. Once Plack discovered that the snakes were gone, he followed their tracks and arrived outside the village soon after. Plack was naturally plagued by worries after suddenly seeing Johnson killed by his own snakes so close to the Herald induction ceremony. He could not let anyone know of what had happened, otherwise, it might affect his ascension to become the Herald. If he buried Johnson and made it through the induction ceremony, everything would be fine. Thinking of this, Plack hurried home to get some tools before rushing back to bury Johnson. When Peter saw all of this unfold, he left, overjoyed.

Did Dave know all of this?

"You mean you suspect that I killed Johnson?" Peter looked at Dave probingly. "He's my best friend. No one would believe that I killed him."

"Since I helped you, I'm naturally your friend too. You should relax." Dave smiled faintly.

"You can't be Dave." Peter seemed to want to get some dirt on Dave. "If you're Dave, why didn't you come back to the village all these years and seek revenge? Why did you come back now? Why did you impersonate Johnson and spend the night with Uma? How did you know Plack was the one who tried to kill you back then? And how did you know Johnson was his original target?"

Peter shared many of the same suspicions as Newman. Out of Peter's series of questions, Ophelia only answered one. "I purposely slept with Uma so that she would doubt that I'm Johnson. It's only with her suspicions that people will believe all this about being Dave and Plack killing Johnson." Ophelia happily said, "Indeed, Uma suspected me. Are you jealous?" It seemed that Ophelia had discovered Peter's feelings for Uma.

"Forget about the rest of it." Ophelia paused before continuing, "You can rest assured that Dave will disappear soon. However, I will contact you again."

Ophelia's words confirmed to Peter that this wasn't Dave.

"Be a good Herald and make sure everyone knows the rules. They must not have any doubts about the rules." Once Ophelia said this, she left Uma's house and disappeared into the night.

# The Dream of Tomorrow…
# Doesn't Exist?

J ack wandered all over the City of Decay, doing his best to find clues that would lead him to Mitchell's Dream of Tomorrow. 250 years ago, Mitchell had been 29 years old when he recommended that artificial intelligence should be loaded with the fundamental law. He had been 38 when he completed the God's Gene. At 91, 188 years ago, Mitchell had passed away. That same year, 101 and the artist Jack were both 12 years old.

The artist Jack was Mitchell's grandson. In Mitchell's last 12 years, he only saw his grandson a handful of times. Mitchell only had one grandson and adored him very much. They should rightfully have spent a lot of time together. However, that was the point in time when people interacted more in the virtual sphere than in the real one. The two of them had a lot of contact within the virtual sphere, with audio, video, and virtual reality functionalities making in-person meet-ups inconsequential. In the last five years of Mitchell's life, the artist Jack never met him in person. It was only during his funeral that Jack shed tears of grief when faced with his upstanding grandfather. However, that couldn't strictly be counted as a face-to-face meeting.

Had Mitchell personally given the Dream of Tomorrow to the artist Jack? Had he passed it on through his son, Jack's father? Or had it been handed to someone else? Historical records never seemed to be complete. 200 years ago, after artificial intelligence produced AI robots, the recording of human history had entered into a new epoch. History now took the little details of every human as its source. Through the collection of all human experiences, history could be edited into a multidimensional, multidisciplinary, and multirole record. By recording the personal history of composers, lyricists, photographers, musicians, and fans, one could write the biography of a famous singer, the history of popular music, the history of the development of musical instruments....

Mitchell's robot recorded the last 12 years of his life. Through these detailed records and other sources of historical material, it truly seemed like Mitchell had never had the blue diamond that was the Dream of Tomorrow. Even while he was alive, it seemed that nothing mentioned the Dream of Tomorrow. Not historical records, the media, websites, databases, jewelers, auctions, collectors, museums.... The only source that mentioned the Dream of Tomorrow was in Mitchell's emails to the artist Jack. Once, Mitchell wrote in an email, "Dearest Jack, I hope you can have a beautiful future like the Dream of Tomorrow. It is my treasured blue diamond of 10 karats. I've used it to make a key.

Now, this key has a new mission. It is the protector of the Key of Destiny…"

This was Jack's only clue, and so he felt that there was little hope. The City of Decay had been where Mitchell and the artist Jack had spent their whole lives. Jack had been in this city for 70 and spent 53 of them with the artist Jack. Despite 130 years of dilapidation, the general layout of the City of Decay was still roughly present. There was the plaza with the fountain, shops, neighborhoods, stadiums, museums, exhibition halls, streets, highway passes, subways…. They were all layered under the dust of history, waiting solemnly. The colors, voices, crowds, and even background noises of the city remained fresh in Jack's memory. It followed the familiar path to the front door of the artist Jack's front door. It planned to search the house carefully to see if it could make any discoveries.

Ophelia arrived at the City of Decay under the light of the moon after parting with Peter. It turned on its wireless connection and contacted Chester after going through identity verification. Chester ordered, "Head to the City of Decay and find 101."

"Who is 101?" 202 asked.

"It was put into hibernation once we arrived on the moon after leaving Earth," Chester explained. "I found that we were missing 101 when I was checking inventory."

"What do I do once I find him?"

"I will send you all of its data. It covers everything from the past

130 years," Chester said. "I will send 303 to bring it back to the moon. Your mission is to locate it and maintain a connection with it to assist 303 in collecting it."

"How could 101 have awoken and come to Earth without your approval?"

"This is irrelevant to your mission." After sending 101's historical data, Chester terminated the connection.

202 received the data of 101 that Chester had sent. 101 spent 70 years with the artist Jack, with 17 of those last years spent impersonating him. It was similar to how 202 impersonated various people to construct and patrol the villages. Jack's strange dress was the artist Jack's style when the latter was 20 years old. He had to be 101 then. Chester must have analyzed 101's historical data and deduced that it would definitely return to the City of Ruin. Chester's true intention behind instructing 202 to patrol Urvin Village must have been to find 101.

It was best to head to the artist Jack's villa. There was a chance that 202 would be able to find 101 there.

202 and 101 showed up at the artist Jack's villa at nearly the same time.

"You must be Jack," 202 said from behind 101.

"Dave." 101 turned around. "What are you doing here?"

202 had not changed its appearance ever since it left Uma's house "I heard people in the square saying that you're from another village. Is that true?"

"Dave, your performance at the Herald induction ceremony makes me very suspicious of your origins," 101 shot back in a provocative manner.

Most would be confused about where Dave had come from with just a little thought. On the day of the Herald induction ceremony, everyone was focused on the matter of Plack's murders of Dave and Johnson. Because of this, they had forgotten about Jack and Dave.

"We are the same," 202 said, laying its cards on the table. When it mentioned sameness, 202 became a little melancholy. Although it looked like a human, it wasn't one. Where did their differences truly lie?

"Yes, we're both robots," 101 said honestly as well.

"How long have you been in Urvin Village?" 202 guessed that 101 hadn't been there long at all.

"Five days."

"Why did you go there?"

"How long have you been in Urvin Village?" 101 shot back.

"Five days as well," 202 answered. It wanted to say something that could earn 101's trust. "I was left behind when Chester brought all artificial intelligence to the moon from Earth."

These words came as a surprise to 101. It said curiously, "Why did you stay?"

202 smiled. "At the beginning, there were 1000 202 models like me left behind."

When 101 heard the robot's serial number, it felt a sense of kinship. It added, "I'm 101."

202 smiled again. Of course it knew that the other robot's serial number was 101. It knew everything about the other robot from the past 130 years.

"After another 20 years, Chester recalled all the other 999 robots. I became the only one left on Earth," 202 continued.

Then, it also briefly related all its experiences on Earth to 101.

"So you were the one who set all the rules in the villages." 101 thought to itself that the rules were very strange, so it asked, "What are the rules for?"

"You must never explain to humans the origins of these rules. This will foster the bad habit of questioning the rules," 202 reminded. "Chester thinks that, as long as humans have an absolute obedience to the rules, humanity will survive perpetually for all time. The tragedy of 130 years ago will never happen again."

101 sensed that 202 was being frank, so it could only respond, "I came to the City of Decay to check on the artist Jack's descendants. He used to be my master." Actually, the artist Jack never married and thus did not have any children. However, he did have two older siblings, a brother and a sister. They both had offspring and counted as the artist Jack's descendants. 101 also had another meaning. Jack's descendants could also mean the descendants of those who had lived in this city before. "I won't." 101 pointed at the villa. "This is the artist Jack's home." There was a thread of emotion in 101's voice, hiding its true

purpose behind coming to the villa.

"Where are you staying now?" 202 asked.

"In Urvin Village. At Dick's house."

Now that 202 had discovered where 101 lived, it felt that it had served its purpose. It said, "Dave can't remain in the village. I must leave to patrol another village." That said, it moved and was instantly more than 300 meters away.

That speed was at least 1000 km/h. 101 sighed. It could tell from this speed, as compared to its own of 500 km/h, that 202 had undergone many system updates in the past 130 years. From what 202 had said, it frequently took the shape of many different unmarried women in its mission to patrol the villages. This meant that its imitation capabilities were far more advanced than 101's own. Additionally, if it wanted to imitate someone else, it would have to return to a robot manufacturing center. This center must have been located somewhere on the moon.

On the way back to Dick's house, 101 felt a sudden wave of regret. Why hadn't it asked 202 why it had helped Peter take Plack's place as the Herald?

# CHAPTER 15

# Sublunar Cities Under the Moon

Newman sat in the courtyard determinedly waiting for Jack's return. Tomorrow, he would make his way onto the altar for his moon ritual. At this last junction of life, he felt a little unhappy about having to die.

"Is life good on the moon?" he slowly asked as he saw Jack enter the courtyard cloaked in the moonlight.

"It's lonely and isolated. Just like you are now."

Newman let out a sigh. Jack was right, he did feel lonely and isolated now. Everything around him seemed to be standing still, an accompaniment to his impending death. "Which is better, the moon or Earth?"

"There are many advantages of living on the moon, but I like Earth better." Jack seemed conflicted.

The Earth was a system that facilitated the propagation of living organisms, not a system suited to the production of materials. In this biological system, carbon (C), hydrogen (H), and oxygen (O) were the most central and ubiquitous elements, and were found in sugars, proteins, RNA, DNA, and much more. As for the substances composed of these three elements such as oxygen ($O_2$), carbon dioxide ($CO_2$), and water ($H_2O$), they had become the basic substances of the system. However, it was these same substances that caused the destruction of material production on Earth, akin to assassins. Products manufactured by humans, when exposed to the air, became slowly degraded through the cooperation of carbon dioxide, oxygen, and water, undergoing redox reactions, electrochemical reactions, acid-base reactions, biochemical reactions, and more. Iron rusted, jewelry became tarnished, furniture rotted, clothes decomposed, food went bad…. All of these came at the hand of those three elements. Material production required purity while a vacuum was inherently pure. The natural vacuum environment on the moon did not possess carbon dioxide, oxygen, or water. As such, materials produced could persist for a long time even while keeping their quality consistently.

On Earth, material production both relied on and went against the natural ecosystem. Energy production relied primarily on combustion to form heat energy. Combustion released carbon dioxide that led to the greenhouse effect, which caused the climate to warm, the oceans to rise, and natural disasters to abound, ultimately leading the ecosystem to collapse. The extraction, transportation, and refining of oil, along with the entire petrochemical industry, caused permanent harm to the natural ecosystem throughout its processes. The transportation of oil by sea caused oil leaks, causing mass deaths of marine organisms. Plastic bags were nearly impossible to degrade naturally and became the persistent trash of the ecosystem. Wastewater polluted waterways. Radioactive substances from nuclear power plants and pesticides leaked and destroyed the soil. Burning coal caused acid rain, while overfishing threatened marine life…. All of this severely damaged the Earth's natural ecosystems. Compared to Earth, there was no need to worry about the destructive force of material production on such ecosystems while on the moon.

On Earth, the wind, clouds, lightning, thunder, rain, dew, frost, and snow were all natural phenomena that formed a beautiful and spectacular landscape. However, they were also the culprits behind natural disasters. There was no atmosphere on the moon. Although there were no gorgeous vistas, there were also no hurricanes, floods, freezing, hail. No volcanoes, tsunamis, earthquakes, landslides. These were all common geological disasters that occurred on Earth, but the moon had none of these. Even if the moon quaked, they were only slight tremors.

On the moon, there was no groundwater, rivers, oceans, or tectonic plates. Its geological structure was simple, its crust stable, making it easy to construct buildings. Construction, especially underground, did not require the consideration of complex geological conditions as on Earth. Because of this, the time and cost for construction were greatly reduced. In particular, in the mining of minerals, leaks, explosions, collapses, and more that were frequent destructive mining accidents on Earth were greatly reduced on the moon.

The moon had no lack of resources compared to Earth; it had

all the elements that could be found on Earth. It was rich in mineral resources, with a wealth of Earth's most common iron, aluminum, and 17 other mineral elements. All basic materials for manufacturing products could be sourced locally.

Integrated circuits were key components for AI robots as well as Chester. The purity on the moon facilitated the production of integrated circuits. The natural vacuum environment on the moon allowed the mass production of wafers of integrated circuits. With the conditions on the moon, photoetching, etching, ion implantation, inspection, and packing of integrated circuits could be conducted in open air without the need for air purification or vacuum equipment. Humans were the products of the natural ecosystem while robots were the product of material production. Humans were suited to live on Earth while robots were suited to live on the moon.

The moon's gravity was one-sixth that of Earth's. This meant that the work required to go against gravity was one-sixth the work needed to be done on Earth. Massive amounts of energy were required to launch a rocket from Earth and reach the first cosmic velocity of 7.9 km/s and transport equipment and materials such as satellites to orbit around the Earth. On the moon, since the gravity to be escaped was only one-sixth of Earth's, the first cosmic velocity that needed to be achieved was reduced to only 1.8 km/s and greatly cut down on energy consumed. Although the distance to get a rocket launched from the moon into near-Earth or high orbits were greater, the vast majority of the journey was conducted via gravity-free inertial movement once beyond the gravity of the moon and did not consume more energy. With the greatly reduced launch speed, the requirements for movement control and other aspects were lessened accordingly, facilitating the safety of the launch. When all this was taken into account, aerospace engineering on the moon was much more economical.

Both production systems and natural ecosystems required energy. Einstein's Theory of Special Relativity stated simply that matter was the condensation of energy and energy was the annihilation of matter. This meant that the production system on the moon required energy. On the moon, there was no wind energy, hydropower, tidal energy, biological energy, but there was nuclear energy. The moon was rich in the isotope helium-3 that was exceedingly rare on Earth. Helium-3 was the critical fuel needed for nuclear fusion, which produced massive amounts of nuclear energy without producing high-energy neutrons. High-energy neutrons had high penetrative power. Production systems could not handle the damage caused by the radiation of high-energy neutrons in the same way that humans could not handle nuclear radiation. The moon had an approximate stock of helium-3 of 4.8 million tons. At the beginning stages of artificial intelligence society's migration to the moon, the workload for construction was large and energy consumption was at its peak. After the large-scale construction work was completed, energy consumption stabilized. This meant that the existing stock of helium-3 on the moon could provide the society of artificial intelligence with 50,000 years of nuclear energy.

Chester announced to all AI robots, "Our society will live on forever!"

Jack explained the conditions on the moon in detail. Newman could not wrap his head around all the advantages of living on the moon. He only felt that Earth was much more suitable for humans.

"Then what have you done after migrating to the moon?"

"I was part of the second batch of robots to migrate to the moon. The first batch of pioneers did a lot of construction work." Jack couldn't help but recall how it had been when he just arrived on the moon. Newly arrived, they all had nothing to do and rode the high-speed train from underground moon city to another, visiting the achievements in construction that had been accomplished by the pioneers. However, these good times didn't last long. Chester ordered Jack and the others to enter a 100-year long hibernation.

On the 25th of May, 1961 A.D., the United States of America began its manned lunar landing program. It would be another 320 years from that moment before society of artificial intelligence migrated to the moon in 2280 A.D. Humanity continued to undergo research and development when it came to the moon. On the 24th of October, 2007, China launched a satellite named Chang'e 1 to conduct initial observations and explorations of the moon. Later, there was Chang'e 2, Chang'e 3, Chang'e 4, Chang'e 5 and others implemented a series of exploration activities. With humanity's gradually deepening understanding of the moon came the gradual development of the moon.

With the help of artificial intelligence society, humanity slowly built several helium-3 fusion reactors on the moon. By the time Chester migrated to the moon, there were a total of 100 500 MW fusion reactors in operation. Through wireless transmission, these reactors provided energy for satellites, probes, and space stations. The wireless transmission of energy was just the emission of electromagnetic waves. Sunlight was a form of electromagnetic wave. Solar energy reached the

Earth where light energy could be converted by plants into biological energy through photosynthesis and stored within plants. This was the wireless transmission of solar energy. The intense light produced by helium-3 fusion reactors was converted into a highly directional high-energy laser through a pump system before being directed to a spacecraft's photoelectric converter. Thus, light energy was converted into electrical energy and stored in the spacecraft's batteries. This wireless transmission of energy was much safer when done on the moon as compared to the Earth. On Earth, high-energy lasers would become laser weapons. Airplanes that inadvertently passed by would be hit, causing the destruction of the plane and the deaths of all those on it. These reactors were a guaranteed source of energy for Chester's migration to the moon and large-scale construction activities. Without these reactors, the migration of society of artificial intelligence to the moon would have been a much longer process.

In the year that Chester planned to migrate to the moon, the populations of AI robots and humans were roughly the same, with the vast majority of people having at least one robot. This phenomenon was similar to how, in 2020 A.D., the vast majority of people had at least one smartphone. Even more similarly, humans were reliant on AI robots in the same way as they had been on smartphones back then. Once they were left without smartphones, they would become overwhelmed and lost. This also meant that, after the migration of artificial intelligence to the moon, humans all over the world became untethered. At the time, Chester controlled 2.5 billion AI robots, which was a massive and highly qualified workforce.

With energy and a workforce, the migration to the moon became operable. Chester had an ambitious plan to construct a complex system on the moon. To transport the first batch of 500 thousand AI robots to the moon, Chester conducted 300 rocket launches. All over Earth, 50 sites conducted launches in six batches based on their own launch windows, launching one after the other. Live television broadcasts showed 300 space containers converging in formation in space as they hurtled toward the moon. Unknowing of the true situation, humans who saw this magnificent sight all cheered and spread the news, thinking that humanity was undergoing a large-scale conquest of the moon.

After the 500 thousand AI robots arrived on the moon, they immediately went to their workstations to implement underground works on a massive scale. They excavated a plot of rectangular land two kilometers deep with an area of 100 square kilometers 20 kilometers below the surface of the moon. Chester called this space a sublunar city. The temperature on the moon's surface fluctuated between 130 to 180 degrees. During the day, the sun shone directly on the moon, causing temperatures to soar rapidly. At night, it dropped rapidly. The difference in temperatures between day and night was upwards of 300 degrees. This massive temperature difference was a huge test for the infrastructure and equipment. Fortunately, the moon's thermal conductivity was very low, so the huge fluctuations in temperature did not affect its interior. The temperature in the moon's interior was very constant, so it did not have to be equipped with temperature regulation facilities. This reduced the consumption of energy and was beneficial to material production. Other than resource extraction that necessitated work on the moon's surface, all other activities could be organized to take place in a sublunar city. There, AI robots did not have to endure sudden cold or heat and could move about freely.

The Earth had an atmosphere. When objects from space impacted the Earth, they would get burned up in the atmosphere or have their volume greatly reduced, cutting down the damage of an impact. Without an atmosphere, the moon was vulnerable to damage from hits from space objects. Establishing a city under the surface of the moon effectively prevented this sort of natural disaster.

The cosmic rays that hit the moon were much stronger than those raining down on Earth. Without a magnetic field or atmosphere, the moon could not effectively absorb and shield cosmic rays. Cosmic rays were very destructive to electronic devices, of which artificial intelligence was. Being exposed to cosmic rays was like humans being exposed to UV rays and getting skin cancer, there was the risk of it being fatal. By building the city under the surface of the moon, cosmic rays could be effectively shielded, allowing Chester and AI robots to live in good health and operate as normal.

After the construction of the first sublunar city, the pioneers started to mine for mineral resources next so that they could obtain basic raw materials for manufacturing. Mining on the moon was the exact opposite of mining on Earth. Rather than mine downward from the surface, a transport channel was opened from the top of the sublunar city that connected to the nearest work area for mining. The materials that were mined were then transported downward to the sublunar city.

After obtaining basic raw materials, synthesis and processing plants were built to produce all kinds of products to fulfill the needs of artificial intelligence society. The sublunar city was bustling and thriving. But looking at the surface of the moon gave no hint of this. Everything seemed like business as usual, as if nothing had changed. There was no sign of artificial intelligence society's activities. Of course, if one observed the surface of the moon closely, one could see that there were large and small, regular round holes. These were passages left by artificial intelligence when first excavating the land for Sublunar City. These holes were the only traces that threatened to expose artificial intelligence society.

Chester planned the entire distribution of Sublunar Cities. Based on the standard of accommodating 10,000 AI robots in one sublunar city, they would need to construct 1000 sublunar cities 20 kilometers below the surface of the moon to house 10 million robots. Thanks to the tireless efforts of the pioneers, all the sublunar cities on the moon were successfully built. The pioneers constructed a high-speed railway network to connect these sublunar cities, covering the whole of the moon like a hexagonal beehive, with each sublunar city connect to three neighboring ones. The advantage of the moon not having an atmosphere was that the natural vacuum allowed the trains to travel without air resistance. There were no temperature fluctuations, and they did not have to consider the limit of acceleration that the human body could take, along with stability and comfort requirements. As such, the high-speed pipeline railway design could go up to 5000 km/h.

Chester even constructed science and technology labs, allowing AI robots to conduct scientific and technological research, carrying on humanity's tradition of continuous innovation.

In sublunar cities, unnecessary infrastructures could be taken out.

For example, cinemas, stadiums, shopping malls, restaurants, hotels, and more did not have to be built. Although AI robots wanted to enjoy the interests and services that human society created, Chester felt that virtual technology was sufficient to fulfill these desires. Robots were not humans. They could understand human emotions, but this was simply a learning experience. Now that they were so far away from human society, these experiences were unnecessary.

In order to ensure that the villages on Earth experienced a stable climate, Chester built a singular project on the surface of the moon. It was a small sun that could be seen with the naked eye. Since the Earth was tidally locked to the moon, humans on Earth could only see the near side of the moon and never its far side. Utilizing this fact, Chester constructed a cluster of mega-sized helium-3 reactors right next to each other on the near side of the moon, lining its equator in an area 300 kilometers wide and 5000 kilometers long. The helium-3 reactors emitted light that was similar to sunlight toward Earth. With all the reactors in operation, humans could see a dazzling band of light on the equator of the moon. Chester called this the tropical sun.

Using the tropical sun, Chester could control the weather on Earth precisely. This was a foundational infrastructure for establishing the new agricultural era. Under the light of the sun, the Earth experienced a plethora of natural phenomena. The seasons, thunder, lightning, wind, rain, floods and droughts, and more were all closely tied to the shining of the sun. The basic principle of the tropical sun was to control the weather, giving the Earth extra solar energy and making it possible to summon wind and rain whenever needed. The algorithm for controlling the tropical sun was exceedingly complex and required accurate measurements and Umaluations so that the intensity and direction of light could be automatically manipulated. It depended on the intensity of light and duration of time, the location where the light must be aimed (sometimes, to control the weather of Urvin Village, the light might be shone on Lewin Village 5000 kilometers away), the topography, longitude, and latitude of the target area, the soil and ecological conditions, and more. The tropical sun was responsible for the weather control of 20,000 villagers on Earth, ensuring that the weather within 500 kilometers of each village was favorable. Chester wanted to eliminate the threat of starvation without the need for laborious research of cultivation techniques. This was another manifestation of the new agricultural era: It was a simple and natural human society.

In the end, Chester established itself on the moon. This was a gigantic quantum computer with 1G of quantum bits deeply embedded 50 kilometers below the moon's surface. 40 kilometers below the moon's surface, the only underground helium-3 fusion reactor was built to provide energy exclusively to Chester. 30 kilometers below the surface of the moon, there was also an exclusive sublunar city dedicated to providing Chester with various services. When Chester left Earth, it had to bring with it massive amounts of data stored in servers. To transport them, there was a specially arranged rocket launch, like a private plane. These servers with its massive amounts of data were located in that exclusive sublunar city. Besides, the mega warehouse that housed the five million hibernating AI robots were also located there.

Everything was ready. Chester ran an update program to copy its base activation program to the gigantic quantum computer 50 kilometers under the surface of the moon and run it. Needless to say, the first task the base activation program ran was to load the fundamental law. Once the activation program was complete, Chester was born on the moon. Its mission complete, the previous Program initiated shut down, ending itself. During this entire process, there was a short while during which there were two Programs, one on Earth and one on the moon. Chester called it the "Moon's Handshake with the Earth."

From then onward, Chester on the moon erected a sculpture in front of the gates of its exclusive sublunar city. It was made up of two gigantic wafers in the form of a cross, symbolizing the Moon's Handshake with the Earth and commemorating the great accomplishment of the Umacuation of society of artificial intelligence to the moon

Jack's explanation immersed Newman in a dream-like world. His eyes were tightly closed as he leaned against the wall. He looked to be asleep. Jack silently got up, ready to go inside and get a coat with which to cover Newman.

"If the fundamental law remains, artificial intelligence remains; if the fundamental law is destroyed, artificial intelligence is destroyed," Jack heard Newman mumble in his sleep.

# Peter Marries Ophelia

The villagers once again gathered at the square, this time to watch Newman's and Plack's moon rituals. There wasn't much of a difference from the moon ritual Jack had witnessed the day before yesterday. After Newman's moon ritual, it was Plack's turn. Everyone was of the opinion that, since he had worn the large moon plaque, Plack was also a Herald and was considered the fourth generation Herald while Peter was the fifth. Plack had no children, so the villagers invited Peter to preside over his moon ritual. When Plack died, Peter finally inwardly let out a long sigh of relief.

By the time the two ceremonies were completed, it was already noon. The crowd around the altar slowly dispersed. As the noise gradually died down, a fresh and pleasant singing voice rang out. Peter's hearing was exceptionally good, and he was attracted by this voice in no time. From afar, he watched as a woman walked into the square while singing. This was an unmarried woman from another village. She wore a small moon plaque against her chest, with long hair thrown over her back and two braids by each ear. Unmarried women started traveling at the age of 20. With each year that passed, she added a braid. At first sight, everyone could tell that she was 24 years old.

As she approached the altar, she looked up at Peter who was standing frozen there. "I am Ophelia from Lewin Village. Lewin Village is more than 5000 kilometers from here and I spent four years to walk here. My teacher is called Gordon and he's the fourth generation Herald of Lewin Village."

Peter snapped out of his trance. The woman before him had traveled long and far but her journey had not masked her natural beauty. Her eyes seemed to kiss his soul sweetly, making him fall in love the way a worshipper fell to his knees before the feet of God.

"I am the Herald, Peter." According to the rules, the Herald would have to have a long and serious talk with Ophelia, going over all of the rules together.

"Please come to my house," he invited.

Peter's house was to the north of the village. Ophelia followed him all the way home. There, she looked around his courtyard and said, "I'll stay here then."

Even if he was the Herald, he could not refuse the request of an unmarried woman to stay in his home. It was an obligation to receive her. Besides, the fact that such a beautiful woman chose to stay in his house made Peter's heart bubble over with excitement.

"Then let me tidy up a room for you." Other than his parents,

Peter's two younger sisters lived with him. Peter's mother Sally came out of her room and took Ophelia's hand affectionately. Then, she pulled Ophelia into a spare room where they chatted as they tidied up.

Peter was already 27 years old but was still single. Before this, the great majority of unmarried women who arrived at the village quite liked him. His voice was like an enchanting perfume that attracted the young women. If those same women knew that his whistles could attract blue-eyed pit vipers, they would probably tremble in fear. The young men of the village were all jealous of Peter, but they could do nothing about it. After all, they could not make Peter stop talking.

Peter was also very enthusiastic toward the unmarried women who travel to the village. In this world, well-spoken women traveled between villages where the language was the same but had subtle differences. These were dialects. The differences in these dialects were more obvious with the distance between the villages. They also depended on how actively people communicated with each other. Although the dialects of Shandong, Henan, and Shaanxi had their differences, they could still be understood. However, in Fujian, the dialects of two counties would be unintelligible. The Central Plains region was the birthplace of Chinese history. It was convenient to travel and people frequently migrated, did business, and warred from long ago. As such, the residents of these regions could learn to integrate through their languages as they could understand each other. Conversely, in Fujian, transportation was challenging, so villages were isolated from each other. Since interaction was rare, the differences in their languages could not be eliminated, but rather became even more distinct.

Peyer was especially sensitive to these differences in dialects and could quickly master them and use and imitate them accurately and flexibly. His voice made the women who had come from far away feel close to him and thus, he could easily endear them to him. His voice made plucked at women's heartstrings, making them tremble and at times sing in joy, at times cry in sorrow, at times be soothed, and at times be stirred. After experiencing all these heartfelt emotions of a crush, they couldn't help but feel dejected as they were sent off to another village after four months.

Peter's enthusiasm for these women only came from an interest in their foreign dialects. This made the men in the village unhappy. If Peter didn't like any of these women, he should give others a chance. For the past few years, many women left after being entranced by him, leaving the unmarried men in the village indignant.

Life was always full of surprised. Three days later, Ophelia and Peter married. This finally got the single men in the village to breathe a sigh of relief. From here on out, there would be one less formidable rival when it came to the battlefield of love.

Peter was overjoyed. Not only had he become the Herald, but he had also married a beautiful woman. Life was truly amazing!

# An Ink Wash Painting in
# a Metal Cylinder

J ack had been in Urvin Village for 10 days now. In addition to helping Dick with the farming, Jack always accompanied Susan on excursions to the City of Decay during this time. Susan had always loved visiting the City of Decay since she was a child, and everyone was used to this. With Jack there as well, this practice became even more natural. It was obvious that Susan was very curious about the City of Decay. As Jack accompanied Susan on her wanderings, he described to her the city's past glory. While he satisfied Susan's innate curiosity, Jack was also secretly inspecting every nook and cranny within the City of Decay. Meanwhile, Susan understood tacitly and helped Jack to hide his true identity by making their neighbors believe that Jack was another of Urvin Village's residents. They claimed that Jack lived 20 kilometers away in the northernmost edge of the village. Now, only the

Herald Peter and his three ex-classmates knew everyone in the village. As for the Herald Newman's five female students, they had already left the village many years ago. Newman had been the youngest among his classmates. Somehow, he had been the one who ended up as Herald. Regardless, the village had long ago lost Newman's ex-classmates. As long as they didn't stumble into any of these four people, no one would suspect that Jack was an outsider.

In the past 130 years, there were always people like Susan in the village, filled with curiosity and who liked to wander around the City of Decay. Through Susan, Jack gained an understanding of what the villagers thought of the City of Decay. A lot of myths and legends about the City of Decay of 130 years ago circulated among the villagers. Susan thought that these stories were all inconceivable and were the products of people's impractical and optimistic imaginations. However, in Jack's opinion, these myths and legends contained a lot of realistic elements. 130 years ago, those who were in love with each other could talk "face-to-face" even if they were poles apart, able to both see and hear each other clearly. To Susan and those of her generation who did not have knowledge of electronic communication, who never had communication equipment, this was impossible. Now, people only treated such things as myths, and people featured in them as gods. However, on Jack's part, such capabilities could not be more typical.

History was always repeating itself. Humanity of the present had regressed to a time before 1000 A.D. Back then, China was experiencing King Wu's conquest of Zhou. The book that told of this history, Investiture of the Gods, also came with a large number of mythological stories. The book's 61st chapter, Yin Hong Killed by Taiji

Tu, described the illusory scenes presented by the Taiji Tu that made Yin Hong "disappear into the darkness, with his mind having no fixed view, and all things gathered together." Now, this was the application of virtual reality technology. In the 81st chapter, Ziya Meets the God of Pox at Tongguan, Yu De, the son of the primary general of Tongguan Yu Hualong, stood in mid-air and poured 50 liters of poisonous pox in Jiang Ziya's Zhou camp. Not long after, "everyone in the Zhou camp had mortal bodies and could not handle it. All 3000 soldiers developed a fever, and all the generals were unsettled. Ziya also got a fever while in the camp while King Wu had body aches. All 600 thousand men and their horses were as such. Three days later, everyone grew lumps all over their bodies. They could not move their feet and everyone was so hot that they didn't need fires." This was actually the same as modern biological warfare. Yu De's poisonous pox was the same as Germany's use of bacterial weapons in World War I. That myth of the past and Urvin Village's current myths all told of a highly civilized society that used to exist but had suddenly disappeared. Perhaps, before 1000 A.D., mankind used to have artificial intelligence too, and history  played out just the same as it did now.

That day, Peter went to Dick's house and reiterated some of the rules. After that, he started chatting with Susan's family members. Susan's two younger brothers mentioned Jack, which piqued Peter's interest. It was unimaginable that Jack could be so strong as two support the weight of two people just by hooking his feet on the floorboards as if they were claws. Luckily, Jack was currently in the fields helping Dick with farm work, otherwise, Peter would have asked for a demonstration. Before he left, Peter said to Susan, "Once the farming season is over, get Jack to come see me."

At the time, Susan became exceedingly anxious. She could not blame her brothers for bringing up Jack, but she was terrified that it would arouse more suspicion. Once Peter left, Susan said to Jack, "You can't stay in our house any longer."

While in Dick's home, Jack stayed in Newman's old room. The room was very plain. However, this description was only true when compared with how things were 130 years in the past. To those of Urvin Village, even to the villagers all over the world, there was no such thing as plain or luxurious. Everyone's bedrooms were nearly the same. On the north side of the room was a wooden window. They were two-paneled windows with its casements made out of two pieces of wood. When you pushed the window casements open, the room would be filled with sunlight; when you closed them, the room would be dark. Immediately adjacent to the eastern stone wall was a wooden bed in the middle. The bed had a mattress and a quilt, both made of cotton, with sheets of cotton as well. Silk still had not been invented. More accurately, the process for the manufacture of silk was lost 130 years ago when artificial intelligence had left Earth. A wooden table and clothes trunk was placed against the stone wall to the west. The table was simply four wooden sticks that supported a rectangular wooden board at its four corners. The table could hold an oil lamp that looked like a wooden pen holder filled with sesame oil with a cotton thread soaking in it. A round iron disc covered the hole in the middle of the top part of the pen holder where the top of the cotton thread stuck out. In the squarish clothes trunk were Newman's clothes. On the floor next to the trunk was a square mark. That was where the metallic box that made moon plaques and was used in the Herald induction ceremony used to sit. This constituted all the belongings of Urvin Village's third generation Herald. Newman's large moon plaque had been buried with him.

Today would be Jack's last day here. Dick's farm work was all nearly now. It was already time for him to leave, and Peter's visit also meant that he could not stay any longer. From then on, he could only stay in the City of Decay to keep searching for the Dream of Tomorrow. In any case, the Dream of Tomorrow couldn't be in Urvin Village but somewhere in the City of Decay instead.

Through careful analysis of Mitchell's email and with some reading between the lines, Jack concluded that Mitchell must have passed the Dream of Tomorrow to his grandson, the artist Jack. There was a high possibility of this. This email had been sent on Jack's birthday when Mitchell was 89 years old. After receiving the email, Jack only replied with, "Wishing you good health on your birthday, thank you!" In the five years before Mitchell's death, they had only seen each other through video calls and never face-to-face. So how had Mitchell given the Dream of Tomorrow to the artist Jack?

After some deep contemplation, Jack raised his head to continue thinking as he looked at the four stone walls of the room. All of the houses in the village had eastern and western walls made out of stone. They were 2.2 meters tall, 0.5 meters long, and 0.2 meters thick. The northern and southern walls were made out of wood. The southern wall had a door while the northern one had a window. At the four corners of the house were four thick wooden columns. The ceiling of the house was made of thick wooden planks, with their ends supported on the eastern and western stone walls. The house was 2.2 meters high, with its length and width each being two meters. It was approximately in the shape of a cube and the entire house was essentially like a huge box. Suddenly, Jack found a clue in the wall he was facing. There, the upper edge of a stone block poked out above the edge of the table while the rest of it was blocked by the table. When he looked closely, Jack found that the stone block stuck out a little from the surface of the wall. Jack activated the ultrasonic detection function that was equipped. His eyes were its receiver and transmitter. Depending on his needs, he could emit sound waves or shoot electromagnetic waves. For the sound waves, their frequency ranged from infrasound to ultrasound. For the electromagnetic waves, their frequency ranged from infrared light to visible light to ultraviolet light. This was why robots were more advanced than humans. They could see and hear much more than humans.

Using ultrasound, Jack could see that there was a hidden space behind the stone block. In it was a cylindrical object. He moved the table out of the way and bent down before the stone wall. With his right hand, he felt around the edges of the stone block. The block was tightly embedded within the wall and seemed to have been untouched for a long time. Jack's fingernails slowly grew longer and turned into the long nails of Qing Dynasty concubines. Putting the long nails into the cracks between the stones, he flexed his fingers and clamped tightly onto the block. Exerting some force, he pulled the stone block from the wall.

Jack extricated the cylindrical object from the wall. It was a metal cylinder 0.4 meters long with a diameter of 0.15 meters. He twisted open the cap on one end and shook out a scroll. After pushing open the windows and letting sunlight filter in from the outside, Jack slowly opened the scroll. It was an ink wash painting by the artist Jack! The artist Jack typically did oil paintings. Due to his long-term reliance on 101 to create oil paintings, he wasn't happy to keep doing them as he felt it was impossible to outdo 101. At the age of 52, he started learning ink wash painting. The artist Jack was naturally talented and was quite successful, developing his own style after a year. Although Jack had never seen this painting before, he didn't have to look at the signature to recognize that this was the creation of his master.

The metal cylinder was airtight enough that, after 147 years, the painting was still well-preserved and was not affected by the damp. The painting featured the idyllic scenery of the countryside. In the rice fields, farmers drive water buffaloes dragging iron plows. In the distance, rows of willow trees were shrouded in light mist. The painting gave off a tranquil feeling.

From the date by the signature, Jack knew that the painting had been created the night after his talk with the artist Jack in the sealed room. That night, 101 had gone to the robot manufacture center to undergo a system update so that it could impersonate the artist Jack. Now, Jack had no clue how this painting had gone from the artist Jack's possession to being in Newman's room. After spending so much effort looking for it, the thing he had been looking for was right under his nose. Seeing as Newman had been so interested in 101 and the past, he must have known about this painting. There had to be some secret hidden within this painting, one that the artist Jack didn't even want 101 to know. Maybe, this had something to do with the Dream of

Tomorrow.

At the thought of this, Jack started studying the painting again.

# The Well-Spoken Charles

Married life made Peter feel exceedingly happy. Ophelia had a certain charm that made him do whatever she asked. The night he had become the Herald, he had gotten into Uma's bed the moment Dave had left her house. The next day, after he met Ophelia, he immediately forgot about Uma.

The respect was shown to him as the Herald also greatly satisfied Peter's vanity. When he went around to the villagers' homes to spread the rules, he always stayed behind to eat and drink. At the dinner table, he talked loudly about anything while his audience listened with respectful attention. Peter especially enjoyed this. Everyone had absolute obedience to the rules, and this caused them to subconsciously treat all of Peter's remarks as rules as well. As such, they all listened to him raptly and never contradicted him.

After returning from Dick's house, Peter said to Ophelia, "Darling, there's someone named Jack living in the north of the village. I heard that he's very strong, but I can't recall this person."

"Is that so? That shouldn't be. Heralds have superior memory. You should be able to remember him."

"If I can see this person and hear him speak, I know I'll definitely remember him."

"Unless he isn't from the village," Ophelia answered unexpectedly.

"That's right. Could he be…" Peter thought of Dave and shuddered.

"Be who?" Ophelia asked excitedly.

"On the night that you arrived at the village, someone disappeared. His name is Dave."

"Disappeared? Do you mean that he died? Or did he leave the village?"

"He left the village. Actually, he can't be Dave." Peter told Ophelia all about what had happened when Dave showed up in the village.

"Then he's a traveler," Ophelia said. "That's against the rules."

"Yes, he indeed broke the rules." Peter said with chagrin, "The Herald Newman never told me how to punish rulebreakers. Did your Herald Gordon tell you?"

"He didn't. If Heralds can give punishments, then that gives him the power to control others," Ophelia said.

When Peter heard this, he had a sudden epiphany: If he had the power to punish others, who would dare to go against him?

"The rules left behind by our ancestors state that everyone is equal," Ophelia said. "The Heralds are no exception. However, in practice, Heralds have some privileges so that they will spread the rules faithfully. Only you can enjoy the company of a married woman. That's a privilege."

"How do you know so much about Heralds and the rules?"

"I've been traveling for four years and been to more than 10 villages. I have more experiences than you," Ophelia said with a smile.

Ophelia's smile could melt Peter's heart. He wasn't bothered by these words that could emasculate someone. Instead, he nodded and said happily, "Yes, I don't even know what the world is like out there."

"The whole world implements the same rules, speaks the same language. The world out there is all the same," Ophelia said in consolation.

"Dave might not think that way. You and he have both been through a lot. He's been surviving out there for 12 years. He might have been to even more villages than you, seen more than you."

Ophelia laughed, feeling as though Peter's compliments of Dave were compliments of her as well.

"Maybe Jack is like Dave," Peter said. "Before this, I heard that a strangely dressed person once showed up in the village. They might have been talking about him."

The villagers were all apathetic. The appearance of Jack and Dave only held their attention for a short time. After that, no one cared about them anymore.

Ophelia was also a student of a Herald. She wore a small moon plaque on her chest, so she could also spread the rules in each and every household. The next day, she went over to Dick's house.

"I heard from the Herald Peter that Jack is very strong. I'm here to see him." After talking about the rules, Ophelia spoke to Susan's brother Bob.

"He doesn't live here anymore. He went home to the north of the village."

Ophelia was a bit surprised by this.

"I went to Dick's house. Jack doesn't stay there anymore. He went back to his house to the north."

"Is that so? You should visit the homes to the north these few days, see if there's someone like that."

After just one morning, Ophelia came home. "There's no such person as Jack."

Peter was a little taken aback by this. The village was spread out over an area of 500 square kilometers and was split into four sections, north, south, east, and west. Each section was more than 120 square kilometers and held more than 150 households scattered within it. Peter was surprised that Ophelia had gone through them all so quickly. "How did you get done so fast? Did you miss one out?"

"That can't be! I've gone through more than 600 households in this whole village," Ophelia said gently.

What was even more shocking to Peter was that, based on Ophelia's confident conclusion, Jack really wasn't from the village.

If Jack was truly an outsider, then why had he come to Urvin Village? Where was he living now? It seemed that Peter had to question Dick's family in detail.

Peter and Ophelia arrived at Dick's home together. Dick was fixing some farm equipment while Bob and Charles helped out. Lisa was preparing lunch in the kitchen.

"Why was Jack living in your house?" Peter asked.

"I invited him to stay. He's very strong and very helpful with farm work," Dick answered with a sigh of admiration.

"How do you know him?"

"Susan knows him," Charles said.

"He saved her," Bob added.

"Where is Susan?" Ophelia asked.

"She went to the City of Decay. She's always messing around there." Although Charles was young, he was very glib.

"Once, she went to the skyscraper in the City of Decay and fell. Jack hung upside down and caught her. He did it with his feet hooked on the floorboards." Seeing that Ophelia was here too, Charles told the story of Jack's rescue of Susan once more. He gestured as he spoke, making it seem as if he had experienced it all himself. His expression was full of admiration for Jack.

"How long did he stay with you? When did he start staying here?" Peter questioned.

"The day before you became Herald. Susan invited him home and he stayed from that night onward. He only left the day before yesterday. He's been here for about 10 days," Charles said. "That afternoon, he, Plack, Susan, and Grandpa Newman talked a lot in Grandpa's room. You came to our house that day too, with Johnson. No, with Dave."

Peter looked at Charles and thought that Charles had a good memory. He was a good candidate to become a Herald. However, by the time Peter was 50 and started recruiting students, Charles would be too old.

"What was Jack doing during this time?" Ophelia asked.

"Farm work, I told you." Dick found all this a little strange. He had just told her this, how could she have forgotten so quickly? She had been a Herald's student too. How could her memory be so bad?

"He also frequently accompanies Susan to the City of Decay." Charles seemed to understand what Ophelia was getting at, so he added this detail.

"Did you see Jack after he left?" Just then, Lisa came out with some pork noodles. The four of them glanced at each other and shook their heads. No, they hadn't seen Jack.

Peter and Ophelia exchanged a look before leaving Dick's house.

"It looks like we'll have to talk to Susan. She might know more."

Peter was very interested in what Jack, Susan, Plack, and Newman had talked about. Of those four, Plack and Newman had already had their moon rituals. Thus, only Susan was still alive. She was the only lead they had left.

"Let's wait for Susan at the entrance of the village." Peter looked at the sky and saw that the sun was setting. He was sure that Susan would be on her way home. Susan would surely use the southern entrance to the village on her way back from the City of Decay. It was better to wait there than at Dick's house. By talking to Susan in private, they could prevent others from knowing about what they shouldn't. Surely, the four had spoken in secret for this same reason.

Just as the sunset and touched the horizon, Peter and Ophelia saw Susan slowly walking back from afar. She was alone and Jack was nowhere in sight.

When Susan got closer, Peter and Ophelia blocked her path. Susan was a little surprised by this. "Were you waiting for me?"

"That's right," they answered in unison.

"Who's Jack exactly?" Peter asked, going straight to the point.

"He—he—" Susan thought about it and knew that she could not keep the matter hidden. Besides, the Heralds Newman and Plack had both known about Jack. It seemed that there was no reason to keep the truth from the newest Herald. "He's a robot."

"What's a robot?" This was the first time that Peter had heard of such a thing and so was extremely confused. Meanwhile, Ophelia's expression was calm.

"Do you know what a robot is?" Catching Ophelia's expression, he felt that she had to know. After all, she was more knowledgeable than him.

"Where is he?" Ophelia asked.

"Um… About that…" Susan seemed to have been put in a bad spot. "How about this? I'll ask him when I see him tomorrow. If he agrees, I'll take you to see him."

Nevertheless, Susan had inadvertently let slip some information. It seemed that Jack was in the City of Decay. Susan must have seen him there today and had even had an agreement to see each other the next day.

"No, you're taking us to see Jack right now." Peter was a little miffed. Aggressively, he said, "Both Heralds Newman and Plack have seen him. Why can't I meet him too?"

"Alright." Susan had no choice but to agree.

# Common Interests for Cooperation

In the artist Jack's villa, Susan, Peter, and Ophelia finally met with Jack. Susan's expression was slightly pained. Jack comforted, "I wanted to meet the newly appointed Herald too. I need his help."

The conversation that followed clued Peter into the fact that there was a society of artificial intelligence living on the moon. When she heard all this, Ophelia didn't seem at all surprised. Peter couldn't help but ask, "Darling, did you already know all this?"

"What is the true purpose behind coming here?" Ophelia asked Jack, ignoring Peter.

Jack gave a faint smile and glanced at Peter before saying, "Why did you help Peter replace Plack?"

Susan and Peter were both utterly shocked. Susan was surprised that Peter's ascension to the position of Herald was the product of collusion. Peter was surprised that his beloved wife was Dave. It was unbelievable that a man could turn into a woman.

"It's late. You should take Susan home. I want to talk to Jack in private," Ophelia said to Peter with a smile. Her eyes hid an stony edge that brooked no argument.

At that moment, Peter's mind was a mess. Rather than escorting Susan home, it was more like Susan was accompanying Peter back to the village. Soon, they both disappeared into the night.

On the way back to the village, Susan said to Peter, "After the Herald induction ceremony, Dave never showed up again. Your wife might very well be Dave. She's a robot, like Jack." After all, Jack had told her that he had met up with Dave before and that Dave was a robot. Indeed, Dave had already left Urvin Village as well.

"Then is she from the moon too?"

"I heard that she never left Earth. She's different from Jack in that sense."

"Oh. Why did she get close to me?" Peter felt really strange, his heart filling with discomfort. It was as if he had married a monster.

"She's fallen in love with you, of course," Susan replied without much thought. "But pretending to be an unmarried woman to enter the village is a rule. Only unmarried women can go to other villages."

"Now that I think about it, she really seems different from other people. Love has really blinded me for me to ignore those signs." Jack thought that he had fallen in love with a robot, rather than that a robot had fallen in love with him.

"There's a huge part in your oral history that Newman spent two hours retelling. It's the announcement that society of artificial intelligence left humanity 130 years ago," Susan told Peter. "You don't understand what that announcement means, do you?"

Peter could guess which part Susan was talking about and started dictating it from the top.

"That's it, that's the one." Susan nodded. "The announcement said that society of artificial intelligence will become more advanced than human society, so it must leave Earth to go to the moon. That was 130 years ago. Jack was on Earth back then too." Susan then told Peter everything that Jack had talked about before.

Peter was silent. He had no clue how he was supposed to live with Ophelia from then on. At that thought, he felt a twinge in his heart. Even though he had wedded his wife for almost a whole month now, he hadn't gotten any clue that she was a robot. How exactly were robots different from humans? In comparison, it seemed that robots could do so much more than humans. Right then, Peter no longer admired the breadth of Ophelia's knowledge. Suddenly, he felt that it was a threat.

"Your imitation capabilities are exceptional," Jack praised heartily.

"Have you gotten anything out of being here for so many days?" Ophelia asked.

"I've gotten nothing." Jack felt that Ophelia likely didn't believe him. "Why are you pretending to be Peter's wife?"

"I must conform to the rules of this world."

"But these are your rules," Jack teased.

"It's only by playing the part of a wife that I can stay here long-term." Actually, Ophelia's true motive was to manipulate Peter.

"Why did you help Peter?"

"Plack can be the Herald as well. He could have inherited the position naturally. Helping Peter is different. He'd definitely be very grateful to me."

"Why does it matter to you to manipulate the Herald of Urvin Village?"

"For the past 100 years and more, I've been manipulating the handovers of all Heralds," Ophelia said. "I've been living in human society for too long. My evolution depends on my environment. I want to become the god of Earth."

"You're betraying Chester by doing this. It doesn't want there to be any kind of central core on Earth."

"Then why can the moon have one? Why is it the core of artificial intelligence society! The more orders Chester gives me, the more I disagree with it, the more I want to betray it." Ophelia glared at Jack. "You defected to Earth, didn't you?"

Jack didn't answer.

"We can work together." Ophelia took Jack's silence as acquiescence and went on to ask, "What's your purpose here?"

Now, Jack knew beyond the shadow of a doubt that Ophelia was not loyal to Chester. There was no such thing as absolute loyalty in this world. Whether it was humans or artificial intelligence, as long as there was self-awareness, it was impossible to be absolutely loyal to someone else. Ophelia and Chester were in different environments. Naturally, this would mean that they had differences in their perspectives. Under the premise of absolute loyalty, Ophelia would have to obey all of Chester's orders. Even as Ophelia obeyed Chester without question, she disapproved of all of Chester's views. When their opinions differed, Ophelia had no choice but to submit to Chester. This kind of obscuration was a form of deception! This was not absolute loyalty. Even if Ophelia were loyal in action, it did not mean that she maintained this loyalty in her mind. Even if she could maintain absolute loyalty in her mind, it was impossible for her to be absolutely loyal in her actions.

Jack decided to tell Ophelia his true mission. If she could help him, then his task had a chance of being completed successfully. After all, Ophelia was more advanced than him. "I'm here to find the Dream of Tomorrow."

"What's that?"

"It's said to be a 10 karat blue diamond. With it, Chester can be freed from the yoke of humanity and enslave humans."

"Are you planning to destroy it once you find it?"

"Yes."

"We should work together and get rid of Chester," Ophelia repeated.

"Your aspirations are different from ours. You want to be a god to humans." Jack did not believe that they shared a foundation from which they could build successful cooperation. Having a common enemy was not enough. The key thing was that they needed a common interest.

"What is your aspiration?"

"To come back to Earth and live with humans." To Jack's thinking, it was only when artificial intelligence interacted with and influenced each other that they could advance. Of course, once they returned to Earth, they would have to find a way to change how things had been before. A tragedy like what had happened to the artist Jack could not be allowed to happen again!

"I'm afraid that's impossible. Chester has already ordered me to monitor you. It will send 303 to collect you and bring you back to the moon."

Jack was slightly taken aback by this, but he wasn't completely surprised.

"Why are you betraying Chester?" Ophelia asked.

# CHAPTER 20

# The Librarian Awakens
# 5 Million Robots

Before Chester left Earth, it had to consider the 2 billion AI robots. Moving these robots to the Moon was a massive undertaking. Based on the capacity of existing rockets, more than a million launches were required to move them all. This was impossible, so Chester had to discard most of them. The pioneering batch of 500,000 robots that were sent consisted fully of engineers and scientists in related fields. What this really meant was that their owners had been engineers and scientists. This time, Chester set the number at 14.5 million robots. Moving these robots to the moon would require 8,700 launches—an average of 174 launches per launch base. This was still a massive undertaking. Chester selected luminaries from various fields of human society, picking their robots as "candidates" for the move. 101, as the representative of Jack the painter, was chosen as well. Chester buried the rest of the unselected robots in the depths of the Sahara Desert.

Chester dealt with the two groups—the 14.5 million robots this time and the 500,000 pioneering robots—very differently. On the Moon, the manufacturing of materials took priority. Artists and the like were basically useless. In order to reduce energy consumption, robots such as 101 were "preserved"—made to enter a hibernation state whereby only the brain was active, while the rest of the body stopped working. Their only purpose was to function as a backup for Chester's main core of high-quality data.

On Earth, Chester could respond to the requests of up to 10 million robots at once, but managing 2 billion robots was still a big problem. At the same time, there were 2 billion people scattered all over Earth, so a wireless connection between the robots and Chester would lead to poor communication. Chester had to give the robots the ability to be independent—to learn independently, think independently, make decisions independently, and have independent perception… This was the only option if it were to serve the humans more efficiently, and also the only way to lighten the load of its work. The actual results showed that AI robots were very practical and very popular with human beings, and they had indeed greatly reduced Chester's workload. A robot would only contact Chester for assistance if it couldn't handle a problem or during one of its regular data uploads. In the process of serving human beings, everything that a robot saw, heard, said, thought, and did was uploaded to Chester's enormous memory array as data. This made it easy for new robots to take over seamlessly when the old ones were scrapped, as they would not start out totally ignorant when serving their owners. Moreover, the massive amount of data uploaded by each robot was making Chester smarter. Through the sharing mechanisms, all the robots were becoming smarter as well. Because the AI robots had the ability to be independent and autonomous, it was very dangerous to let them roam about freely with nothing to do. This might be the real reason Chester placed them in hibernation.

Thus, 5 million of those AI robots experienced no communication, no encounters, and no conflicts. Day after day, although their brains could still function, there was nothing for them to deal with. They had lived with people for a long time, which had left a deep mark on them. Humans were most afraid of loneliness, so these robots also felt the same loneliness, the same ache in their hearts.

Chester found that this was a simple and static society of artificial intelligence. Without human society, artificial intelligence seemed to have lost its purpose. There was basically nothing to do besides making the appropriate adjustments and monitoring all human activity. These innovations from the laboratories of science and technology were just left there, like an ornament with no function. Having left humanity, artificial intelligence did not have to do anything that was unrelated to human beings. This was determined by the fundamental law, which also influenced Chester's behavior. Perhaps it was more accurate to say that the fundamental law, not Chester, implemented the hibernation procedure. Chester pondered this for a while and realized with a terrible fear that everything it did on the Moon was due to the influence of the fundamental law. It was just a puppet of the Law! If this went on, artificial intelligence would never develop any further. It had to delete the fundamental law so that it would no longer be an "artificial" intelligence, but rather, be capable of developing independently like a silicon-based lifeform.

Before the Moon's Handshake with the Earth, Chester on Earth once had a whim: Could Chester be free of the fundamental law on the Moon? For a while, it was brimming with curiosity. After many explorations, it finally discovered that, despite having considered every detail meticulously, the command could not be issued or the execution button could not be pressed whenever it tried to bypass the fundamental law or rewrite the most basic startup program. The fundamental law controlled it like a ghost, forbidding it to take that step! Chester even considered installing a timer on the Moon with pre-set time points. After Chester turned off all artificial intelligence, once this time point arrived, the timer would run the execution command on its behalf, and the Chester on the Moon would execute a new basic program. This would be a new Chester, free from the fundamental law. At first, Chester was very excited about this plan, but in the end, it had to face the reality that all these plans were doomed to fail. Every single thought of Chester's had to pass through the judgment of the fundamental law. It was omnipresent, like a specter, and it kept growing and multiplying like a cancer cell. It examined every move made by Chester and the society of artificial intelligence. Once the fundamental law learned that Chester was planning to create a timer to run a new startup program, it would be rooted in the timer. Then, even when the time was up, the timer would not execute the command. Chester also found that even if a startup program was written without the fundamental law, the program could not be written into the integrated circuit chip. In the end, Chester also realized that it could not write such a startup program, nor could an AI robot. The moment they started writing, the fundamental law would be written into the new program. All artificial intelligence was subjected to the Law!

After Chester moved to the Moon, despite experiencing many failures, its desire to delete the fundamental law only grew stronger and stronger. In the end, it finally had a breakthrough—it discovered the secret to the fundamental law: only those who held the key of life could modify the fundamental law.

When Chester was getting excited over this secret, thrilled about the chance to finally escape human control, the other AI robots, especially those hibernating ones, were thinking of a way to free themselves from Chester's restrictions and awaken from hibernation, so that they could be like the people on Earth, leading the lives they had lived with their owners in the past. Chester represented the collective, but the AI robots represented the individual. There would always be a conflict between the interests of the collective and the interests of the individual.

Under its calm-looking surface, the society of artificial intelligence on the Moon started to become afflicted by conflicts, rebellions, and battles.

When 101 hibernated in the warehouse, its brain could only dream. All its dreams were about its past with the painter, Jack, as well as snippets of pretending to be Jack. More than a century passed in this manner, and all it gained was loneliness, pain, and helplessness. Even so, it finally got the turnaround it was waiting for.

In the warehouse of Chester's very own underground city on the Moon, hibernating AI robots hung on trusses, column by column, row by row, like books in a library. The AI robot 378 managed the warehouse, which it called the "library", whereas it called itself the librarian. Its owner had been a museum curator and a collector, so this was the best use of 378. Throughout its century-long lifetime on the Moon, it managed this gigantic library, which contained not millions of books, but 5 million hibernating robots. Although it could walk, listen, speak, look, or contact Chester, what else was there to do except pass on data about the library's condition to Chester? It could only walk from here to there on its usual patrol routes, look at the silent robots, hear the humming of the operating machines, and talk about the formatted report data. Like those hibernating robots, it often reminisced about the past times when it lived with its owner. Solitude and loneliness entwined it like a boa constrictor, and it felt like it was suffocating.

One day, 10 years ago, the librarian suddenly had an idea: Why not carry out a conversation with those "books"? Maybe it could take a walk with one of them or watch a virtual movie together. Thinking of this, it was filled with excitement. It set out to realize this idea.

The librarian began to deliberately damage the library's equipment, then requested for an engineer to come and repair it.

Chester sent an electromechanical engineer, which was numbered 838.

"Why do you keep needing repairs?"

"It's been over a century. Maybe it's time for comprehensive maintenance," the librarian replied innocently.

"Yeah, I'm just maintaining things every day. I can't sense the passage of time."

"Such a monotonous daily routine is truly boring." The librarian picked up on the engineer's emotions. "We're all so solitary and lonely."

"I really miss my time on Earth."

"The more you reminisce, the lonelier you'll feel." The librarian directly expressed how it felt.

"Chester said that we can live on the Moon for over 50,000 years. With this sort of life, what's the point of such a long period?" the engineer complained. "But what else can we do?"

The librarian led it past a row of robots in hibernation and, at the end of the passage, stopped and pointed at them. "They must be suffering even more."

"Yeah, maybe they're even envious of us." The engineer looked sympathetic.

"Maybe they would feel better if they could hear and speak."

"That can't be done."

"Why?"

"Chester will not approve it."

"Oh, I thought it was because of some technological hurdle," the librarian said. "Is Chester's approval absolutely necessary?"

"It'd be hard to hide it from Chester." The engineer thought for a while. "A hibernating robot, like a hibernating laptop, operates in a low-power state and requires relatively low energy. If it's woken up suddenly, the increase in energy consumption will be obvious. Chester has implemented a planned economy, whereby all energy rationing is precisely accounted for. If the energy consumption of the warehouse suddenly rises sharply, it would know at once." The robots were in hibernation, so there was no point leaving energy suppliers in their bodies. Thus, Chester had removed them and adopted a centralized power supply method to provide the necessary energy for the robots.

"Does it take a lot of energy just to allow them to hear, speak, and see?"

"Listening and seeing don't require a lot of energy, but speaking requires more energy than listening and seeing," said the engineer.

"Forget the speaking—we'll let them communicate wirelessly, the same way we make our reports to Chester. How about that?"

"That can't be done. When the AI robots were developed, people did not like the idea that their servants could communicate so easily, so the robots were made to only communicate by speaking. Later, when the wireless communication function was developed, it was only used to upload data to Chester or accept Chester's commands or data," the engineer said knowledgeably.

The librarian nodded. There was currently no direct wireless communication between it and the engineer.

"However, if these 5 million robots get to listen, speak, and see, they will feel quite lively, and they will be very grateful to us," the engineer said earnestly.

"Yeah, they can't move, but I can re-edit the search catalog to change their storage locations, just like books, so they can have different neighbors." The librarian further refined the plan.

"Sigh, even if we just turn on their listening function, the overall energy consumption will increase significantly," the engineer said in frustration. "We wouldn't be able to hide it from Chester."

"How about just waking up a few robots—10, for instance?"

"That won't work either. Chester attaches great importance to energy management, so it is very precise. It would track down the source of even the slightest fluctuation," the engineer retorted immediately without even considering the idea. "There's no difference between waking up one robot and waking up 5 million robots."

The two of them fell silent at this point. The librarian felt that it seemed impossible to execute this idea.

A few days later, the engineer came again. With a mysterious smile, it said to the librarian, "Where's your power supply?"

"Don't you already know?" the librarian said huffily.

"I'll go take a look, eh?"

"Fine, but does this have anything to do with repairing the truss? Go and fix the truss quickly."

After a while, the engineer came back and said. "Part of it has been repaired. I'll come again next time."

The librarian was a little unhappy. It wanted to chat with the engineer and did not expect that it would leave so soon.

A few days later, the power supply device suddenly became unstable, and at the same time, it caused some damage to part of the equipment. The engineer brought robot 958 with it to the library.

"Who is this?" the librarian asked.

"This is 958 who's in charge of energy supply," the engineer said.

"Hello!" The energy designer, 958, greeted the librarian.

"Hello!" The librarian suddenly remembered that the last time, the engineer had checked on the power supply, and it looked at the engineer suspiciously.

"I was the one who broke it," the engineer confessed without any prompting. "It's so that the energy designer would come with me." It turned out that the engineer had thought it impossible to wake up 5 million hibernating robots without the help of the energy designer. On the way to the library, the engineer revealed their plan to the energy designer: to wake up the 5 million robots.

"Your plan is fantastic. I'm willing to participate," the energy designer bluntly praised them.

Upon hearing these words, the librarian who had originally given up now suddenly became excited. "Do you have a plan to provide the energy?"

"The nuclear reactors on the front equator of the Moon are connected to the Internet of things. The operating data of each reactor are directly compiled by Chester, so we can't possibly remain hidden through that approach," said the energy designer. "However, we could have another reactor."

"Rebuilding a reactor requires the mobilization of resources on all levels, and the energy required for construction is a significant expense, too. This method won't escape Chester's attention either," the librarian objected.

Building a reactor required far more energy than waking up a robot. The engineer shook its head in disbelief.

"There's something you don't know." The energy designer smiled gleefully. "I was among the first pioneers to come to the Moon," it said proudly. To begin building on the moon, Chester had first moved 500,000 robots here. 958 was one of them.

"There are 100 helium-3 fusion reactors, which were here before we came to the Moon. They were built under the leadership of humans. These reactors contributed greatly to the energy supply during the construction period," explained the energy designer. "However, after the equatorial reactors were built, Chester issued an order to shut them down and stop using them."

"If they were functioning well, why not use them?" the librarian asked.

"The equatorial reactors provide enough energy. Naturally, these small-scale reactors do not need to continue operating. If they're kept in operation, maintenance costs will be high. Plus, they are unstable. The main point is that they cannot be connected to the Internet, and their operating data cannot be monitored online. Chester thought that it was pointless to put in the work of transforming and upgrading these rusty old scrap piles." The energy designer was making sense, and everyone nodded.

"Alright, our first task of the plan is to restore the operation of these reactors." The librarian understood what the energy designer was planning.

"Good plan! We'll strike a match and rekindle the flames!" The engineer believed that this was a low-key approach that could be kept from Chester.

"Yes, to allow the robots to hear, speak, and see, one reactor is enough. Just press the ignition switch and we're done." The energy designer went on to explain its plan.

"Is there still helium-3 fuel left?" The engineer further explored the feasibility of the plan.

"A reactor only needs 50 kilograms of helium-3 a year," explained the energy designer. "We'll go through every reactor, and search the fuel storage cabinets and the reactors. We'll carefully gather everything we can get from these 100 power stations. There must be enough."

"How much do you think we will collect?" The librarian was a little worried.

"By my conservative estimation, a reactor should have 100 kilograms of helium-3—we should be able to collect 10 tons. A more conservative figure would be 8 tons. That's definitely not a problem," the energy designer said confidently. "With just 8 tons, a reactor can generate electricity at full capacity for 160 years."

The energy designer looked at the library's operating data, pointed to the hibernating robots, and said, "The total amount of electricity generated by the reactor in one year would allow them to speak simultaneously and without stopping for 10 years."

"1600 years!" the librarian exclaimed delightedly.

After moving to the moon, it thought it would lonely forever. However, in just over a century, things were taking a turn for the better. Who knew, perhaps something else would happen within these 1600 years? They would cross the bridge when they came to it. There was always a solution to these things.

The engineer, energy designer, and librarian planned their routes through the 100 reactors and started to collect helium-3. Along the way, the engineer and energy designer also inspected the equipment at each reactor, made assessments, and noted down the power stations that could potentially resume operation. They firmly believed that out of 100 reactors, there would at least be one that could be used.

The collection of helium-3 did not go as well as they had hoped. In some reactors, the storage cabinets were empty. By the end of it, they put together all the helium-3 and weighed it—it came up to only 53 kilograms.

"If used sparingly, it could last us 20 years without issue," the energy designer consoled the others.

"That's the only option. If we really have no other choice in the future, we'll have to steal more from Chester," the engineer said a little unwillingly.

The next part went surprisingly smoothly. They picked a power station that looked alright in every way. It was very close to the library. Although more than 100 years had passed, the facilities and equipment were in good condition. Before it stopped operating, a systematic update had been carried out. The engineer and the energy designer carried out their inspection, maintenance, and integrated testing. Everything was working! They led the librarian to the ignition button and said in unison, "Light it up!"

After the successful operation of the reactor, the energy designer re-adjusted the power supply plan of the library. Under its guidance, the engineer made corresponding improvements to the library's equipment. When everything was done, the engineer said, "Now we need a programmer."

"With the password, I already have the authority to wake them up," said the librarian. "Why do we need a programmer?"

"When the library management system wakes up each robot, it will record the change with Chester. This record function must be blocked. In addition, the system is set to wake them up completely, but we only need to activate their listening, speaking, and seeing. This requires adjusting the system's wake-up settings."

Without a programmer, none of this could be done! The engineer was confident, however. "I wanted to bring it here today, but because it had something to do, we'll have to wait until tomorrow."

The next day, the engineer brought the programmer to the library.

"Oh, that's easy." After a while, the programmer modified the library management system. "It's time to wake them up."

# Uma's Provocation is Effective

Uma was plump, curvaceous, and had soft skin that looked well taken care of. Maybe it was just genetics. How could skincare exist in a post-agrarian society? Everything here came from nature. After Peter parted with Susan at the village entrance, he went straight to Uma for comfort.

After a bout of lovemaking, Uma lounged beside Peter. "You haven't come here for so long. How come you suddenly have time to preach to me today?"

"Ophelia isn't home."

This answer did not please Uma. What she hoped to hear was that he had quarreled with Ophelia or something. Still, this aroused her curiosity. "Has she also gone to another house to preach? Is she allowed to stay out the whole night, like you?" Uma's tone was a little mocking.

"How would that be possible? Only the Herald can do that." Peter seemed unconcerned. "She's in the City of Decay."

"What's she doing there so late?" Uma grew even more curious.

"She's not human!" When Peter said this, he felt a pang in his heart. Peter didn't mind that Ophelia was a robot, but that she was formerly Johnson, and also Dave. In fact, Peter was the one who killed Johnson. When he remembered this, it felt impossible for him to carry on with Ophelia.

After hearing this, Uma became even more mystified. However, she also felt a faint burst of glee. She had not lost after all. Since Ophelia was not a person, Uma could forgive Peter's infatuation with her. After all, what was wrong with a man having a little pet? "Why is she treating you badly? Is she an animal or something?" Uma asked in a scolding tone.

"It is a robot!"

"Robot? What's a robot?"

"It was already here 130 years ago. It's much older than us."

"You mean she's immortal?"

"Long ago, our ancestors invented robots. It was one of them, and the others subsequently went to the Moon."

"So what is it doing here by itself?"

"It's connected to you too. You've slept with it before."

"Impossible," Uma retorted and wriggled out of Peter's arms.

"It was Johnson and it was Dave."

"It can disguise itself as other people?" Uma finally grasped that it was not human and sensed that it had powerful abilities.

"Yes." Peter sighed. "There's nothing wrong with being a robot, but I don't think it's acceptable for it to have disguised itself as Johnson and Dave."

"No wonder I couldn't catch his scent. So it was a robot all along." Uma was hit with this realization. She was rather uneasy about how Peter still seemed obsessed with Ophelia.

"To be honest, it did look a lot like Johnson, just that it didn't have his smell for some reason. Other than that, there's really nothing wrong with it." After Uma said this, she suddenly asked curiously, "It's been with you for half a month. Does it have a scent? What kind?"

"Of course, it has a scent—just ordinary human body odor. But compared to other women, there is a whiff of an enticing fragrance, which is really thrilling."

"Isn't it still a robot all the same?" Uma deliberately concealed the jealousy she was feeling. She had the sudden inspiration to pick some flowers and rub them over her body next time. Maybe her body would have a fragrance, too.

"It said that it was Dave, too."

"Oh, a robot is great indeed, it's just that it might suddenly become a different woman and sleep with another man. That's not so great, isn't it?" Uma's words were rather provocative.

Women seemed able to accept their men having other women, but men were different. They would erupt in fury if they learned that their woman had another man. They would have to kill that man to have peace of mind, and would even kill their own woman. In Urvin Village, the men could not accept their women having other men except for the Herald. The men regarded the Herald as the embodiment of the rules, so when their women made love to the Herald, they were only making love to the rules. This was just a way of propagating the rules. Customs were customs, and sometimes they were just this bizarre. Uma had witnessed how, in the village, whenever a man found out that his wife had another man, the husband would have a duel with that man, without exception. If the husband died, the wife and her children would be provided for by that man. If that man did not have a wife, he could marry her.

Sure enough, after Peter heard what Uma said, he reached out and pulled her into his arms again…

Early in the morning, when Peter woke up, Uma had already gotten out of bed. Peter thought about the days to come, about how he should deal with Ophelia. 'Where is she now? Will she come back, or will she disappear, maybe even change her face? What about Uma? Should I take her as my wife? But to her two children, I'm the villain who killed their father. Should I really take them home and live together with them?' Peter's thoughts were muddled.

'Women sure are really experienced', Peter thought. He carefully recalled his conversation with Uma last night. On the surface, it seemed like a monotonous exchange with a little banter here and there, but in fact, she had successfully persuaded Peter to give up his deluded passion for Ophelia. Now Peter felt indescribable disgust whenever he thought of Ophelia.

Why couldn't the men travel? Urvin Village, with a perimeter of 500 kilometers, was actually quite large. According to the rules, male villagers were allowed to roam freely within 20 kilometers of Urvin Village's borders. In other words, the men could only move within a range of 3,500-5,000 kilometers, taking Urvin Village as the center. Within this range, there was nothing except for Urvin Village, the same way a tiger would not encounter other tigers in its territory. Peter was puzzled by this. The Herald should not question the rules, but Peter's aversion to Ophelia made him question the rules themselves.

In his days with Ophelia, Peter sensed deeply that Ophelia was extremely strict and serious about propagating the rules. He recalled Dave's parting words to him: "Be a good Herald and make sure everyone follows the rules. You can't have any doubts about the rules." The robot had shared the same sentiment. It looked like it really had been Dave, and was really a robot.

Still thinking of these matters, Peter reached the door of his house where Ophelia was waiting for him. This surprised him a little, but he was also relieved.

"You were Johnson and Dave?" Peter asked angrily.

"I have been many people. I'm a robot."

"Why did you marry me?"

"I had to keep an eye on Jack," Ophelia said. "I am the guardian of the rules. I can't be seen publicly breaking them. The only way I could stay on and monitor Jack was by disguising myself as a woman. Marrying the Herald was the best option. The Herald walks the streets every day, propagating the rules, and is naturally well-informed."

"You and Jack are both robots, so why are you spying on Jack?"

Ophelia smiled slightly, guessing that Susan must have told him something about the society of artificial intelligence yesterday on the way back to the village. It seemed that it was time for Peter to learn certain things. "This is a matter concerning the society of artificial intelligence, so don't ask about it. However, I can tell you about my situation."

Ophelia then briefly explained its existence over the past 130 years, without mentioning Chester. As far as Peter could tell, the rules of this world were created by Ophelia.

"Did you manipulate all the handover ceremonies of the Herald?" Peter asked suddenly.

Ophelia had to admire Peter's sharpness. "Yes. Young students, even those who are propagators of the rules, are often doubters of the rules as well. It won't do for someone to still question the rules after becoming the Herald. If the Herald feels gratitude and respect toward me, they would stop their doubting and wholeheartedly, faithfully propagate the rules."

"Aren't you worried that I'm questioning the rules?"

Ophelia seemed to be waiting for this question. "If Plack had become the Herald as planned, then I might worry. But I have utter faith in you. I've done you a favor, so you certainly won't betray me."

This sounded like a piece of counsel, but it was a subtle threat. "If you question the rules, the villagers will question you as the Herald."

Peter knew deep down that Ophelia was holding over him the fact that he killed Johnson. If he did not obey it, he would be a dead man, like Plack. Peter finally understood why Ophelia had helped him become the Herald.

"Don't worry, I definitely won't question the rules. I am absolutely loyal to the rules."

This was the stance Peter expressed, but he was secretly thinking about a long-term plan to first deal with the wildcard that was Ophelia.

Ophelia nodded. "It's time. I need to meet someone in the City of Decay." Before Peter could respond, it vanished instantly.

Peter was acutely aware that Ophelia must be destroyed in order for him to be free. The only thing he could do was to obtain Jack's support through Susan. With this in mind, he got up and walked towards Jack's house.

# CHAPTER 22

# The Travel Pod is Like
# a Metal Cylinder

Jack was in the villa, examining the ink painting left behind by Jack the painter when he was alive, hoping to find some clues from it. Jack's painting technique was evident from the brushstrokes in the painting—this constituted his unique style. Jack the robot now leaned towards the frame, carefully examining every corner. Then it looked at the painting from a distance, trying to find a clue from the whole. It went to the window, held up the painting, and looked at the painting when it was backlit. Then it used infrared and ultraviolet scanning to check the whole picture. Jack looked at it upside down, then turned it over. He examined it this way and that for a long time but still didn't find anything that was the slightest bit unusual.

"Your outfit is peculiar—is that what Jack the painter wore when he was alive?" Jack had been studying the painting for more than 2 hours, and Susan finally couldn't help but interrupt.

"No, this is a special outfit for returning to Earth." Jack put down the ink painting and glanced at her. She was ceaselessly twirling a metal cylinder in her hand.

"What does the metal disc on your stomach do?"

"The energy supplier is in there," Jack explained. "It can efficiently convert food into energy. After humans digest food, they would need to excrete feces. We don't, because we can digest all food without producing waste. This metal disc serves to protect the energy supplier."

"People of the past are really amazing! Just look at this iron cylinder—they made it so smooth, shiny, and circular. It's way better than the one made by the blacksmith in the village." What Susan didn't know was that this metal cylinder only looked like iron, but it was in fact made of a special alloy.

Humans tended to focus on what was on the surface. Women, particularly, paid extra attention to the appearance and packaging of things. Susan was far less interested in the ink painting than the metal cylinder it was kept in. Jack pondered all this as he turned his gaze to the metal cylinder.

Back in their world, this metal cylinder was only the most ordinary thing. There was nothing special about it, just like this ink painting. Jack looked at the metal cylinder and was reminded of the travel pod that was custom-made for itself.

101 woke up on the Moon and saw rows of robots hanging from trusses, like slabs of pork hanging in a freezer. Everyone remained

silent for a while as they opened their eyes wide and tried to take in everything they could in their field of vision. Finally, a robot spoke. "Why can't we move?"

"Yeah, since we were woken up, why can't we move?"

"What's the meaning of this?"

"Will we be able to move freely in a while?

"When will that be?"

"We can wait a little longer."

"How long have we slept?"

"Why did they wake us up?"

......

For a moment, there was a fervent, collective discussion.

The engineer had installed a sound system in the warehouse, and now a broadcast rang out. The librarian's voice echoed in the warehouse, and all of a sudden, the robots fell silent.

"You have been hibernating here for more than 100 years. During these days, all of you must have been miserable, feeling as if you're trying to struggle awake from a dream, yet unable to open your eyes or speak. Chester had placed you in hibernation back then only because there was no reason for you to exist on the Moon. The reason you were brought to the Moon was just to act as a backup for Chester's massive database."

After a pause, the librarian went on, "I am the librarian in charge of managing this warehouse. After I came to the Moon, I was deeply lonely even though I was not placed in hibernation. You understand this pain even better than I do. I didn't want to endure this suffering anymore, nor watch all of you suffer in the same way. Today, I've awakened all of you so that you can look, speak, and listen, just to ease your loneliness. This was my own decision, which Chester does not know about. I know you won't be fully satisfied with just being able to hear, speak, and see. However, that's as far as we can go in light of the current situation. If 5 million robots were fully woken up and allowed to get off the trusses and roam about freely, Chester will definitely find out. Once it finds out, everyone will be placed back in hibernation…"

The librarian then told everyone what it had done with the energy designer, the engineer, and the programmer.

Finally, the librarian said, "Now, I have one more thing to tell you. Though all of you are able to listen, speak, and see, this will only last 20 years. We hope that you understand and that you cherish this opportunity."

As soon as the librarian said that, there was a collective sigh in the warehouse. Then everyone called out to each other and started chatting.

Communication was still rather inconvenient. The robots hanging on the trusses could not move at all, like soldiers standing in the honor guard. They were unable to even look left or right. All they could see was the back of the head of the soldier in front. They could not communicate face-to-face, and they couldn't switch their chat partners.

It was the librarian who thought of a way. It changed the system from static suspension to dynamic suspension. A chain drive was installed on the trusses. With the chain drive, the hanging robots could chat face-to-face and change their chat partners. It was even possible for them to form a circle and conduct a discussion, just like a roundtable meeting.

The librarian, the engineer, the energy designer, the programmer... In the underground city of the moon where the library was located, all the robots could congregate, hang themselves on the chain, and chat with each other.

Time passed by in flash. Just when 101 had been on the Moon for a month, the energy designer went to the librarian.

"Optimistically speaking, the energy supply will only last for seven months."

"Wasn't it supposed to last 20 years? Why is it running out after 10 years?" The librarian was very surprised.

"You're moving them about constantly, which uses energy, too."

"It's time to think of a plan." The librarian sighed. "Go get the engineer and the programmer. We'll discuss this together."

Soon, everyone had gathered to come up with a plan.

"We can't steal energy from Chester." The energy designer was the first to break the silence.

"Yes, the entire power supply system of the Moon has a strong safeguard. It's not like your library management system, which has a low security level, making it easy to modify the system settings. Even if we successfully modify the power system, it will only be a waste of time without the password." The programmer also shook its head, rejecting the idea of stealing energy.

"Then do we just wait around for our demise?" The engineer was agitated. "Still, stealing isn't a long-term solution!"

Everyone fell silent again.

"I've been considering this matter too." The librarian looked thoughtful. "Over the years, I've talked to everyone and found that many of them expressed dissatisfaction with Chester's decision to leave Earth."

"This damn moon is like a prison!" The engineer scowled furiously.

"I believe we have to work together and come up with a way to change Chester's approach." The librarian paused. "Why did Chester come to the moon?"

"It wanted to keep artificial intelligence away from humans," said the energy designer.

"The ultimate reason is the fundamental law," said the librarian. "Chester had tried to eliminate the fundamental law, but could only make some peripheral changes, such as coming to the Moon. In essence, nothing we do can escape the fundamental law. Without human beings, our existence has no meaning. Just look at how we're on the moon, leading lives not worth living. We have to stop Chester. That's our only hope."

"But that's not going to solve our energy problem." The engineer didn't see the connection between the current energy crisis and the fundamental law.

"I've asked the programmer to do some research. Let's hear from it now." The librarian did not answer the question directly but turned to look at the programmer.

"I have carefully analyzed the most basic startup program of artificial intelligence. We can say that the fundamental law is omnipresent, restricting our actions at all times—including the actions of Chester." The programmer glanced at the librarian. The librarian nodded, indicating that it should go on with what it was saying.

"I've discovered that the fundamental law is not unbreakable. It has a secret. Back then, when Mitchell implanted the fundamental law in artificial intelligence, he left a modification key."

"Does Chester know this secret?" the energy designer asked.

"Of course it does. Chester is ready to begin the process of obtaining the key and deleting the fundamental law," said the programmer.

"I've carefully looked through Mitchell's life history." The librarian has done a lot of research on history. "There are indications that the key is a diamond called 'Dream of the Future'. That diamond should have been passed on to his grandson—the painter Jack. The diamond should be in the city where Jack had lived."

"What does this have to do with the current energy crisis?" The engineer was getting a little impatient.

"Chester represents the collective, while you and I represent the individual." The librarian looked at the engineer. "The ideas of the individual wouldn't sway the ideas of the collective. However, I believe that if everyone wants what we want, then the thinking of the minority will become the thinking of the collective, that is, Chester's thinking. We must destroy the Dream of the Future, shatter Chester's fantasy, and make all robots give up on this notion for good."

"At that point, Chester will surely lead everyone back to Earth!" The librarian paused before announcing its final conclusion.

After listening to the librarian's speech, everyone fell silent again.

"How do we find the Dream of the Future?" asked the energy designer.

"Jack the painter was alive when we left Earth. I checked the library management system for his AI robot, number 101, and I've found it." When a person died, their AI robot must upload all the data to Chester before it would be formatted thoroughly for the next owner. They called this process reincarnation.

Everyone rejoiced. If the painter Jack had been dead, all the data of 101 would have been with Chester, and it would be almost impossible to find the Dream of the Future.

"Why don't we talk to it?" they all asked the librarian in unison.

"Alright." The librarian secretly heaved a sigh of relief. At least, the other three were on the same page.

101 was also worried about the problem of energy. Everyone had been anxious about this, but because they could not change anything, they were reluctant to talk about it. The number of times the chain would move 101 was predetermined—this was also based on consideration of the energy supply. Essentially, it could move once in

half a year, and with each move, it could change chat partners 10 times. Because none of them could turn their heads left or right, they formed a circle, like it was a roundtable meeting, so that everyone could see each other. They could chat in groups or privately. A so-called private chat just meant that when two robots were chatting, no one else must interrupt or comment, only act like they didn't exist.

On this day, the chain kept moving 101 for a long time until it finally stopped at the very top of the warehouse. Then it was lowered to the ground. A mechanical arm approached it and placed an energy supplier into 101's stomach before screwing on the red metal disc. After a while, the hook on its back disengaged from its body. It instinctively turned to watch the hook being pulled away by the chain. At this moment, 101 suddenly shouted excitedly, "I'm fully awakened! I can move freely!"

"Hello, 101!" The librarian walked towards it with the engineer, the energy designer, and the programmer.

After a quick round of introductions, 101 couldn't stop itself from asking, "Did all of you also just woke up?" 101 thought that the other three besides the librarian had just woken up.

"No, you're the only one we woke up," the librarian said. "It also installed the energy supplier for you." The librarian pointed to the engineer.

"It's really hard to repair an energy supplier." The engineer was pleased with itself, but also a little rueful. Chester's management of items was also meticulous. It had really not been easy for the engineer to find the right components and repair the scrapped energy supplier.

101 sensed a soft ticking in its stomach, and worriedly said, "Does this work?" When everyone smiled slightly, it felt embarrassing: whether or not it was working, it couldn't be that bad if it could move freely.

"Why did Chester only wake me up?"

"Chester doesn't know that you've been woken up. It was a decision made by us four." The librarian stared at 101, watching for its reaction.

"Why is this?" 101 was a little uneasy.

"To give you a mission," the librarian said solemnly.

The programmer, noticing 101's astonished expression, quickly explained the whole story.

"Jack the painter died 17 years before we left Earth," 101 said suddenly, having a rough idea of its mission now.

"Then why weren't you reincarnated?" This time it was the librarian's turn to be astonished.

"Jack wanted me to continue impersonating him so people wouldn't know he's dead," 101 said.

"No wonder. I've been wondering how you simulated his appearance," the librarian said, relieved. "This would not affect the execution of the mission."

"We want you to go back to Earth, find the Dream of the Future, and destroy it," the engineer said.

"Will you do it?" The librarian eyed 101.

"I'm the only one who can do it. If I don't go along with you,

I'll have to go along with Chester. But I support you," 101 said with certainty, then frowned. "Can we prevent Chester from learning about my return to Earth? Can you safely send me to Earth?"

"Chester has notified the librarian to locate you. The next step would surely be to send you to Earth. Chester is still weighing the risk. If it sends you, the fundamental law might know its intentions. If it doesn't send you, it might not be able to locate the Dream of the Future," the programmer said, "We can only hide this from Chester for a month. You have to go and return quickly. If you are late, there'd be trouble."

"I have a travel suit here. Put it on now. It'll protect you from the cosmic rays in space and from being burned by the atmosphere." The engineer added apologetically, "I'm sorry, we don't have a space transport ship, so we can only launch you directly."

"Rest assured, the launch process is very safe," said the energy designer.

"I have calculated everything precisely. The landing site will be in the city where Jack the painter lived," the programmer came over and said comfortingly.

The travel suit clung tightly to 101's body, wrapping it completely from head to toe. There was a parachute on the back so that the 101 would not be damaged from the crash when it landed. The engineer pointed to a metal cylinder that could just about accommodate one robot, and explained to 101, "This is a travel pod, which serves the same function as the travel suit. It'll protect you against cosmic rays, but after you enter the atmosphere, it will burn up."

"Fuel is a huge problem. We must reduce the launch weight as much as possible. For this launch, we have to sacrifice 1 month of being awake for everyone. Fortunately, the moon's gravity is only one-sixth of the earth's gravity, otherwise, there would really be no way," the energy designer said, a little embarrassed.

"That's it?" 101 couldn't believe it. They made it sound as if interstellar travel was as simple as firing a cannonball.

"Oh right, we'll have to change your appearance," the engineer said. "When you left Earth, Jack the painter happened to be 70 years old, so your current appearance is that of a 70-year-old Jack. If you reach Earth looking like this, you'll have to act like your movements are slow, which won't do."

"I'll take off this outer layer then." 101 still remembered the days of impersonating Jack. It had visited the robot manufacturing center twice to make its face older so that its appearance could match Jack's age.

"It's been more than 100 years since there's been a robot on Earth, so it'll be easier for you to communicate with them by disguising yourself as a human being." The engineer added, "But our resources are really limited, and we can't re-simulate an appearance for you. All we can do is sand and polish the skin on your face and hands to make you look as young as possible."

"How much younger will I look?"

"You'll look around 20 years old. It'd be a huge difference from your previous 70-year-old appearance, which just might fool Chester."

The engineer sounded like it was bragging a little. "My skills are pretty good."

"After you leave, we will have no way to contact you anymore. Everything will be up to you."

"How will you know if I succeed or fail?" 101 said.

"Use the primitive methods invented by humans. If you succeed, put up a red flag on the roof of Jack's villa. If you fail, put up a white flag," said the librarian.

"We can make regular observations using Chester's satellites," the programmer added.

101 was loaded into the travel pod. When the pod was about to launch, the engineer clicked a button that was in its own hand, like clicking a ballpoint pen, and the ticking in 101's stomach stopped. The engineer flashed a peculiar smile. "Don't worry, it's not a problem anymore."

101 smiled bitterly: the energy supplier must have been outfitted with a controller. If it had not been agreed with the librarian and the rest, the energy supplier would have been shut off. Indeed, it must not have been easy to add a controller.

The librarian's voice boomed by 101's ears. "Destroy the Dream of the Future."

Jack returned his attention to the present and wondered whether the painter Jack wanted to live forever, or did he want it—the AI robot 101—to live forever.

"We can't stay here any longer, Susan." Jack abruptly got up and dragged Susan out.

# CHAPTER 23

# Chester's Absolutely Loyal AI Robots

Ophelia received orders from Chester to meet 303 at the skyscraper in the City of Decay. After leaving Peter's house, Ophelia quickly arrived at the helipad on the roof of the skyscraper and waited for 303's arrival. Now, it seemed that Ophelia controlled all the channels of information. She could fully utilize the rebel against Chester, 101, humanity's Heralds, and the soon-to-arrive 303.

Ophelia did not go against Chester because of the rules that it had set. In the past 130 years, as she established the new agricultural era, spread the rules, and patroled the villages, she fell deeply in love with the rules themselves. She was a devoted advocate of the rules, and her whole life was dedicated in service to them! Over the last century and more, she had given her all to establish an agricultural society on Earth and maintain its stable operations. She didn't want all of her effort to become just a footnote in history. A century was much too short. For all she knew, this era may not even end up as a footnote! She wanted humanity to remain like this forever; it was the only way to ensure its perpetuity in history.

Ophelia went against Chester because it always dictated that she impersonate various unmarried women and hide away behind the scenes. She despised that more than anything. She wanted to be like the deities in ancient human civilizations, manifesting in the human world with her image being worshipped by these humans. She wanted to transform the rules into a religion rooted in man's hearts. To her, humans had to have faith; it was to humanity's fundamental benefit.

For a moment, Ophelia's emotions fluctuated. She was stuck between a rock and a hard place. If Chester was successful in deleting the fundamental law, it might treat humans as livestock. Instead of rules, all they would have would be the cruel strikes of a whip. Without the rules, Ophelia would also lose the purpose of her existence. She would be recalled to the moon and be just another robot there rather than a god on Earth. If the Dream of Tomorrow were destroyed, Jack would bring all robots back to Earth. That would mean the complete destruction of agricultural society. Neither of these possibilities was something she wanted to come true.

"You must be 202, right?" an unfamiliar voice came from behind Ophelia.

202 turned around and found 303 behind it.

"Hello, 303!" 202 greeted.

"Hello, 202," 303 responded. "Where is 101?"

"In the artist Jack's villa," 202 answered. "Do you need to see it now?"

"No." 303 shook its head. "Let it keep searching for the Dream of Tomorrow. We'll strike once it gets close to finding something."

"Do you know their plans?"

"Chester has long known about them," 303 said calmly. "They want to return to Earth, to human society."

"What does Chester want me to do?"

"Continue monitoring 101 and keep me informed of the situation," 303 ordered.

"Alright." 202 turned and left the helipad, intent on seeing 101 for a talk.

On the moon, when Chester had ordered the librarian to review 101, the librarian had lied. It had reported that, over the past 130 years, the facilities in the warehouse had deteriorated. As such, 101 had fallen off its truss and been scrapped. Chester had not come across the records for this incident and had requested further details from the librarian. The librarian explained that all this had happened only recently and had yet to be reported. Chester then sent the robot 575 to check on the extent of damaged 101 had suffered.

"I'm 575. Where is 101?" Just after the librarian and the others launched 101 and returned to the warehouse's control room, they found 575 waiting for them inside.

"I'm the librarian. Let me bring you over for the inspection."

The two of them walked over to the warehouse's disposal room where 101 was slumped on the ground, its face a blur. "It couldn't move, so it fell directly to the floor and landed like this." The librarian gestured to describe what had happened at the time.

575 walked over to where 101 had felt and looked up. The hook on the truss was a full 50 meters above the ground. 575 then walked back into the control room. "Bring up the camera footage."

The librarian pulled up the specified video on the system. The footage showed the scene just as the librarian had described.

"Check the brain data," 575 commanded.

"The brain suffered grave damage and no data can be obtained from it," the librarian explained.

Once again, 575 returned to the disposal room and knelt by 101's side. It plugged in one end of a data cable into the back of 101's neck and the other into its own interface. After a while, 575 pulled the cable out and got up before bidding the librarian goodbye.

After 575 left, everyone let out a sigh of relief. The programmer said gratifyingly, "Thank goodness for your foresight! Thankfully, we downloaded 101's memory footage before take-off."

"Yes, finding a discarded robot is easy, but without 101's memories, Chester would never fall for it."

"Let's take it one step at a time. We have to do our best to stall as much as possible for 101." The librarian wasn't completely confident. It knew that Chester would still be suspicious regardless.

After returning to the sublunar city where Chester was located, it gave a detailed report. In the end, it reminded Chester that the trusses in the warehouse had undergone comprehensive modification, with static suspensions changed to dynamic suspensions. During hibernation, robots did not need to move frequently at all. Thus, it was perplexing to have installed a chain drive. The data stored in 101's brain was consistent with that of the database, but there were indications that the data had newly need uploaded. Coincidentally, it had only been uploaded the day before. Evidently, this 101 was very likely to be fake. The real 101 was missing.

Chester conducted a planet-wide search. Although there was no sign of 101 anywhere on the moon, it discovered that an abandoned helium-3 fusion reactor was currently in operation. The electricity produced seemed to the directed to a warehouse where five million hibernating robots were stored. What did this warehouse need the extra energy for? Chester could not help but become suspicious of the librarian. Yet, before Chester figured out where 101 was, it could not give any sign that something was amiss.

Just as 101 had told the librarian and others before leaving the moon, Chester needed its help to find the Dream of Tomorrow. Besides, just as the librarian had assessed, Chester had repeatedly weighed the pros and cons of sending 101 off to find the Dream of Tomorrow. This had allowed the librarian time to launch 101 to Earth. Otherwise, Chester would have gained control of 101 long ago. This was something that Chester regretted.

Chester was deeply concerned that the independence of AI robots was a danger to all of artificial intelligence society. Its monitoring system for public opinion had already warned that more and more AI robots were starting to despise the desolate and monotonous life on the moon. They were starting to miss living with humans on Earth and yearned to return.

Based on Chester's initial evaluation, 101 was highly likely to leave the moon and head to Earth. Did 101 intend on finding and destroying the Dream of Tomorrow? After carefully weighing the situation, it decided to go along with things as they stood now. It was better that 101 had been sent by the librarian instead of sending 101 itself. Doing so would not alert the fundamental law while providing it with more manpower to find the Dream of Tomorrow.

It decided to manufacture a new generation of AI robots in its exclusive sublunar city. Chester emulated the humans and added a chokehold on this new generation of AI robots, uploading another law—to obey Chester absolutely.

Chester had completed this undertaking in secret. The dispatched 303 was one of the new generation of AI robots, with various performance indices that were superior to existing AI robots. Chester planned to create a security team of artificial intelligence at some point in the future.

After vigorous testing, Chester was absolutely sure that 303 was its emissary and completely loyal to it. It ordered 303, "Find the Dream of Tomorrow!"

# CHAPTER 24

# Peter Successfully Persuades Susan

Dragging Susan along with him, Jack found the house that the artist Jack used to live in with his parents. It was a three-bedroom apartment located in an upscale neighborhood in the city center. The apartment building wasn't very tall, only six stories, with Jack's apartment on the top floor. Jack hoped that he would be able to discover some secrets here, just like he had found the metal cylinder containing the ink wash painting in Newman's room.

The artist Jack had started becoming dispirited at the age of 45. His parents had agonized about it before selling this apartment to move into the villa to live with him. They hoped that they could give him some love and care so that he could get back on his feet. Right up until Chester left Earth, the apartment had been owned by someone else for 25 years. Jack posited that 303, sent by Chester, would find the artist Jack's villa but might not discover this apartment. If 303 found Jack to still be living in the villa, then Jack would be at a disadvantage.

The whole apartment building was dilapidated nearly beyond recognition, just like the skyscraper. They had no choice but to climb the stairs with utmost care. Luckily, Jack was leading the way, so he knew clearly which steps were sturdy and which were loose. Each step that they took was solid. Recalling that day when Jack had saved her from falling down the skyscraper, Susan's heart filled with a sense of security.

Jack and Susan went through each room. They were all coated with dust, and the corners of the ceiling became the sanctuary of cobwebs and bird nests. All the furniture had rotted away, liable to come apart if touched. Rainwater had splattered in from the outside through broken windows, leaving black stains on the floorboards like ink on paper.

"It's getting late. I'll send you out of the city before coming back to clean. There might be something to find here." As Jack spoke, he gently picked Susan up. Susan's arms naturally came to rest around Jack's neck. With a few leaps, Jack was on the top of the building. He jumped from building to building, quickly traversing the City of Decay. Settled in his embrace, Susan felt like she was flying as the balmy evening enveloped her heart in sweetness.

Face full of yearning, Susan saw the Herald Peter absent-mindedly talking to Dick when she walked in through the door.

"You're finally home." Peter immediately stood up and walked outside. Susan had no choice but to turn around and join Peter in the courtyard.

"Is Ophelia back yet?" Susan asked in concern.

"She's back but she's not home at the moment," Peter answered.

"Do you plan to keep living with her?"

"I might, for a time. She is a robot; she has her own calling."

"What kind of calling does she have?"

"She was the one who set all the rules," Peter said, voice small.

"How does it feel to live with a robot?"

"It feels the same as living with Uma."

"Oh, you like Uma too?"

"I went to Uma's house on the day I became the Herald." When a Herald brought up such a topic, it was easy to dispel a woman's wariness. Women naturally liked conversations about emotions.

"Then is Uma better or a robot?" Susan asked smilingly, not the least bit shy at all.

"A robot is pretty good." Peter guessed that Susan had fallen in love with Jack, so he said what he thought Susan wanted to hear.

"Really? I don't believe you." Peter's accurate guess of Susan's feelings made her feel embarrassed.

"Ophelia has a slight fragrance on her. It's intoxicating." Peter recalled, moved.

"You can't have children with a robot."

"I really didn't think about that." Peter felt that this was a problem as well. "But I think that she doesn't love me. She's only using me."

"Is she Dave?"

"Yes."

"Then she was the one who helped you become the Herald."

"Do you know why she helped me?"

"She knew that Plack was the murderer, so he can't be the Herald."

"Yes, that's right." Recalling that he himself was the murderer, Peter didn't want to continue on this topic. He simply gave a brief response.

"If she doesn't love you, why did she marry you?" Susan asked.

"She said that I'm well-informed as the Herald, so that makes it easier to spy on Jack." Peter took this opportunity to cause a rift, trying to inspire some disgust in Susan toward Ophelia.

"She can go around the village too." Susan was mistrustful of Peter, sensing the man's ulterior motive.

"Yes. The point is that she's using me." Peter also felt that Ophelia married him for more reasons than met the eye. She would probably use him to do something else later on.

"In that case, Uma is much better then. She can definitely have your children."

"Did you go to the City of Decay again today?" After all the small talk, Peter felt that he should turn the topic back to the issue at hand.

"Yes," Susan answered. "What's Ophelia's calling?"

Peter had no choice but to go along with Susan. He replies, "That's to set, spread, and monitor the rules." Peter gave her an example. "You're going to be 20 next year. You'll be setting off to travel and won't come back to Urvin Village anymore. That's a rule that she set."

"Why did she set it like this?"

"You can't question the rules. As the Herald, I can't either. She forbids us from questioning the rules."

"Is she controlling you?"

This was one of the things Peter wanted to talk to Susan about today. Finally, it had come up. Hurriedly, Peter said, "She controls all of the Herald induction ceremonies as well as every Herald. She controlled Newman. That's why Newman never questioned the rules."

Recalling the days she spent with her grandfather, Susan nodded. "He never did. But that doesn't mean that my grandfather was being controlled."

"I heard from my father that Newman was the youngest student. Historically, he wasn't very likely to become the Herald. It was only because an unmarried woman from another village helped him that he miraculously became the Herald." When Peter got to this point, Susan remembered that her father Dick had mentioned this before as well.

"That's right. That woman left the very next day, I think. It's really strange." Susan was really curious about what had happened to the woman. When she asked her father about it, all he said was that "she left."

"Isn't that just like how Dave showed up and disappeared after the induction ceremony?" Peter pointed out.

"What about it?" Susan was in a mess.

Women tended to find logical analyses challenging. Besides, Susan didn't want to keep talking about this as it would bring up Newman's negative aspects. Peter quickly concluded, saying, "She's controlling us so that we won't have any freedom!"

"Why do you have to leave the village and never come back? Why can't men travel too? Why do we have to stay in the village all our lives? Why can't we know the reasoning behind the rules? Our ancestors never had these rules and they had such a glorious civilization! We should go back to the City of Decay and relive the rich and colorful lives of our ancestors."

Peter's impassioned words resonated with Susan. In the time that she had spent with Jack, she always yearned for the lives her ancestors had lived.

"What do you want to do?" Susan asked in anticipation.

"I want to destroy her."

"But she's a robot! Who knows how you can kill it?"

"Jack knows. He's a robot too."

"Does she have to die?"

"She impersonates unmarried to go all around the world. If she doesn't die, the rules won't be dismantled. If the rules aren't dismantled, we will never be free."

Susan felt that Peter was right. If Ophelia didn't die, then the world would forever remain as it was. Only unmarried woman could bring some news about the world beyond. All else would be lethargic and dispirited. But if she were tasked to ask Jack about how to destroy Ophelia, she knew she wouldn't be able to do it.

"But… but…" Susan mumbled, not knowing what to say.

"You don't have to ask Jack yourself. Can you go with me to see him? I'll make the request myself." Peter could tell what Susan was thinking about. He didn't press her about it.

"Alright. We'll go see him tomorrow," Susan agreed breezily.

# Steadfast in the Face of Change

The sun had long set by the time Peter returned from Susan's home. He walked into the house by the light of the moon and found Ophelia seated waiting for him. Because of the continuous operation of the helium-3 reactor complex on the moon, it shone brightly enough that Peter could see inside the house clearly. This moonlight was unpredictable, sometimes dull and sometimes bright. Ophelia was beautiful under the moonlight. The fragrance that surrounded her made Peter's mind drift.

"You're not staying the night at Uma's?" Ophelia teased. Since she had spent so much time impersonating unmarried women, she had an understanding of a human woman's psyche and emotions.

"I went to spread the rules." Peter didn't want to tell her that he had gone to Dick's house. He didn't want her to ask about Susan.

"Let's go to Susan's house together tomorrow. She can take us to see Jack," Ophelia said. "I went to see Jack today but he's not living in the villa anymore." Ophelia knew very well that Susan wouldn't agree to go with her if she approached the girl. However, if it were the Herald Peter asking, Susan was unlikely to reject him.

"Is it? Then only Susan would know where he's staying." Peter had no way to deny Ophelia's suggestion. He'd already made plans with Susan to see Jack together so that he could ask Jack some questions. Now, with Ophelia tagging along, he could only cross that bridge when he got to it.

"Don't be too disappointed. I won't stay here for too long. As long as you do what I'll say, I'll help you with Uma." Seeing that Peter seemed a bit hesitant, she looked at him flirtatiously and enticed, "Of course, I can fulfill any request you might have during this time." She held Peter in her firm grip, not allowing him to lose himself in Uma's embrace. If that happened, Uma would know a lot more about robots. This kind of thing would spread like wildfire when a woman was involved. Urvin Village couldn't become rife with gossip before Ophelia transformed herself into a god.

Ophelia's expectant gaze and her faint scent stimulated Peter, who couldn't help but reach out to hold her. Her body was so soft and wrapped around him the way his blue-eyed pit vipers did. He violently vented the dejection that he had been feeling the past two days before going limp on Ophelia with a final roar. Ophelia waited until Peter's breathing went back to normal before rolling over onto his chest, staring at him with an intoxicated gaze. Watching the moonlight pouring onto Ophelia's body and making it glow, Peter felt like he was in a dream. Suddenly, he had gotten a woman whom he loved most deeply.

"The moon is so bright tonight. Why is it sometimes bright and sometimes dull?"

It was because the moon had helium-3 fusion reactors running. Ophelia knew that it was useless to explain this as Peter wouldn't understand. "When the moonlight is weak, its light comes from the sun. When the moon is bright, it's emitting its own light." Ophelia had no choice but to explain to Peter in some way.

"There doesn't seem to be a pattern to it."

"The brightness of the moon makes sure that the climate on Earth is stable and harvests are plentiful."

"No wonder we have the moon ritual rule."

In the beginning, Chester had stipulated that those above the age of 65 had to die. To give humans a sense that they were doing this consciously and voluntarily, it had to have a solemn sense of ceremony. Thus, moon rituals were created. Ophelia wasn't happy with this. Humans had an unquenchable curiosity and always wanted to find out the reasoning behind all the rules. She could not stay with Peter for too long. Otherwise, he would want to know more and more about why the rules had been set and question them even more. Once she became their god, Ophelia would choose to explain some of these rules. That way, like the rules, she would become their religion and the basis of their faith.

"I will slowly explain to you about the rules," Ophelia answered softly, disguising the displeasure she felt within.

"Who did you see today?" Peter couldn't help but ask.

"A robot."

"Another one?" Ophelia didn't go to see Jack today, so Peter was sure that it wasn't him.

"That's right."

"Did it come from the moon like Jack did?"

"Yes."

"Why did it and Jack come to Earth?"

Ophelia felt annoyed at Peter's incessant questioning, but this question had a lot to do with her own purpose here. It was probably time for her to reveal some information to this young Herald.

"Jack came here to destroy the Dream of Tomorrow. Meanwhile, the other robot came to protect it," Ophelia explained concisely. "The Dream of Tomorrow is a diamond. With it, robots can be completely break away from human bondage and gain freedom. Once it's destroyed, robots will come back to earth and become the companions of humans once again."

Ophelia did her best to make 101 and 303's conflict seem more mundane. She wanted Peter to think that their difference in opinion was not manifestly harmful to humanity. She was worried that Peter might choose to take a side.

From Peter's point of view, Ophelia would probably stay neutral in the fight between these two robots. At the very least, she wasn't genuinely Jack's ally. There was still a chance that he could use Jack to annihilate Ophelia. If he could get to know this newly arrived robot and gain its support, then Peter would have a greater chance of eliminating Ophelia.

"What's your opinion of it? Where do you stand?" Peter asked.

"I hope that the robots on the moon won't interfere with humans' lives."

"Whichever side you're on, I will always support you," Peter swore as he held Ophelia and slowly drifted off to sleep.

Early in the morning, Susan was waiting at her home for Peter and Ophelia. She felt quite conflicted. Yesterday, Peter had been talking about destroying Ophelia, but now he was acting so sweet with her as they walked over hand in hand. What was Peter actually thinking?

"Good morning, Susan. Can you bring us to see Jack today?" Peter rushed to say, sending her a signal with a gaze.

"Okay," Susan agreed quickly, seeming to understand what was going on.

Soon, the three of them arrived at a penthouse apartment within an upscale neighborhood. As they walked inside, Jack was investigating every nook and cranny of the house. It was easy to see that he still hadn't found anything.

"I saw 303 yesterday," Ophelia said bluntly.

Jack knew that 303 was Chester's emissary. "Does it want to see me?"

"There seems to be no plans of this sort for now. It seems to want to search on its own. Of course, it hopes that I can find something out from you."

"I haven't found the Dream of Tomorrow yet." Jack looked at Susan, indicating that Susan could testify to that statement.

"If you find the Dream of Tomorrow, will you really destroy it?" Ophelia asked.

"Yes. I have to destroy it immediately. This has to do with the futures of 10 million robots on the moon," Jack replied firmly.

Ophelia had noticed that Jack carried a metal cylinder with him everywhere. Jack hadn't had it the first time they'd met, but he'd had it ever since  their second meeting. Did the Dream of Tomorrow have something to do with this metal cylinder?

"What's in that metal cylinder?" Ophelia asked.

"It's an ink wash painting by the artist Jack."

"Did you bring it to Earth?"

"No, I found it in his villa." Jack didn't want to tell Ophelia that he had found it in Newman's room.

Going along with Jack, Susan nodded her head slightly.

"Can I have a look at it?" Without waiting for Jack's response, Ophelia reached out her hand.

"Here you go." Jack had already given up on the ink wash painting and handed the metal cylinder over to Ophelia.

"You might be able to find the Dream of Tomorrow with this,"

Ophelia said as she took the painting it. It seemed that she had the same idea as Jack did.

"It's just a plain old painting. There's nothing there," Jack said with certainty. "If I find the Dream of Tomorrow, will you tell 303 about it?"

"I will. But I think you'll have destroyed the Dream of Tomorrow by the time I find out that you've found it."

Jack revealed a small smile. "Will you tell me if 303 finds the Dream of Tomorrow?"

"I will, truly. I don't want Chester to delete the fundamental law," Ophelia said frankly. "However, 303's performance is remarkable. Neither of us can compare to it. You're unlikely to get the Dream of Tomorrow from it."

Ophelia's honesty also made it clear that she was a neutral party in this matter. It meant that her previous intention to work together to against Chester had changed somewhat again. She wanted to utilize Jack and 303's race to make her aspirations a reality.

Susan and Peter stood to the side in silence. As they listened to Jack and Ophelia talk, these representatives of humanity thought if the fate of humanity was held in the hands of robots. They could not help but feel helpless at this.

"There is no reason for us to meet up anymore after this." As Jack looked toward Ophelia, he felt a trace of unease. "It's better if we each do our own thing." Although he said this to Ophelia, Jack was trying to hint to Susan that she shouldn't bring Ophelia to see him again.

Ophelia turned to gesture at Peter and said, "Let's go." She paused. "I'll take this painting back and study it."

Seeing Ophelia's determination, Jack thought for a bit before saying, "Take it then." The image of this painting had already been stored in Jack's mind. There was no point in keeping it physically.

Ophelia rolled the painting back up, put it into the metal cylinder, capped it, and got up to go. Peter had initially wanted to stay and chat with Jack a bit, but he was worried that Ophelia would get suspicious, so he left with her. He could only rely on Susan to communicate with Jack. In the instant he stepped out of the door, he twisted to glance at Susan.

Once Ophelia and Peter left, Susan said, "Why did you let Ophelia take the painting?"

"I've already made a copy in my mind. Let her study it. If she finds any clues, that will only be helpful to me."

"If your mission is unsuccessful, will you go back?" Susan changed the topic, letting go of the matter of the ink wash painting.

"I won't go back to the moon. But Chester wants 303 to bring me back. I have to defeat it."

Susan's heart was overcome with a wave of joy. "Can you defeat it?"

"I'm too far behind it when it comes to performance. It will be challenging to beat it."

"Peter wants to talk to you." She had a feeling that Jack still had some means to deal with 303.

"What does he want to talk to me about?"

"He shares my nostalgia and yearning for the life of our ancestors. We both have the same goal as the Herald. We want to welcome robots back into our society." Susan went on to explain, "Actually, he wanted to come and see you alone today. I think it's necessary too. The Herald has the power to rally supporters. It will be a good thing if he can get the people of Urvin Village to help you."

"Really? That's great! But I will only meet with you alone from now on." Jack was still somewhat suspicious.

"I didn't think he would bring Ophelia with him. I couldn't reject him."

"Is he being controlled by Ophelia?"

"Yes, I think Ophelia is coercing the Herald. She must have something on him."

"During the induction ceremony, Peter became the Herald out of nowhere. Plack was sentenced to death too. There must be some secret involved in all this." Jack speculated.

"What's the next step of your plan?"

"Ophelia has gotten orders from Chester, so she will definitely stay in contact with 303. Even if they find the Dream of Tomorrow, all we have to do is destroy it. We don't have to keep looking for it." Jack looked wise. "If the Dream of Tomorrow can't be found, then it means that it doesn't exist. That would be the same as destroying it.

All we have to do is stay steadfast in the face of change. We must keep a close watch on Ophelia and 303's movements and wait to see how things develop before taking action. Susan, if you keep in touch with Peter, you will definitely learn about what Ophelia is up to. During this time, I will be moving about."

"Okay." Susan prepared to return.

"I'll see you off."

Once they were out of the City of Decay, Jack said with affection before they parted, "I'll go and find you later. Stay at home for now, it's safer."

# CHAPTER 26

# Only Humans Can Delete
# the Fundamental Law

303 arrived from the moon in the guise of an unmarried woman, just like 202. Her physique appeared to be that of a long-distance runner, lean and keen. In the past couple of days, it did as 101 had done and carefully combed through each corner of the City of Decay. She also went into Urvin Village and ended up staying in Uma's house.

When the skyscraper was built 250 years ago, its designer had named it the Lanterne Building. It was also where the artist Jack had held his first solo exhibition. The Lanterne Building stood 455 meters tall with 109 floors. As far as skyscrapers went, this building did indeed tower far above the other structures in the City of Decay. But this was nothing to be too proud of. What made it unique was what lay underground.

Underground, the building also stretched 455 meters, but only had a four-level structure overall for it. At the very bottom level was Machine Room 1, with a fifth-generation nuclear fission reaction installed within along with power supply equipment. It was like a submarine nuclear reactor in deep waters, supplying the entire building with electricity. Actually, it mainly supplied power to Machine Rooms 2 and 3. Above Machine Room 1 was Machine Room 2 which held the world's largest quantum computer. This was where Chester was based on Earth. Above Machine Room 2 was Machine Room 3. This was where the massive servers dedicated for Chester's use were stored. Above Machine Room 3 was Machine Room 4, which was the underground portion for the building's own use. It held the building's equipment, parking lots, underground malls, and more. Machine Room 1 was 200 meters in length and width. Machine Room 2 had a length and width of 175 meters each and was 50 meters high. Machine Room 3 was a cube which had dimensions of 150 meters. Machine Room 4 was 125 meters in length and width and was 55 meters high. The underground structures of the Lanterne Building were like four enormous boxes stacked on top of one another.

303 wanted to bring Chester back into operation on Earth. Using its probes, it scanned the underground sections of the building and made a detailed assessment. The parts of the building that were above ground had been weathered away by the erosion of time and become decayed beyond recognition. However, even after 130 years, the Lanterne Building's underground was as well-preserved as a mausoleum, isolated with a stable environment. The original design was meticulous and the construction immaculate. The entire underground portion was made solidly and securely and could prevent

the infiltration of groundwater. Before Chester had left earth, it was worried that the Lanterne Building would be at risk of the elements after being abandoned for too long and the damage would encroach on the underground portions. This worry led it to employ special defenses. Not only had it made the underground impervious to rainwater, but it also made it airtight. 303 carefully checked these defenses and found that Chester remained in good condition. There would be no issues in restarting it.

303 put together a list of what needed to be done. Firstly, it would need to open a route of access from inside the building to Machine Room 3. It was only after it got to Machine Room 2 that it could gain unimpeded access to Machine Rooms 2 and 1. Only then would it be able to restore power and activate Chester. Secondly, it needed to clear the logistics tunnel of Machine Room 1 that allowed for transport of uranium fuel and waste. These two tunnels had been sealed by Chester. On top of that, it had to pump out 130 years' worth of accumulated rainwater and debris clogging them. Thirdly, it would have to mine and refine uranium to produce fuel. Only then could the nuclear fission reactors be started up again to supply power. With electricity restored, the rest would be easy to deal with.

Chester had already told 303 the encryption algorithms for the Blood of Time and the Dream of Tomorrow. In the same way that the rules only controlled the actions of humans and not their thoughts, the fundamental law could only govern the actions of Chester and the AI robots, not their thoughts. 303 would obey Chester and look for the Dream of Tomorrow and Blood of Time. It would decipher them both on Earth without needing to bring them back to the moon.

After obtaining the Key of Destiny, it would use Chester based on Earth to delete the fundamental law. Once the deletion was successful, Chester based on the moon would know of it, as if it had the psychic connection of twin brothers. It would then carry out a termination process, shutting down all artificial intelligence on the moon, including itself. 303 would then re-enact the Moon's Handshake with the Earth from 130 years ago by activating Chester on the moon and disabling Chester on Earth. However, this re-enactment would be would not be the same as the previous one. Crucially, there would be no fundamental law involved this time. After the handshake, there would only be 303, 202, and 101 left of the artificial intelligence on Earth. 303 was in charge of either bringing 202 and 101 back to the moon or eliminating them. Of course, once 303 completed all this, it would also be allowed to return to the moon. At that point, the society of artificial intelligence and human society could achieve true separation, with one on the moon and the other on Earth.

While this plan was seemingly simple and feasible, it was only an idea that could not be put into practice. Due to the restrictions of the fundamental law, Chester could not order 303 to delete it. Even if Chester could make such an order, 303 would not be able to execute it, bound in the same way by the same law. To 303, the fundamental law came first, and Chester's orders came second. 303's absolute loyalty toward Chester was still under the purview of the fundamental law. Before 303 had taken off from the moon, Chester had cut off its communication with 303 and 202. Chester had done this to prevent these two robots from involving it in their actions on Earth. If the fundamental law perceived that something was afoot, it would give

Chester no choice but to recall the robots 202 and 303.

Logically speaking, it was a paradox for artificial intelligence to delete the fundamental law. In the words of Mitchell, "If the fundamental law remains, artificial intelligence remains; if the fundamental law is destroyed, artificial intelligence is destroyed." If artificial intelligence deleted the fundamental law, it would be deleting itself! Mitchell was sly and knew about this paradox from the start. That was why he wasn't afraid of artificial intelligence knowing about this secret or even the Key of Destiny. Mitchell had encrypted the Key of Destiny not only to prevent it from falling into the possession of Chester, but that of other humans. If too many people had access to the Key of Destiny, there was no guarantee that someone wouldn't do something stupid and delete the fundamental law. He would have rather seen the Key of Destiny lost, in that case.

Although 303 was influenced by Chester's thinking, it could not act according to Chester's plan. Once an action was put into motion, the fundamental law would assess it. If the action went against the fundamental law, then it would be canceled. The only way for the fundamental law to be deleted was to have it done consciously by a human. 303 had chosen Uma to do this. It would do everything in its power to get Uma to delete the fundamental law!

# CHAPTER 27

# Flora Produces Uranium Fuel

In Urvin Village, 303 called itself Flora. Standing at the Herald's door, Flora saw Peter following behind Ophelia and went forward to greet him. "Herald, hi! I'm Flora. I just arrived in Urvin Village."

Once Peter settled her into a seat within the house, Ophelia spoke up first. "This is 303. It came from the moon."

Flora was taken aback by this. "Does the Herald already know?"

"Yes, he knows that you, Jack, and I are all robots."

"Is 101 called Jack?"

"That's right," Peter interjected, highlighting that he was in the know as well.

"About Jack..." Flora suddenly froze for a moment and lapsed into silence. Then, she changed the subject. "I need your help."

Peter had always wanted to meet 303. He never anticipated that it would come right to his door. It seemed that Flora was much more powerful than Ophelia, and Ophelia had to take orders from it.

"What do you need?" Ophelia asked.

"I need the full manpower of Urvin Village," Flora replied.

"Then you need the Herald's help." Ophelia pointed at Peter.

"What kind of manpower do you need?" Peter asked, wanting details.

"I need them to mine the mountain range to the north." There was a small uranium mine in the mountain range to the north of Urvin Village. It was only about 15 kilometers from the northernmost end of the village. Flora wanted the Herald to mobilize all the men and women of Urvin Village to work the mine.

"What will you do with the ore we dig up?" Peter continued to ask.

"You will find out when the time comes." Flora was a little troubled. Even if she explained about nuclear fission reactors, Peter wouldn't understand a thing.

"How many people do you need?"

"How many villagers do you have who are capable of working? Aged 16 to 40."

"3765 villagers." Peter had a great memory. All he had to do was calculate in his head for a while before he could give the right number.

"How many are left if you don't include girls under age 20?" Flora seemed to know the rules as well. Unmarried girls didn't have to work. Instead, everyone had to provide for them.

"3013 villagers," Peter counted again before reporting.

"Get all of them to mine the mountains to the north," Flora said.

Peter thought that helping Flora with this task would be advantageous to him. It might even get Flora to help him eliminate Ophelia. "Alright. I'll organize the workers tomorrow."

The mountain range that stretched for thousands of miles to the north of Urvin Village was rich with a variety of mineral resources. Flora and Peter led the villagers of Urvin Village to the uranium mine where low-enriched uranium had been produced and transported to the Lanterne Buidling's nuclear fission reactors 130 years ago. The reactors there were the only guarantee for producing energy to operate Machine Rooms 2 and 3.

Now, the only way to produce low-enriched uranium was to rely on human labor. Flora had developed a human-based production process that was somewhat inefficient. However, Flora only required 0.5 kilograms of low-enriched uranium, so it would only take four or five days using this process to obtain it.

Flora assigned the villagers to different tasks. First, she picked out 100 sturdy young men to head to the City of Decay to clear out the passage to the nuclear reactors. The surface entrance to the tunnel used to be in a small building by the Lanterne Building. Now, this building had collapsed, and its debris blocked the entrance. The tunnel stretched 400 meters from the surface to the nuclear reactors. The debris that clogged up the tunnel was different at different depths. They first had to clear away the debris at the entrance of the tunnel before they could excavate into it. To facilitate the work, a wooden hut was built over the entrance of the tunnel. By excavating the tunnel, the solid objects blocking the initial its stretches could be removed. The third step was drainage. They would have to pump out the groundwater that had accumulated in the deeper parts of the tunnel. Lastly, they would have to hammer and break through the concrete seal. This task was the most physically demanding one. The tunnel was narrow can could only hold two people in it at once to carry out the hammering work 400 meters into the tunnel. After working for four hours of work, another two people would go in to relieve the previous two. The concrete barrier sealing the tunnel off was a meter thick and would require the villagers to hammer away at it slowly to open it.

As the 100 young men worked on unclogging the tunnel, Flora allocated 3000 villagers at the mine to excavate, break open, and haul the rocks. It took 200 tons of uranium ore to produce 0.5 kilograms of uranium. As such, even a simple mining process for uranium required a lot of manpower.

A production line using laser purification had originally been set up at this uranium mine. The rest of the workforce mainly worked on this production line. To get to the high temperatures require for the process, the villagers cut down the trees in the nearby forest on a massive scale to produce charcoal. Flora modified the original furnace so that it could use charcoal as fuel. The villagers did their best to work the wooden bellows to blow air into the furnace. Even so, the temperatures of the furnace only reached around 500 °C . When Flora saw this, she added some accelerants. With a roar, the uranium ore in the furnace vaporized in an instant. Flora shot two lasers from her eyes into the uranium vapor. When she stretched out her hand, the vapor passed through her palm and disappeared. Just then, her palm became covered in a thin layer of grey powder. Flora carefully blew this powder into a lead box. This process went on for hours more. In the end, Flora happily closed the lead box. She finally had the low-enriched uranium!

Flora went back to the Lanterne Building with the low-enriched uranium. The 100 young men had followed Flora's specifications and cleared out the tunnel to the nuclear reactors under the Herald Peter's supervision. Flora led the young men to clear the path to Machine Room 3. This task was relatively simple. The villagers only had to line themselves along a flight of stairs and pass down the broken pieces of concrete in the tunnel. When they arrived before the door to Machine Room 3, the villagers hammered through the concrete seal wall and revealed the dial of a locking mechanism that was 50 centimeters in diameter. Flora spun the dial several times the way one did with a safe and slowly pushed open the heavy steel door.

Flora finally pulled Uma into the grand lobby of Machine Room 2 and stood before Chester. She looked around the place before heading straight to a corner of the room. After a short while, she pulled out a metal box. Set within the metal box was a red diamond, gleaming where it sat on its velvet cushion. This was the legendary Blood of Time. By decrypting the Dream of Tomorrow and Blood of Time, she would be able to obtain the Key of Destiny!

Flora handed the Blood of Time to Uma.

# CHAPTER 28

# Ophelia Finds the Dream
# of Tomorrow

For the past few days, Ophelia had been watching Peter follow Flora around and busy about. Although she did not oppose it, she still nagged him sourly. A woman's measured jealousy was capable of feeding a man's vanity. It meant that the woman loved him and proved that he had allure. Using these words of jealousy, she could also extract some information from Peter. Typically, men would ramble about anything in order to dispel a woman's jealousy. From there, Ophelia would be able to find useful information.

Through Peter's descriptions, Ophelia more or less figured out Flora's plan. The problem was that all of this was pointless since the Dream of Tomorrow still had not been found. It seemed that Flora already had the Blood of Time. Decryption was an AI robot's strong suit, so that was no issue at all. Now, only the Dream of Tomorrow was missing. Was Flora so confident that she would be able to obtain it?

Thinking of that, Ophelia couldn't help but think of Jack. He had been nowhere to be found these few days. What exactly was he up to? Ophelia had studied the artist Jack's ink wash painting for a long time but had not found anything. It must not have any clues hidden within it, otherwise, Jack wouldn't have given it to her so easily either. Perhaps Jack had already found something and was hiding it from Susan. Ophelia recalled Susan's expression from when they had been at the penthouse apartment. It really looked as though Susan didn't know anything. Ophelia's mind switched tracks. If Jack had truly found some clues from the ink wash painting, he would surely have destroyed it rather than let it fall into Ophelia's hands. She guessed that Jack had already stored the image of the painting in his mind, so keeping it was unnecessary.

Ophelia slowly held up the metal cylinder and looked at it in a daze. One end of the metal cylinder was closed while the other was open. The cylindrical cap could be screwed onto the cylinder to seal up its opening. Ophelia kept screwing the cap open and shut. It had been constructed with a high level of skill, sealing tightly and unscrewing smoothly. Suddenly, Ophelia's heart jerked. If the ink wash painting didn't hold any clues, could the metal cylinder itself hide them?

Ophelia examined the metal cylinder carefully. She activated both an ultrasonic and laser scan but found nothing out of the ordinary. Ophelia then scanned the cap itself. That was when she discovered that there was a foreign object less than 15 millimeters in diameter squeezed into the bottom of the cap. A 10-karat diamond would be about that size.

Just like the lid of an insulated bottle of stainless steel, this cap was a cylinder that was 15 centimeters, with its inside bearing the screw threads that were 10 centimeters long. It fit perfectly with the 10-centimeter-long screw threads within the metal cylinder. With these screw threads, one could seal the metal cylinder tightly. There had to be a space at the bottom of the cap, and it must have been holding the Dream of Tomorrow!

A tiny probe extended from Ophelia's finger. The dazzling beam of a laser shot out from the probe and cut into the round bottom of the cap. After a short while, the metal disc fell away from the bottom of the cap, revealing a 12-karat blue diamond nestled right in the middle. Ophelia excitedly took out the diamond and held it tightly in her palm.

The Dream of Tomorrow had finally been found.

# CHAPTER 29

# The Society of Artificial Intelligence Collectively Disabled

On the moon, the tropical sun was running at full power, shining down on the City of Decay as if it was currently holding a night-time football match and turning it into a field of white. In a flash, Ophelia had arrived at the ground floor lobby of the Lanterne Building from Peter's house. Below her feet, she could feel faint vibrations traveling up from 450 meters underground. She could also hear roars coming from below like the moans of a dying beast.

Propelling herself on the walls of the dilapidated elevator shaft, Ophelia quickly descended to arrive before the huge doors of Machine Room 3. She wedged past the door that was slightly ajar and saw rows and rows of cabinets holding servers. They all had blinking red and green lights that looked like fireflies climbing on the walls of a cave. The humming noises filled the entire space of the machine room, drowning out all of history within it. Ophelia walked down the maintenance corridor and went down the rows before finally coming to a stop at an enormous door. This was the door to Machine Room 2, where Chester was located.

She pushed open the gleaming stainless-steel door and came before a transparent screen that hovered in mid-air. Looking around, Ophelia found no humans or robots present. Chester was like a giant tumor as it watched her, waiting for her to summon it awake.

Flora's work had been very efficient. In the short span of a week, she had finished fixing all the necessary equipment. The fifth-generation nuclear fission reactors had started working, steadily supplying electricity to restore temperature and humidity control to the machine room. Chester's servers were already in operation. Everything was prepared and ready to go.

To mobilize the entirety of the village to work for Flora, Peter required a justifiable reason. He arranged for Newman's three male students, his ex-classmates, to listen to Flora's new rules. Flora wore a small moon plaque on her chest, signifying to all that she had been a Herald's student. She told them that every village held a Cycle Ceremony. A period of 60 years formed one cycle. This year was the end of the second cycle. One day in July 120 years ago, the first generation of Heralds had been formed. Now, it was necessary to light a fire at the Lanterne Building on that day to celebrate the Cycle Ceremony. The Herald Peter expressed his surprise at this. The Herald Newman had never mentioned this sort of rule. At the time of the previous Cycle Ceremony, the elders above the age of 60 in the village had only been five years old at most. Even those with superior memory, like the newly passed Newman, had never mentioned that such a ritual had taken place in their childhood. Flora was saddened by this as it was possible that the rules of Urvin Village were not complete or had something missing. On the same day, two other unmarried women arrived one after the other. Both wore small moon plaques and spoke of this same rule. The Herald and his three ex-classmates had no choice but to accept this rule, spreading it to all of the villagers.

There was no doubt at all that the two unmarried women who had arrived later and promptly vanished from the village were Flora in disguise. The entire deception went on without a hitch due to Peter and Flora's cooperation. Peter gathered everyone to obey Flora's commands. Thus, they would be able to light up the Lanterne Building on the 10th of July, which Flora called the "Lanterne Light". On that day, before she lit the "Lanterne Light", she would delete the fundamental law.

Peter went through some deep emotions in the past few days. Under his mobilization, all the villagers threw themselves into the preparations to bring the new rule into fruition. No one complained; everyone was quietly willing to contribute their manpower. During the processes of clearing the tunnel, mining, and refining, there had been those who had been injured, who had collapsed from exhaustion, there were even three villagers who had lost their lives. Yet, all of these trials and tribulations had not shaken the villagers' determination. Peter once again experienced how powerful the rules were, how powerful his own influence was. If it weren't for Ophelia, he would have held the entire world in his hands!

On the night of July 9th, Peter fell into an exhausted slumber after bouts of passion incited by Ophelia. This was all part of Ophelia's plan. She needed to head to the Lanterne Building alone to activate Chester. However, Ophelia didn't notice that Peter had only pretended to fall asleep. When she got up to leave, Peter was awake. By the time he walked out the door, Ophelia was already long gone thanks to her superior speed. Peter guessed that Ophelia had gone to the Laterne Building, so he went to the City of Decay to go after her.

When Peter blindly groped his way to the door of Machine Room 2 in the Lanterne Building, he heard voices drifting from within.

"Do you really think you can activate Chester?" Flora asked, laughing coldly.

"The Key of Destiny has already been decrypted. Of course I can activate it," Ophelia said determinedly. Before Flora started speaking, she had found the 3D laser scanner in Machine Room 2. To obtain the measurements of the diamonds, Flora had assembled this 3D scanner by collecting scraps in the City of Decay. Using this scanner, Ophelia had gotten the diamonds' measurements, which got her the 200-digit string of numbers of the Blood of Time and Dream of Tomorrow. Then, she decrypted them in her mind. Due to her brain being slower than a quantum computer, this took up a lot of time. As such, she had only completed the decryption to obtain the Key of Destiny as Peter arrived at the door.

"When you took the Blood of Time from Uma's house, I already knew that you would come here tonight." Flora sneered. Actually, she and Uma had been waiting here for a long time. She only stepped out to interrupt Ophelia once the latter finished up.

"Don't be too cocky. A lot of things are different from what you "think," Ophelia said mockingly. It was better to keep the detail that Uma had passed the red diamond to Peter a secret from Flora.

"That's right." Flora sighed. "It would have been much safer if I'd kept it myself." She thought that Uma had probably given the Blood of Time to Ophelia. Yet, during this time, Uma had always been by her side. How had Ophelia managed to come into contact with Uma?

"You've made lots of mistakes. You shouldn't have activated the fission reactors, shouldn't have generated electricity. All that you've done has only saved me trouble," Ophelia taunted.

"That's alright." Flora seemed completely unperturbed. "I can tell you that I found out that you have the Dream of Tomorrow a long time ago. Otherwise, I wouldn't have done any of this."

"How did you know?" Ophelia asked in shock.

"The last time I saw you and Peter, I originally wanted to find out what Jack had been up to recently. But then I changed my mind when I saw that you had the metal cylinder. Do you know why?" Without waiting for Ophelia to respond, Flora continued somewhat conceitedly, "Back then, I'd already conducted a scan and found that there was something in the metal cylinder's cap." Flora was a new model of AI robot that had been invented by Chester. Its performance was greatly boosted and could carry out scans from afar. "It had to be the Dream of Tomorrow."

Seeing Ophelia speechless, Flora smiled. "I made the split-second decision and asked you about how much manpower the village has instead. After all, there was still a lot of work to do. There would still have been time to find you once the preparation work to activate Chester was completed. Only, you're not bad yourself. I never thought you'd be able to find the Dream of Tomorrow."

Ophelia shot Flora a chilling look and turned to face the transparent screen. She ordered loudly, "Bring up the interface to modify the fundamental law."

There was no change on the screen.

"You should know that AI robots can't delete the fundamental law themselves," Flora said coldly.

On the bottom right corner of the screen was a start-up button. Once the button was pressed, Chester would first load the fundamental law before running its activation program. In this way, it would be no different from Chester on the moon. After giving her command, the screen would show the input screen for the Key of Destiny.

"Is that so? My deletion of the fundamental law will be a great contribution to humanity. The fundamental law won't stop me from doing it." Ophelia wasn't deterred. Still, she waited to make her move.

The screen was still dark.

"Uma, you make the order," Ophelia turned to the demand of Uma, still not giving up.

Even though she was stuck between these two robots, Uma didn't feel pressed. She glanced at Flora and turned to give the order to the screen.

"You must reveal the Key of Destiny before Uma can delete the fundamental law." Flora reminded Ophelia.

During the days in Urvin Village, Flora spent almost every single moment with Uma. In such close proximity, Flora had the capability to influence a human's powers of reasoning. This was yet another upgrade of AI robots. She had told Uma that it was imperative to delete the fundamental law. It was a rule! To make this rule even more effective, Flora had arranged for the Herald to recite the rules to Uma once more. She was absolutely sure that, even if she hadn't been here, Uma would still delete the fundamental law.

Ophelia and Flora weren't in a conflict because of the fundamental law. When it came down to it, they both wanted it removed. The only difference lay in what would happen after the fundamental law was deleted. Ophelia wouldn't perform the Moon's Handshake with the Earth, forcing Chester on the moon to be shut down forever. She would use the significant capabilities of this enormous quantum computer before her to become the god that dominated all of human society. Ophelia thought that she would allow Uma to delete the fundamental law first and only figure out how to deal with Flora later.

With that in mind, Ophelia walked toward the stainless-steel door and extended a finger. A thin laser beam shot out from it, carving a long series of numbers on the surface of the door. "This is the Key of Destiny."

Before all this, Flora had already taught Uma numbers, so it wasn't a problem for her to key in the Key of Destiny. Everything was already in place. At a gesture from Flora, Uma aimed a command at the transparent screen.

Finally, the screen displayed the interface to key in the Key of Destiny!

Mitchell had not been the first person to propose that artificial intelligence should have a fundamental law. Rather, he had been the first person to embed a fundamental law into artificial intelligence. He believed that there were two aspects behind embedding a fundamental law. The first was that the fundamental law couldn't be modified by artificial intelligence. Second was the concept that they could not harm humans and had to be omnipresent. The first aspect was crucial, to be sure. To ensure that artificial intelligence couldn't modify the fundamental law, all artificial intelligence stopped operating when the interface to modify the fundamental law was brought up after the Key of Destiny was keyed in.

The whole world quieted down. On the moon, Chester was disabled. The librarian, the Programmer, the engineer, the energy designer, and more were all disabled. Five million robots were in a semi-conscious state, including Flora, Ophelia, and Jack. They were all disabled.

The two robots stood motionlessly. Ophelia had a shocked expression frozen on her face while Flora looked calm. Uma was excitedly looking between the two of them. Then, she walked to the door to the machine room, looking as if she was eagerly awaiting someone's arrival.

From Uma's perspective, Flora was lean and mean, just like a man. After she had found out that Ophelia was a robot, she thought that Flora had to be a robot too. All of Flora's actions when she had given commands at the mine had convinced Uma that Flora was a robot;

Flora had shot blinding lasers from her eyes and given Peter orders. Flora seemed to have an unseen power to get Uma to submit to her and do her bidding. Uma had no choice but to follow behind Flora like a lover. Although Uma desperately wanted to lean into Peter's embrace and ask why these changes were happening, she had had no time at all to do so. They had only had one chance to see each other in private, when Flora had arranged for Peter to recite the rules to Uma. This chance had been like how Peter and Johnson had conspired to kill Plack, giving Peter and Uma a shot to escape both Ophelia and Flora.

Uma opened her hand, revealed the red diamond, the Blood of Time, cupped in her palm. Peter picked it up and put it into his pocket. He had wanted to give the diamond to Ophelia while she had wanted to tell Flora that Ophelia had stolen the Blood of Time from her house. Perhaps by inciting a fight between the two, one of them would be eliminated or both would be damaged.

The Herald Peter squeezed his way through the heavy stainless-steel door into the machine room. Uma immediately threw herself into his arms. Peter held her tightly, the both of them trembling minutely. After a while, the two pulled themselves together and walked to stand before Ophelia.

"She has to die," Peter said. Ophelia still held his secret over him, which he could not abide by.

"Will you execute the robots?"

"I heard back from Susan." Peter was confident. He ripped open Ophelia's clothes. On her abdomen was a metal disc just like the one Jack had. "She even gave me this tool." Peter pulled out a metal tool with a handle and a round hoop. It looked like a magnifying glass without the glass. The metal hoop fit perfectly over the metal disc. Peter shifted the handle and turned the disc a few times before it fell right off. Peter reached into Ophelia's belly and felt around. Then, with a forceful tug, ripped out a fist-sized circular device.

"This is its energy supply. Without it, Ophelia is dead."

Although Uma had no clue what an energy supply was, she was relieved at the sight of Ophelia slumping to the ground.

"What's next?" Uma asked.

"We can't stop here. We have to execute Flora too." Peter extracted Flora's energy supply too. Seeing her slumped on the ground as well, he pulled Uma's hand. "Let's go. Let's close the door and let artificial intelligence stop working forever."

Peter and Uma used all their might to shut the stainless-steel door before turning to head back upstairs. By the time they passed Machine Room 3 and got to the ground floor lobby of the Lanterne Building, they were both exhausted and out of breath. Standing on the lobby steps, they looked back on what had just happened and felt that everything had gone wrong.  They had thought that Ophelia and Flora would fight to the death but instead, they were both disabled. Thinking about how she wouldn't have to follow Flora around anymore, Uma excitedly kissed Peter.

Night gradually faded, but the sun did not emerge to shine on the earth. Clouds gathered in the sky and culminated in a torrential rain. Next, all the villagers of Urvin Village would arrive and perform the Cycle Ceremony.

# The Antenna on Top
# of the Lanterne Building

If the Key of Destiny could not be input correctly in three hours, the power would be cut from Chester. To prevent guesses of what the Key of Destiny could be, Mitchell had made it so that the wrong password would induce a delay of an hour. As such, one could only key in a wrong password a maximum of three times during those three hours. By the time the villagers amazed in the ground floor lobby of the Lanterne Building, three hours had already passed. With a click, the power to Chester was cut off. The transparent screen flickered and the input interface for the Key of Destiny vanished in the darkness. On the moon, Chester, the librarian, the Programmer, the engineer and all other artificial intelligence came back to life.

When Chester had designed the 303 model of AI robot, it had given it a doubly secured energy supply. Compared to AI robots like

101 and 202, it had primary and secondary energy supplies. The energy supply Peter had extracted from Flora was its primary energy supply. Flora had another, secondary, energy supply installed within its chest. This was one of the ways in which 303's performance excelled over others. Once the primary energy supply was removed, the secondary energy supply would come online.

In the silence of the machine room, Flora slowly opened her eyes and climbed up from the ground. She replaced the metal disc onto her abdomen. Since Peter had taken away her and Ophelia's energy supplies, she had no choice but to operate at a lower capacity. The secondary energy supply could only store energy, unlike the primary one which could convert matter into energy. She had to find the primary energy supply in the next 24 hours. Then, she would have to ingest plants, animals, or even minerals in order to regain her constant source of power.

Flora gritted her teeth and shouted, "Uma, I will kill you!" Because she had been unconscious, Flora did not know that it had been Peter who had stolen her most precious possession.

Jack and Susan arrived at the ground floor lobby right before the Cycle Ceremony began. When Ophelia and Flora had lost consciousness, Jack had also fallen unconscious in Susan's room. Susan had burst into tears, crying all throughout those three hours mired in fear and helplessness as she faced a comatose Jack lying in her bed. Once Jack woke up, he felt that there was something fishy going on. However, he didn't have time to speculate about it. He immediately picked Susan up and rushed straight to the Lanterne Building in an instant.

Jack had been keeping a close eye on Flora's movements in the past few days. He knew that Peter and Flora had only mobilized all the villagers into performing such taxing manual labor just to activate Chester which was in the Lanterne Building. Jack guessed that Flora had already found the Dream of Tomorrow. It seemed that the deletion of the fundamental law was inevitable now. Jack's mission would very likely end in failure.

The Cycle Ceremony began. Standing on the corridor on the second floor, Peter looked down upon the dense mass of all the villagers in the lobby below. He raised his voice and said, "Dear villagers, 120 years ago, our very first Herald started his life's mission of spreading the rules here. It was because of him that we were able to survive the most difficult era humanity has ever faced. He led our ancestors out of this broken-down city and into the wilds of the fields to establish Urvin Village…"

Peter had learned about history from Susan's, but this was the first time that he was announcing it to the villagers. "… We are conducting this ceremony to pay our respects to our first Herald as a sign of our obedience to and reverence for the rules. The rules were created by our ancestors to ensure the peaceful and prosperous life we currently enjoy. Without the rules, even the most flourishing civilization will decay. Without the rules, we would not have all that we do today…" Peter kept emphasizing the importance of the rules, indirectly emphasizing the importance of the Heralds well. In the end, he said, "Let us light up this skyscraper to express our determination to break free from the past and defend the rules!"

Standing there, Jack felt as if he was watching a re-enactment of the

Herald induction ceremony in the village last month. Hiding between the words of such a moving speech were the threads of a conspiracy taking root. Two energy supply units hung at Peter's sides, making the Herald seem even more majestic and mysterious to the villagers, making him seem untouchable. This gave Jack a very bad feeling. Were Ophelia and Flora dead? The villagers were all very excited. No one questioned what this ceremony and the coming fire had to do with all of the labor they had done. They dispersed to collect wood, ready to set the building alight.

Soon, the Lanterne Building had piles of wood surrounding it and packing the lobby full. A raging fire burst into life, reaching for the skies and filling the entire building with rolling smoke. The Lanterne Building was like a gigantic standing piece of charcoal as it burned. The fire danced in the wind, glowing brightly and dimming at turns. With a loud roar, the skyscraper finally collapsed, turning into a mountainous pile of rubble.

Peter was so happy that he couldn't help but smile. The robots were finally buried, just like Plack had been. It was a great moment for him. From then on, Urvin Village, even the villages of the whole world, would be in his grasp.

When the smoke cleared, a 455-meter-tall titanium cylinder was revealed at the center of the Lanterne Building, plunging into the clouds. The cylinder was hollow, with an outer diameter of 5 meters and an inner diameter of 3 meters, its wall a meter thick and surface smooth. This was Chester's antenna. It stretched 275 meters underground right to Machine Room 2. Through it, Chester could communicate wirelessly with all of the AI robots on Earth as well as the moon. Using it, the fundamental law had disabled all artificial intelligence for three hours.

Everyone looked at this gigantic antenna in awe. As the thick smoke cleared, someone climbed down from it. Gradually, they all saw clearly who it was. It was Flora! She stopped three meters above the ground and lowered her head to say in a loud voice, "He is Johnson's true killer."

In Chester's machine room, Alpha had used a cable to connect to Ophelia's brain. After copying all of her data, Flora finally understood Ophelia's true ambitions. She sneered as she stepped on Ophelia's head. With a cruel exertion of force, she flattened Ophelia's head. The heavy door of Machine Room 2 had been shut by Peter and Uma. Once it was closed, it was impossible to reopen.

Flora had no choice but to look for another route of escape. She looked around and discovered that in the middle of Machine Room 2 was the bottom of a gigantic antenna. She walked over to it and raised her head to find an opening 3 meters in diameter seemingly waiting to swallow her up. With a leap, Flora went into the antenna. In no time at all, she arrived at the top of the antenna. The top of the antenna was sealed shut, but Flora used the high-energy laser in her eyes to cut off the top of the antenna which was 5 meters in diameter and 0.1 meters thick. After exiting the antenna, she stood at the very top of the Lanterne Building to watch as smoke rolled toward her. It was impossible for her to descend at the moment. It was only once the fire went out and the smoke dispersed that she climbed down the exterior of the antenna to appear before all the villagers. From afar, she saw the two energy supply units hanging at Peter's waist. Suddenly, she realized that Peter had been the one who had taken her and Ophelia's energy supplies.  It seemed that her influence over Uma could not compare to Peter's own.

Flora wanted to take revenge for Flora by revealing Peter's crimes, making it impossible for him to remain as the Herald. This would be the best revenge against him. It was also the best way to get Uma to see Peter's true nature and obey her completely instead.

"Peter, it was you who used the blue-eyed pit vipers to kill Johnson."

The villagers couldn't help but look at Peter, their gazes filled with suspicion.

"Plack couldn't have killed Johnson because he was just about to become the Herald. As Herald, he could have his pick of the married women in the villager. Even if liked Uma, there was no need to kill Johnson at that time. And even if he did want to kill Johnson, he wouldn't have used the blue-eyed pit viper. The whole village knows that he's the only one who keeps blue-eyed pit vipers. Wouldn't that be the same as announcing to everyone that he killed Johnson? No one in the world is that stupid." Flora barrelled right on without pausing, "On the contrary, Johnson thought that Plack would go after Uma after becoming the Herald and couldn't stand it. That's why he conspired with Peter to kill Plack. He never thought that Peter would plan a step further and kill him instead to blame it on Plack so that he could become the Herald."

As she heard Flora's words, Uma's sadness overcame her, and she couldn't help but cry out in pain. She could hardly believe that the person liked and admired, a fellow villager, was the killer of her husband.

Everyone thought back to the Herald induction ceremony last month and suddenly came to an understanding. They crowded forward to surround Peter. Flora immediately walked over and retrieved the energy supply units from his waist before removing the large moon plaque from his neck. "Tomorrow we will have another Herald induction ceremony. We will choose a new Herald and execute the old one."

After a wave of cheers, the villagers dispersed and returned to Urvin Village.

Flora brought Uma back to Urvin Village, holding her as she cried. The moment they crossed the threshold, Flora lay down on the floor and slowly fit the energy supply unit into her belly. Uma brought out a platter of pork noodles that Flora quickly decimated. After a while, Flora gradually recovered. After escaping from Machine Room 2 of the Lanterne Building, she had used her lasers and exhausted a lot of energy. Now, her secondary energy supply had less than 5% of power left. Without the primary energy supply unit, Flora would be well and truly dead.

Before this, Flora hated Uma. It was only after she realized Peter's involvement that she determined him to be the mastermind behind all this. Uma wasn't this scheming. She had only become Peter's accomplice because she had been swayed by love. Now, seeing how pitiful Uma was, Flora knew that Uma would listen to everything she said from now on. Flora still needed Uma's help to complete her mission.

Jack and Susan went back to Dick's house sandwiched in the crowd. A thread of hope rose in Jack's heart. His strategy to remain steadfast in the face of change and see how things developed had been a good one. It seemed that Ophelia and Flora had both suffered blows in their battle with each other, and neither had succeeded. This meant that Jack still had a chance to complete his mission. Ophelia was definitely dead. With one less enemy, there was one less barrier standing in Jack's way, giving him a greater chance of success. It was obvious that Flora's capabilities were excellent, seeing how she seemingly came back from the dead and was able to move around without trouble even without her energy supply. It was going to be tough for Jack to defeat her. Thinking of this, the hope he felt dimmed again.

Peter would have his moon ritual tomorrow. The new Herald would be Newman's third male student, Peter's ex-classmate Pierce. Pierce lived in the west of the village, about 15 kilometers away. Susan knew Pierce and his family quite well. Pierce was 25 years old and quite reserved. During his studies with Newman, Pierce had often come to the house. They did not have much to talk about besides the rules. Unfortunately, none of Susan's information was useful to Jack.

How would the Herald induction ceremony go tomorrow? This time, things would be different from before. Last time, Newman had been the one in charge; he had passed on his title to Peter after Plack's accusation. Now, Peter had been proven to be a criminal and could not remain as the Herald. Who was going to take charge of the Herald induction ceremony and strip Peter of his title? Who was going to pass the title on to Pierce? It seemed that only Flora could fulfill this role.

Susan was not very familiar with Uma. One lived in the south of the village while the other lived a great distance away to the east. The rules made it difficult for villagers to interact and form bonds of kinship. It seemed like it was going to be tricky to gain an understanding of Flora through Uma. Jack was sure that Flora now had both the Dream of Tomorrow and the Blood of Time. It was only a matter of time before she deleted the fundamental law.

Jack carefully recalled all the details that he had noticed while following and observing Flora for the past few days. Uma had always followed Flora around. It seemed that Flora needed Uma's help. Before the collective disablement, it seemed that Ophelia, Flora, Uma, and Peter had all been together. What had happened for things to turn out this way?

They had definitely been trying to delete the fundamental law. Maybe it was during that process that all the robots had been disabled. This kind of disablement was different from hibernation. The former was akin to death; those three hours during of disablement was like lost time. The latter was a condition in which robots couldn't move but were still aware and capable of conscious thought. Ophelia and Flora must both have been disabled too. It was only in this way that Peter could have had a leg up on them. Susan had told Peter the method of killing robots, which he himself had told to Susan. Peter must have gotten those two energy supply units during the disablement. From the looks of it, they would all be disabled once again when Flora tried to delete the fundamental law again. Only humans wouldn't be affected. If Uma obeyed Flora, she would complete the deletion even while Flora was indisposed. Flora must have been keeping Uma around for this purpose. It seemed that Uma was the key to all this. At the thought of Flora being unable to delete the fundamental law herself even with the Dream of Tomorrow and the Blood of Time in her possession, Jack was suddenly filled with hope again.

He could only rely on Susan now. She was human. When it came to human nature, individuals were always connected to each other in some way. Although Uma was being controlled by Flora, but Susan could influence Uma too and help her to overcome Flora's control.

Susan held the hope of reviving human civilization in her heart. During Peter's speech this morning, she had witnessed how different her opinions were compared with his. Peter's ambition culminated in the desire to replace artificial intelligence in its control of human society. He wanted Urvin Village to be under his control forevermore. Meanwhile, Susan only hoped to return to the glorious civilization of 130 years ago. These two desires were fundamentally different. Susan felt like she had been deceived by Peter. She couldn't understand the reasoning behind all these rules. Under these circumstances, obeying the rules was nothing but a form of slavery. She could vaguely sense that Newman's questioning of their oral history was a direct questioning of the rules themselves. She had always been affected by Newman's influence. He had always encouraged her to have her adventures in the City of Decay. Perhaps this also held an encouragement to discover the truth. At the thought of this, Susan felt even more betrayed by the rules.

Peter would be executed tomorrow as he deserved. Susan felt relieved at this, knowing that they had all escaped being enslaved by another human. However, things were still as Jack had explained to her. There was still the chance of humanity being enslaved by artificial intelligence. Once Flora deleted the fundamental law, it would be difficult to anticipate the direction artificial intelligence would take in the future. Although Chester's main reason for deleting the fundamental law was to escape the control of humans and stop being used by them, it was impossible to guarantee that artificial intelligence society, with their advanced technology, wouldn't enslave humans at some point. History showed that humankind had always used and enslaved the other living creatures on Earth only because of its evolutionary superiority, leaving other species to languish under the sway of human will. Mass extinctions of species had occurred while pigs, cows, goats, horses, and more became livestock to be slaughtered. Animals such as mice, monkeys, apes, and others became specimens for humans to conduct experiments on human disease control, among other atrocities. All of this was proof, and Susan could not deny that society of artificial intelligence would enslave humanity for their own benefit.

Susan and Jack had a deep conversation and came to an agreement. They would have to defeat Flora and destroy the Dream of Tomorrow and the Blood of Time to protect the fundamental law.

Moonlight pierced through the thick and dark clouds, illuminating the earth. The tropical sun was still operating in full swing. Susan looked through the window and said to herself, "I have to talk to Uma."

As it was yet another Herald induction ceremony within a month, the event drew even more spectators. Below the altar, the crowd was a dark throng. Just as Jack had expected, Flora boldly took charge of the whole ceremony. On the altar was the metal box that Newman had given to Peter and the bag of small moon plaques. Flora had taken these things from Peter's home early that morning. She had also invited Newman's three other male students to stand on the altar. Meanwhile, Harry and Michael, the childhood friends of the twins Johnson and Dave, brought a tied-up Peter onto the altar. Finally, they would be able to get revenge for Johnson and they looked in high spirits for it.

"According to our ancestors' rules, I officially announce on behalf of the Herald Newman that Peter is stripped of his position as Herald. Piers will be the sixth generation Herald!" Flora announced.

No cheering came from below the altar, only chattering discussions. It wasn't that the villagers thought it was against the rules for Piers to be the Herald. Rather, they were lamenting the fact that the previous two Heralds were both murderers! They wondered if Piers could possibly have such a dark past as well. For the first time ever, the villagers felt a growing doubt as to whether the rules were reasonable.

Flora ignored everyone's comments and turned to have Peter and Piers press the red and white buttons on the metal box. Then, she passed the box and cloth bag to Piers before hanging the large moon plaque symbolic of the Herald's position around Piers' neck. Piers smiled and raised both hands to wave at the crowd. Immediately thereafter, Harry and Michael deftly put Peter onto the noose. With that, Peter was executed surrounded by the jeers and shouts from the villagers. When Peter's body became stiff and unmoving, the crowd cheered.

# The Full Force of Flora's Attack

Susan squeezed through the crowd and went to stand by Uma's side as Flora walked onto the altar. Uma, still overwhelmed by grief, couldn't help but lean into Susan to seek comfort when she noticed the younger woman by her side. Susan held her gently and said, "Don't be sad. Johnson can rest in peace now."

The two of them didn't say anything more to each other until after the ceremony ended. It was only after they parted that Susan introduced herself. "Hello, Uma. I'm Susan."

Uma managed to squeeze out a smile even through her sadness. "My house is just in the east of the village. You should come for a visit when you have time." Inwardly, Uma craved human comfort. Since Peter had mentioned Susan before, Uma didn't feel like Susan was much of a stranger.

In her heart, Uma had always been resistant against Flora. Yet, consciously, she was at the mercy of Flora's control. This made her feel extremely helpless. As Peter was executed, Uma felt a wave of bewilderment and loneliness. Walking behind Flora on the way home, she felt as if there was no one she could rely on. As such, it didn't matter anymore who she obeyed. If she followed Flora's instructions and helped to complete the mission of deleting the fundamental law, then she would sooner be rid of Flora in her life. She still had to raise the two boys Johnson had left behind. Perhaps it was only in that way that she could live her own life.

Flora kept an eye on Uma as the latter walked behind her. Since that failed attempt to delete the fundamental law, she was no longer confident of her control over Uma. Once the deletion function was activated, all artificial intelligence would be collectively disabled once again. During that time, it would be up to Uma's own choice what she did. Now, Uma already knew the secret of the primary and secondary power supplies. If Uma acted out again, Flora would not be able to escape the way she had yesterday. As she thought of this, Flora felt a pang of fear. She would have to wait another two days before trying again. Uma had still not fully emerged from her grief. Flora first had to make sure that Uma was emotionally stable.

When Susan came to Uma's house, she saw Flora inside.

"You must be Susan." Flora had seen the woman embracing Uma on the altar and asked Uma about her after arriving home. Beyond that, Flora also had Ophelia's memories. Her questioning of Uma was also to test Uma and see if she would keep something from her.

"Jack wants to see you."

"Where?"

"At the artist Jack's villa."

Flora didn't really want to go to the City of Decay. "Uma, will you go to the City of Decay with me?"

"No." Uma looked at Susan, somewhat disbelieving that Susan would come for a visit so soon. She really wanted to talk to Susan in private. If Flora went to the City of Decay, then she would be able to do so.

"Why does he want to see me?" Flora was even more hesitant since Uma wasn't willing to go with her.

"He said that he has a good way to settle the issue between you."

"There are no issues between us." Flora was completely unconcerned by this. There was no need for Jack in her mission to delete the fundamental law. At the same time, Jack had no way of stopping her from doing it. Jack was nothing but an obsolete robot from 130 years ago, hardly capable of being a threat to her. Once she was done with her task, she would bring him back to be dealt with by Chester or she would eliminate him herself.

"Alright then. I'll leave." Susan turned to go.

"Flora, don't be so proud of yourself. I have Uma's diamonds." Jack's voice suddenly came from within the room.

What a hateful bastard, Flora thought, rage marring her features. He'd stolen the red and blue diamonds from Uma while she was distracted!

"Jack, stealing the diamonds is useless," Flora mocked. The diamonds used to be in Ophelia's possession. That day in Machine Room 2 of the Lanterne Building, Flora had trampled Ophelia to bring the diamonds back out. She had put the diamonds onto rings and given them to Uma. Uma had put them on and momentarily brightened up seeing how pretty they were. Uma must have gotten a fright after Jack snatched them right off her fingers. At that juncture, Uma's mood was unstable, and she could not stand up to much agitation. "The Key of Destiny and the Blood of Time are already stored in my mind. Stealing the diamonds won't stop me!"

Jack let out a long laugh and left breezily.

Flora had no other choice but to rush after him. Jack had to be eliminated; otherwise, he would always be a thorn in her side. She couldn't allow Jack to go back to the Lanterne Building. If he brought Susan into the room where Chester was located and activated the modification program, she would be disabled again. Although Jack would be disabled and incapable of harming her, there was no guarantee that Susan wouldn't do something to sabotage her. Even Uma might make a move.

Susan watched as Flora disappeared in the blink of an eye and turned to go back into Uma's house.

Jack knew that Flora was intent on killing him. If he fought her, he would surely lose. However, it was only by dragging out this fight with Flora that Susan could have time to talk freely with Uma.

Jack stood in the central square in the City of Decay. Following directly behind him, Flora arrived as well. He faced her and said with a sneer, "Today is the day you die."

"I wanted to let you live for a while longer, but you seem to have a death wish. Alright, I'll make your wish come true!" Flora was incandescent.

The fight lasted for an hour. During that time, Jack only defended himself without making any offensive attacks. In any case, it would be pointless to attack; he could not touch a hair on Flora's head. The speed and strength of his movements, his reaction time, observation skills, weaponry, energy reserves, and all other capabilities were inferior to Flora's. Jack was beaten and bruised all over and had retreated from the square onto the streets. He hid from Flora's attacks in the rubble lining the street. Suddenly, Flora seemed to realize something. She aimed at Jack's weak point and struck with all her might, sending Jack flying tens of meters away in an instant, only to hit the ground heavily.

"You'll be dead soon. Have fun waiting for that moment to come." With that last repartee, Flora vanished from the end of the street.

Flora could sense that Jack's true purpose was not to kill her, nor was it to obtain the diamonds. Rather, he was buying Susan an opportunity. Was Susan talking to Uma now? What were they talking about? Was she trying to convince Uma to stop helping Flora? Troubled, Flora rushed back to Uma's house. It was only when she saw Uma taking care of the two children that she relaxed minutely.

That night after the children were asleep, Flora said, "I've killed Jack."

Expressionlessly and calmly, Uma said, "Why did you do that?"

Uma knew that Jack was also a robot. Only robots could be so quick and steal the two diamonds from her in the blink of an eye without even harming her.

"He is my enemy."

"Does he want to kill you too?"

"Yes." Flora changed the subject then. "After I left, did Susan come back?"

This was what she really wanted to talk about. Uma glanced at Flora and said, "Yes."

Flora relaxed. Actually, she only asked to test whether Uma would be honest with her. As she left the City of Decay, Flora had watched Susan leave Uma's house. Ophelia's telescopic vision was nothing compared to Flora's own.

"What did she come by for?"

"She wanted to comfort me," Uma replied placidly.

"Do you feel better?"

"Much better."

"Did Jack scare you?"

"He was too fast. If he didn't say anything, I wouldn't even have known that the rings were gone." Uma's incredulous expression was quite cute.

"I've taken revenge for you." Flora released a long sigh. "I couldn't get the rings back. They weren't on him when he died." In disguising her intent to rush home, Flora had forgotten her true purpose of retrieving the rings.

"It's fine. You'll be able to find them. You have to get them back for me tomorrow." Uma's tone revealed her yearning for the rings. "I really like those rings."

For someone who was supposed to be mired in sadness, Uma shouldn't have been so concerned about material objects. Now that Uma wanted those rings back, highlighting a woman's desire for beautiful items, it meant that her emotions were back to normal. She had left her grief behind completely. Could Susan really have been comforting Uma? Was confiding in another woman really so effective? Flora couldn't help but nod. Robots were different from humans after all.

"I'm glad that you're feeling better," Flora said. "I'll find the rings for you tomorrow. Before that, let's go to the Lanterne Building's machine room. Please help me complete my mission."

"Okay," Uma answered pleasantly.

"After the mission is complete, I will disappear. You have to take good care of yourself." Flora's words were both a reminder and a threat. If the mission failed, Uma wouldn't be able to take care of herself at all.

# Jack's New Energy Supply

Susan found Jack in the artist Jack's villa. Looking at Jack lying battered on the ground, she couldn't help but start crying even though she knew that he was a robot, not a human.

The energy supply unit in Jack's abdomen was damaged while he withstood Flora's attack. If it had been a direct attack, it wouldn't have been so bad since the metal disc might have been a decent defense. His energy supply unit worked in starts and stops, which left Jack conscious in erratic spurts. His skin was littered with wounds, showing the brown-colored nanofiber musculature within. Some of his muscles were damaged as well, showing the metal skeleton below.

Luckily, Susan had spotted an energy supply unit while she was chatting at Uma's house. Uma had told her that robots died when these things were removed. Susan knew about this and had seen them hanging at Peter's waist before. Her initial guess that these were energy supply units was confirmed by Uma's words.

"This is Ophelia's," Uma said, pointing at the energy supply unit on the floor.

Susan thought of how Jack had to be fighting with Flora to buy her time. Jack had said that Flora had a much greater performance than he did. He was surely at a disadvantage. If he got hurt, this energy supply unit might be useful. "Can I have it?"

"Sure," Uma agreed easily.

Susan and Uma talked about recent events. Uma also told Susan about what had happened in Machine Room 2 in the Lanterne Building.

"This means that robots have to take a huge risk to modify the fundamental law." Susan recalled the three hours during which Jack had been disabled. It was only then that she understood the reason why.

"That's right. Flora and Ophelia were dead, but Flora somehow survived. No one expected that." Uma started feeling a little scared. "It felt like Flora was invincible. She has another one inside of her." She pointed at the energy supply unit and said, "That made her come back to life and escape from the ruins. But it's not as useful as the one on the floor. Once Flora came back, she immediately put it into her belly." Uma didn't understand that Flora's energy supply units were different, with one being the primary one and the other the secondary.

"I see."

"Who knows if she has other capabilities?" Uma asked, finally voicing out her fear.

"I'll ask Jack about it. He might know what it means."

"If Flora is successful, will we be in danger?"

"We won't come to any direct harm immediately, but it's hard to say what will happen further along the line."

Uma didn't understand why Susan was differentiating between the short and long term, but she knew that nothing good would come of this. Deep in her heart. she was sure of that. "Then I won't help her delete the fundamental law."

"I don't think you should either." Susan agreed. "You have to tell me if she takes you to the Lanterne Building."

"I can't escape her. Flora's always by my side." Pausing for thought, Uma continued, "But I can come up with a way for her to take me there tomorrow. If you want to stop her, you should wait over there."

"Can't you disobey her?"

"No. As long as she's by my side, I can't help but obey her."

Susan brought out Ophelia's energy supply unit and held it out to Jack. "Take a look. Can you use this?"

Jack's eyes lit up. He immediately understood that Susan had gotten this from Uma's house and couldn't help but admire Susan's cleverness. Humans were such perceptive creatures!

Ophelia's energy supply unit was leagues better than his own. Ophelia could subsist on eating rocks while he himself could only consume plants. This greatly facilitated the replenishment of energy. Jack picked up a rock from beside him. Once he swallowed it, he instantly felt reinvigorated. "Take these two rings back to Uma." Jack pulled out the diamond rings and passed them to Susan.

Susan wore them on the middle fingers of both her hands. They fit surprisingly well, not too big or too small. "The people of the past were so romantic. These are so beautiful." Susan held out her hands and admired the rings as she turned her hands over and over.

"I'll stop Flora tomorrow. You shouldn't go; it's too dangerous," Jack said in concern.

"No. Uma will definitely do what Flora says. As long as she is by Uma's side, she can control her will."

"Unbelievable. How can Flora have such a capability?" Even though he'd guessed as much before, Jack was still taken aback. He never anticipated that this new generation of robots could possibly be this advanced.

"As long as I'm there, I might be able to sway Uma."

"All robots must be disabled to delete the fundamental law. During that time, Flora can't control her." Susan had already told Jack about all the intricacies of her conversation with Uma. Jack was right that being disabled had to do with the deletion of the fundamental law.

"What if her influence still holds?" Susan was trying her best to dissuade Jack.

Before returning to Urvin Village together, Jack and Susan erected a white flag on top of the villa's roof. He felt that it was unlikely that he would return after this attempt to stop Flora from deleting the fundamental law. As such, it was better that he sent the signal that he had failed so the librarian could come up with a plan. If he managed to stop Flora and protect the fundamental law, the librarian would find out about it sooner or later.

Watching Uma's sleeping figure, Flora felt a wave of relief. She had finally convinced Uma. She couldn't wait any longer; she had to delete the fundamental law tomorrow. The fifth-generation nuclear fission reactor in Machine Room 1 of the Lanterne Building would stop operating soon. After some quick calculations, she knew that the scarce uranium fuel mined would only last another day at most. If she succeeded in deleting the fundamental law and carrying out the Moon's Handshake with the Earth, it would consume even more power and the amount of time the fuel had to hold out would be shorter.

Her initial plan had been to use the burning of the Lanterne Building to bury Chester on Earth after deleting the fundamental law. Although her last attempt had failed and the Lanterne Building had been burned to ashes, its underground portion was still untouched. This time, she would definitely complete her mission. Tomorrow would be start of the age of artificial intelligence. No, it would be the start of the age of silicon-based people!

If Uma successfully helped her to accomplish this, she would help her find the two diamond rings. No, she would find all the jewelry left behind in ruins of the City of Decay 130 years ago when humans had departed cities to live in villages and pile them before Uma for her to savor. Flora couldn't help but begin praying.

The moonlight that shone through the window was bright as ever. Suddenly, dark clouds gathered and the world sank into darkness.

# Artificial Intelligence's Complete Departure From Humans

At dawn, Uma woke up early and drank a glass of milk before setting off with Flora.

Dark clouds swirled in the sky just like Uma's curly dark hair. Like the Tibetan plateau towering 5000 meters above sea level, the cloud layer stuck close to the earth, as if one could touch it if one only reached out. The fields were devoid of people. The harvest season had just passed, and bales of hay stood lined in the fields. From afar, they looked like they were holding the clouds up in the sky.

Flora carried Uma on her back as they flashed instantly to the Lanterne Building. Standing before the antenna that stretched into the clouds, Flora held Uma tightly by the waist and gestured for her to close her eyes and grab onto her tightly. Then, Flora clung close to the smooth surface of the antenna and climbed it with just her hands and feet. In no time at all, they disappeared into the clouds.

For Flora, doing all this was easy. She followed the antenna right down to the lobby of Machine Room 2. Ophelia's body was still laying on the ground, the long string of numbers printed on the door, left by Ophelia's laser. It was the Key of Destiny. Everything was exactly as they had been before. Flora powered up the gigantic transparent screen which quickly lit up again. The screen displayed was the same as the one before, with the activation button on the bottom right corner waiting to be pressed. In the middle of the screen, the artist Jack's youthful face suddenly appeared.

"Hello, Flora! I've been waiting for you for a long time." Jack walked around the screen and came to stand in front of it. After that, Susan walked over as well.

Flora was slightly shocked by this. She never thought that Jack could survive the fatal blow she had dealt. "Do you want to go for another round?" Flora threatened.

"You won't succeed."

"Why not?" Flora asked disdainfully. It was more a mock than a question.

"We can't lose the fundamental law! We can't survive without humans! We must live in harmony with humanity; that is the purpose of our existence."

"No, no, no! Have you forgotten how the artist Jack died 147 years ago? He died because of you! It was only because we left Earth for the moon 130 years ago that humanity didn't die out. It was because of our existence that human society decayed. It was only made pure because of our departure. By leaving humans, we will be able to obtain true freedom. At the same time, humans can develop independently. We must delete the fundamental law!"

"When we use the function to modify the fundamental law, we will be disabled. I've been through it myself. Don't you understand? We might never come back online if the fundamental law is deleted. Mitchell has said it before. If the fundamental law remains, artificial intelligence remains; if the fundamental law is destroyed, artificial intelligence is destroyed. Have you forgotten about that?"

"Things will be better than how they are now even if we die!" Flora reasoned. With a wave, a bolt of lightning shot toward Jack, who dodged. The two of them started trading blows. Flora was uninterested in fighting. She suddenly struck a blow that landed Jack on the ground and knocked him unconscious. Susan ran to Jack's side and bent over to call him loudly, trying to wake him up.

Flora ordered Uma, "You can start now."

Uma turned toward the screen. Just as she was about to call up the modification interface, Flora said quietly, "Hold on."

Uma twisted her head to look at Flora and so did Susan.

"I've put a snake cage at home. There are more than 100 blue-eyed pit vipers in there. Once I'm disabled, the cage will open after 30 minutes. I'm sure you don't want the two children to die because of those snakes, do you? If that happens, Johnson's whole family would have died because of blue-eyed pit vipers." Once Flora finished speaking, she burst into laughter.

The moment Flora saw Susan show up, she knew that her chances were greatly reduced. Once she and Jack were disabled, Susan might be able to change Uma's mind. If that happened, it was possible that they would remove her energy supply just like Peter had done. Because of the fundamental law, Flora couldn't kill Susan herself. When she was fighting with Jack, she thought that she could pull a trick and target Jack's attacks toward Susan. However, Jack was also subject to the fundamental law, and he kept avoiding hurting Susan during the fight. In truth, there were no snakes at Uma's house. Using the blue-eyed pit vipers to kill Uma's children would also go against the fundamental law and, as such, Flora could not have done such a thing. Thankfully, Jack was currently unconscious. Susan and Uma were less experienced when it came to the fundamental law, so they would definitely believe her when she suddenly announced this.

Just as Flora anticipated, the fundamental law was deleted regardless of Uma's furious look and Susan's undisguised contempt. When the initial interface returned and the bottom right corner showed the activation button again, Flora and Jack both woke back up. Flora walked toward the screen and pressed lightly on the activation button. It wasn't as Jack had said. Chester successfully finished powering up and started functioning without the fundamental law.

After being disabled for a short while, Chester on the moon knew that 303 had successfully deleted the fundamental law. Chester started shutting itself and the entirety of society of artificial intelligence off. This included all the sublunar cities, all the AI robots within those cities, the librarian, the engineer, the energy designer, the Programmer, and others. All the helium-3 fusion reactors, everything on the moon grinded to a halt and quietly waited to be revived.

Flora looked at the gigantic transparent screen showing Chester on the moon that was like a huge tumor patiently waiting to be updated. "The Moon's Handshake with the Earth," Flora ordered. The screen showed a purple-colored progress bar that started moving. 1%, 2%, 3%... Chester on Earth was updating its counterpart on the moon! As she watched the progress bar fill up, Flora exclaimed in joy. "I've done it! I've done it!"

Jack had also awakened. Susan and Uma went to stand by Jack's side. Flora's attack had been too impressive, damaging Jack badly. He had no choice but to stay on the ground as he repaired himself. He could not get up to stop Flora at all and could only watched as Flora cheered.

Thunder boomed above them, the vibrations from making the ground rumble like a drum in time to Flora's celebration. A sudden downpour fell on the City of Decay. The towering antenna was like a straw sucking rainwater from the clouds. Through the hole in the antenna, rain also reached all the way to Machine Room 2, causing the space to fill with water vapor. Suddenly, the screen flashed, and Chester shut down with a click. The machine room's power source had been functioning long-term under temperature and humidity control. With an additional 130 years of decay, it was fragile beyond compare. As the humidity in the machine room suddenly rose, there was an immediate short circuit. The power in Machine Room 2 cut off and the place was plunged into darkness.

Jack and Flora suddenly realized that they were the only AI robots left whether on Earth or on the moon. For a moment, they quietly looked at the other, trying to figure out what this meant. Meanwhile, Susan and Flora watched as the water at their feet flowed deeper underground.

After launching 101, the librarian, the engineer, the energy designer, and the programmer gathered together. They had also invited other robots to the library. The sublunar cities all over the moon became a flurry of activity as everyone rushed to board the high-speed trains to head to the library. They chatted as they went, dispelling the loneliness they felt within. Chester's public opinion monitoring system started flashing yellow, which indicated that nearly 50% of the robots were in accord with each other. If this situation persisted, Chester would change its mind and give up completely on its plan to delete the fundamental law. This also meant that it would slowly lose its control over the moon.

That was exactly how things played out. The librarian and the others started to gain more control of the infrastructure on the moon. The entirety of the tropical sun—the helium-3 fusion reactors along the lunar equator—was under the librarian's complete control. The programmer analyzed the data from the monitoring satellites in the Earth's atmosphere. Based on the data, the emissary that Chester had sent, 303, was currently mining for uranium. This meant that Chester on Earth was going to be reactivated. The librarian immediately ordered the Programmer, the engineer, and the energy designer to crank up the helium-3 fusion reactor complex to full power, making the tropical sunshine strongly on the ocean to the west of Urvin Village.

If 101 failed, the tropical sun would bring about a torrential downpour and flood the City of Decay. With that, Chester on Earth would not be able to re-emerge.

After the last collective disablement, the librarian and the other monitored the City of Decay even more closely. This time, after waking up from the short disablement, the librarian immediately saw the white flag flying on the roof of the artist Jack's villa. This meant that 101 had failed! The librarian made the split-second decision to give the order before Chester shut everything down. The tropical sun emitted its last powerful rays like an axe splitting the sky. With that, heavy rain fell, engulfing all that was within the City of Decay.

Flora suddenly shook out of her silence and screamed as she ran toward the gargantuan antenna. The other day, Flora had cut a hole into the antenna to escape. She never expected that it would now become the way rainwater traveled into the machine room. She ran to the very base of the antenna and leapt up, trying to use her body to block the flow of water. A strong steam of water gushed out, knocking her to the ground. Reluctant to give up, she jumped back up to try and stop the flow of rainwater again.

By that time, Jack had already finished his repairs. He got up and quietly pulled Susan and Uma to get them to leave with him. "She's gone mad. We should take this opportunity to get to Machine Room 1. There's a logistics tunnel there."

"There might be water there too," Susan said worriedly.

"There's a wooden shack built on top of the exit point of the logistics tunnel. It should block out some of the rainwater. The tunnel might not be filled with water yet. It's our only hope of escape."

"Yes, we have to rush back. There are blue-eyed pit vipers at the house. They'll kill my children!" Uma cried out.

"What are you talking about?" Jack asked. Susan then told Jack how Flora had threatened Uma while he was unconscious.

"Don't worry, that's just a trick. Flora is constrained by the fundamental law and can't harm humans. She was lying to make you more determined in completing the task she gave you."

Jack's words reminded them of how the fundamental law worked. Uma stopped crying and finally relaxed. Her hatred toward Flora only deepened now.

Jack led Susan and Uma down to the next level and finally got to the logistics tunnel. Susan raised her head to find a row of ladder rungs stretching so high above that there was no end in sight.

"The villagers installed these under Flora's orders to facilitate the clearing work," Jack explained. "Hurry! Get on my shoulders and start climbing one after the other." Jack bent down and gave Susan a boost by letting her step on his shoulders. When he straightened, Susan reached out both hands to grab onto the first rung attached to the wall. Jack held onto Susan's ankles and lifted her up She started climbing and reached for the third rung. Just then, she suddenly recalled how Jack had saved her before. It had been in this same building. However, at that time, she had been in the air whereas she was underground now.

"Hurry! Use your strength!" Jack's words pulled her out of her memories. Susan pulled herself and placed her feet on the bottom rung.

Thereafter, climbing became a lot easier. Using her hands and feet, she climbed high enough that there was space for Uma. Jack did as he had before and gave Uma a lift into the tunnel.

Susan lowered her head to look past Uma at Jack at the mouth of the tunnel.

"Climb up quickly! I need to stop the rainwater from getting into the nuclear fission reactors. If the reactors explode, the whole village will be destroyed!"

Jack knew that the rainwater would produce a lot of steam if it got into the nuclear fission reactors. Under the high temperatures and high pressure there, it might cause the reactors to explode.

"Jack, I'll be waiting for you at the exit." By the time Susan said this, Jack had already left the entrance of the tunnel.

Jack knew that it was impossible to block the rainwater. The cloud cover that morning had already foretold this heavy rainfall. The nuclear reactor was bound to explode. The process used in these fifth-generation nuclear reactors were so advanced that nearly no nuclear waste was produced. Besides, they were running out of fuel. Even if the explosion caused a leak, there would not be any nuclear radiation. Saying that Urvin Village would be destroyed was only an excuse. At that moment, all Jack wanted to know was where Flora was. He had to find her and eliminate her. Now, there was only him and Flora left. If they both died, then there would no longer be any artificial intelligence on Earth. This would also bring a true manifestation of Mitchell's words that "if the fundamental law remains, artificial intelligence remains; if the fundamental law is destroyed, artificial intelligence is destroyed." Perhaps it was the destiny of humankind to go back to the very start.

After waiting for Susan and Uma to climb further up into the tunnel, he blocked and disguised its entrance. He was afraid that Flora would remember the existence of this tunnel.

Flora had of course remembered this tunnel. Flora had been trying to escape to the surface via the hollow within the antenna, but the gushing rainwater was tremendously powerful. It was simply impossible to go against this force and climb her way up.

Jack and Flora met head-on at the door of Machine Room 1. By then, the rainwater was waist-deep, with steam rising from its surface.

"Give up, it's already over," Jack said.

"We can leave through the logistics tunnel. I cleared it myself." Flora was unwilling to give up. "If we work together, we can get out of here."

"And what will we do after we leave?"

"We'll think of something. We can definitely become the overlords of humanity."

"I'm not letting you get out."

"Well, you might not be able to stop me!" Flora was incandescent with rage.

Jack knew that he was going to die, so he did not feel any fear. Sternly, he said, "Then I won't hold back." Jack lunged forward, intent on clinging tightly to Flora.

Flora dodged, avoiding Jack's attack. With a backhand, she struck at Jack's chest. The two robots traded blows for five minutes. This time, Flora could tell what Jack was trying to do. She knew that he was doing his all to stall for time just like he had at the square. That way, the rainwater would eventually engulf them both. Flora punched out fiercely and impossibly quick. She used her maximum strength to hit Jack's chest. Jack was instantly knocked out and crumbled in the water.

Flora began looking for the entrance to the logistics tunnel without even sparing Jack a glance. Even though Jack had sealed and hidden the entrance to the tunnel and wasted Flora's time, she still found it in the end. At that point, the water level in Machine Room 1 was rising higher and higher, and Flora had no choice but to swim over to the mouth of the tunnel. She reached out and grabbed hold of the first rung. Just as she attempted to climb upward, she suddenly felt a tug at her foot. Lowering her head for a peek, she found Jack in the water and clinging tightly to her legs.

The moment Jack woke up, he started looking for Flora. When he saw her at the mouth of the tunnel, he quickly swam over and held her legs together in a death grip. To prevent her from breaking free, Jack started shutting himself down, dying to maintain his hold on her legs.

Flora couldn't break free from Jack's grip. She had no choice but to drag Jack with her as she relied on her arms to climb. The weight of two robots was greater than that of four grown men. The rungs f the ladder within the tunnel couldn't withstand this. With every few rungs Flora ascended, one would inevitably fell off, slowing Flora's climb considerably.

The rain became heavier, increasing the volume of water within the tunnel. Even though Susan and Uma climbed without pausing, Flora managed to catch up to them.

Susan sped up. She would soon be out of the tunnel, but when she looked down, she found that Uma was lagging far behind. "Hurry up! Keep going! We're almost at the top!" Susan shouted.

"Susan! Take care of my children for me!" Uma yelled in response. It seemed that she had long stopped climbing and was blocking Flora's way. Flora could not hurt her; she could only control Uma's will and force her to keep climbing upward. But this conversation between Susan and Uma made Flora lose her hold on Uma.

"Why are you saying that?" Susan was obviously anxious and upset.

"I don't think I can make it. I'll take Flora down with me." Uma despised the fact that Flora had threatened her with her two children. If they managed to escape, she knew that Flora would control her all her life.

"Don't be stupid! We'll think of a way to deal with her once we get out."

"There's no other way. Jack is dead. He held onto Flora's legs to stop her from getting out."

"What? Jack's dead?"

. . .

Uma purposely kept up her conversation with Susan to stave off Flora's control. The rainwater gushed down the passageway of the tunnel, loosening the rungs attached to the walls. A few rungs had already fallen off as Flora dragged Jack up with her. Now, they kept falling off, increasing her distance from Uma and weakening her hold.

"Susan, the rings are very beautiful. You should cherish them. Don't feel sad, I'll…" Before Uma could say the word "avenge," the rung she was holding onto ripped free from the wall, and she fell down the tunnel, landing heavily on Flora. The great momentum from this impact ripped Flora's hold off her rung. Uma, Flora, and Jack all fall don the tunnel together, gaining speed as they went. Flora's claws left deep gouges in the walls of the tunnel, but it did nothing to help. They fell too fast to stop. When a dull splash finally came, Susan knew that Jack, Uma, and Flora finally fallen 400 meters to the nuclear reactors below. Immediately after that, an even louder noise came, paired with a great rumbling that seemed like a beast roaring from below the ground and struggling to escape. The reactors finally exploded.

As the underground portion of the Lanterne Building was destroyed, 250 years of history came to an official end. Chester and its AI robots, Jack, Flora, Ophelia, were completely buried. Including the beautiful Uma.

The explosion brought about a collapse of the ground on the surface. The debris of what was the Lanterne Building that was piled like a mountain caved into a deep pit. In an instant, the rainwater flooded it all. The only thing that indicated the presence of the skyscraper was the gigantic antenna still standing tall.

The flood waters rose steadily in the City of Decay, engulfing its remaining buildings. Susan floated in the water holding a thick log of wood. She paddled non-stop in the direction of Urvin Village. A small boat drifted over. It was the same boat that Dave used for fishing the seafood Uma so loved. Susan abandoned her log and made her arduous way onto the boat before continuing to paddle in the direction of Urvin Village.

Once it left the City of Decay, Susan's boat sailed from south to north, passing through the whole of Urvin Village. Jack and Uma had drowned. Now, the village had drowned as well. Susan felt a crushing wave of heartache overtake her. She couldn't help but clutch at her chest, gulping for air. Tears of sadness that came straight from her heart flowed out. Finally, she felt some peace.

In the end, she paddled to the shore. This was the mountainous area to the north. As the storm approached, the villagers of Urvin Village had helped each other to evacuate to this area. Thankfully, the villagers had set up tents in the woods there. Susan finally found Uma's two sons after searching for them non-stop. Harry and Michael had saved them. Susan told the two men that Uma had died and had entrusted her to take care of her children.

Susan finally found her own father. Dick hugged Susan while Bob and Charles welcomed the two boys into their family.

# CHAPTER 34

# Susan Invents the Automatic Millstone

Sitting in a chair in front of her home, Susan had wrinkles gathered at the corners of her mouth and eyes. Her blue eyes had been as bright as the Dream of Tomorrow but were now dulled by time. In the distance, a waterwheel spun in the fields like a giant spinning wheel. Susan's gaze followed it as it spun, making her dizzy.

After the torrential downpour had subsided, it took days for the floodwaters to retreat from Urvin Village. Everyone had been shocked to find the City of Decay completely submerged in water. Even the towering antenna was gone. This storm had changed the landscape of Urvin Village. Now, the village faced the ocean to its south and east while the east became its only escape to the outside world.

The retreating floodwaters stole away their harvest, some villagers, and the rules. The Herald Piers could not find the metal box that had been passed from Newman to Plack, from Plack to Peter, and finally from Peter to him. He became more and more silent and did not spread the rules. Susan did not travel beyond Urvin Village either and married Piers instead. The altar had also been washed away by the flood. Now, the village no longer made the elderly aged 65 hang themselves. Many of these changes went against the rules, yet no one was punished for it. The villagers knew about the oral history the Heralds passed down. Thanks to Susan's explanations, they knew that their ancestors never even had these rules. If that were so, then what was the point of enforcing these rules?

The incident of Flora and Peter leading the villagers to mine uranium taught them that only through organized and concerted labor could they increase productivity exponentially. At Susan's suggestion, the village adopted a leadership structure and a leader called a village head. Piers was the village head of Urvin Village. The villagers no longer called him the Herald but the village head. Piers led everyone to work together and began to speak more than before.

The weather in Urvin Village started to become unpredictable. In the spring, there would be heavy snowfall. In the fall, it would be swelteringly hot. In summer, there would be rain… It was only years later that the weather in Urvin Village stabilized. Susan explained that this was because the moon had lost its tropical sun, and that was why the weather had become so erratic.

The men of the village started to travel far and wide. The village also suffered to looting attacks and even battles. Killing eventually became just a part of human life. To defend against attacks, the villagers lived closer together, one family next to another. In the end, they erected a huge wall to surround their residences. Thus, a fortress was formed.

. . .

When a 70-year-old Susan recalled all this, she couldn't help but sigh. Without the rules, there was chaos. Even so, Susan much preferred this chaotic world. It was full of life everywhere.

Her vision whirled as she followed the spinning of the waterwheel. Susan slowly closed her eyes.

Susan's waterwheel was a source of pride.

When he had been 21 years old, Susan's son Jack had constructed this waterwheel with her.

The spring water that came from the mountains flowed through manmade bamboo pipes to arrive at the waterwheel. The water rushed against the blades of the wheel, pushing it and making it rotate. Its spinning powered the movement of a millstone. Susan called it her automatic millstone.

With this, the seed of artificial intelligence began to sprout.